Book One of the
NOTHING IS WHAT IT SEEMS Quartet

Confusion

Peter de Vos

Matador
9 Priory Business Park
Kibworth Beauchamp
Leicestershire LE8 0RX, UK
Tel: (+44) 116 279 2299
Fax: (+44) 116 279 2277
Email: books@troubador.co.uk
Web: www.troubador.co.uk/matador

ISBN 978-1783064-014

British Library Cataloguing in Publication Data.
A catalogue record for this book is available from the British Library.

Typeset in Aldine by Troubador Publishing Ltd
Printed and bound in the UK by TJ International, Padstow, Cornwall

Matador is an imprint of Troubador Publishing Ltd

Also by the same author:

The *NOTHING IS WHAT IT SEEMS* Quartet:

Book Two - *Clarity*
Book Three - *Commitment*
Book Four - *Confinement*

With thanks to my friend Jelte for encouraging me to start writing
and to my wife Silke to push through with it

MAIN CHARACTERS

Elena Lee
A young Filipino woman; spoiled by her proud mother, Cornelia, and her wealthy, much older father Zhiheng Lee.

Robert William Delsey-Cauloyne
A rash Englishman with a past shrouded in clouds. Manager of the Bayun Beach Resort. Women were his downfall in England and history repeats itself in the Philippines…

Zhiheng Lee
The islanders refer to him as old Mr. Lee or plain Mr. Lee. A Chinese immigrant who amassed a fortune with trading, possibly in less than legal ways. He is also the owner of Bayun Beach Resort. Married to Cornelia and father of Elena.

Cornelia Lee
Daughter of an impoverished Spanish-Filipino aristocratic family. Married to Zhiheng Lee and mother of Elena.

Yunlin Lee
'Little brother' of old Mr. Lee. One of the heads of the Hong Kong triads, specialising in drug trafficking.

Juan Aldones
Filipino dive master at the Bayun Beach Resort; bon-vivant, self-proclaimed playboy and admirer of Elena Lee.

Jonathan Sy

A bright and correct inspector connected to Central Headquarters of the Philippine National Police. He acquired the highest success rate of the whole force, due to his multiple qualities that he modestly tries to hide. Second generation Chinese Immigrant, but ingrained with English virtues.

Daniel Arozo

Middle-aged chief of police on the island of Siquijor. A troubled and emotional bachelor who loathes being unjust in order to uphold the law.

Uncle Joe

A former American GI, who decided to stay on Siquijor after the war. Bright, inquisitive and loved by the local population. But also unmarried, quaint and meddlesome.

Teresa Zampata

The young head waitress at the Bayun Beach Resort. Cheerful and kind, although she is pregnant from a man who ignores his coming fatherhood.

Eulogio 'Nonoy' Negrito

Resort guard at Bayun Beach Resort. Servile and observant. Loyal to his masters, but mainly to himself.

Antonia 'Tony' Gambana

The much older 'wife' of the guard Eulogio; fat, quarrelsome and demanding.

Sergeant Ramos

Former marine and second-in-command at the small police force commanded by chief Arozo.

Dr. Gonzales

The local physician, who also acts as a coroner on call. Unruffled by death and murder, even when it concerns people who were too young to die.

ONE

Siquijor, Philippines, Summer 1978

There is an island in the Philippines called 'Siquijor'. The island is part of the central 'Visayas' area and was the first part of the Philippines to be colonised by the Spaniards in the 16th century. The island is not big, nor small. It's just a well-sized tropical island with dazzling, white, tropical beaches, lots of small villages scattering the coastline and gentle rolling hills covered by coconut groves and pristine jungle deeper inland. The island does however have a rather mixed reputation in the Philippines, because some superstitious souls – and you will find many of them in the Philippines – whisper that the local voodoo witches can conjure up forces from the dark to throw a spell on victims of those who are willing to pay a price to hurt their enemies. And since emotions can run high in the Philippines, there seems to be a good market for the witch doctors from Siquijor...

But to us outsiders, who have grown up under the dark and rainy skies of the Northern hemisphere, Siquijor looks like pure paradise; idyllic bamboo huts scatter the hillsides and fat, green jungle that rolls down to the blinding white beaches of powder-fine coral sand, brushed by the lazy waves of the azure-blue Sulu sea. It is a magnificent sight to approach the island from the west. In summer, large, billowing thunderclouds erupt in the deep-blue sky behind the green hills of the interior. Sometimes they unload their cargo of lukewarm tropical rain onto the island; more often they do not, and only show a nightly spectacle of heavy, tearing flashes of lightning in the distance. You can try to count the time between flash and thunder, but often the thunderstorms that seem so close are actually too far away to be heard.

In the late afternoon of this particular day, a girl, or rather a young woman, is standing on the beach, shielding her eyes against the glaring sun, which is about to disappear behind the dormant volcano craters of the large island opposite. Behind her rises a cluster of well-maintained buildings in a setting of palm trees, trimmed tropical bushes, shrubs and heaps of flowering bougainvillea. Some smaller buildings, which seem to be staff accommodation, line a winding path leading to a large house with a columned veranda on the top of the hill. The house has the look of a grand, old-fashioned yet comfortable colonial home of a plantation owner, which it actually used to be before the site was converted into a resort. On top of the building perches a rather vulgar sign, lined with a row of eroded metal floodlights, saying *Bayun Bay Resort*.

A small *banca*, the typical local outrigger boat that has been used for centuries by Philippine seamen and fishermen alike, is approaching from the distance, its small diesel engine noisily puttering along. For the girl it's still just a white dot on a sea of glimmering, silver wave tops, but it is closing the gap to the beach fast. Its bow dips into the wave tops with lazy regularity, reflecting the mood of the dark-skinned crew sitting on the grubby deck. When the little vessel approaches the beach, the girl recognises an equally dark-skinned man who is holding the tiller pin in his large hands. His features are not Asian, but distinctly European. The man is tall, at least 1.85, and his broad, muscular frame has not yet acquired any fat, which it undoubtedly will with approaching years. Bright, blue eyes pierce from below heavy-set eyebrows and his almost too full mouth is set in a concentrated line as he aims the little boat for its final approach through the surf. Nobody on the island is aware of the fact, nor would it interest them if they had known, that the ancestors of this man were Portuguese Jews who fled to England during the *Estafa*. Robert, as the man was baptised by his parents 39 years earlier, hardly ever loses a thought about the origins of his ancestors. He feels through-and-through British; born and raised in the town of Huntingdon, England, where his father owned the family wine-store facing the River Ouse; being the former captain of the local youth cricket team and a graduate in ancient languages at nearby Cambridge. Ah, Cambridge… As little as Robert thinks about his origins, the more he ponders about his time in Cambridge. Cambridge; a period of great exaltation, joy and success. But

2

also the period which presented him with the greatest disaster and embarrassment in life. A disaster which led to his more or less voluntarily exile to the Philippines.

But on this very day, Cambridge is far from his mind. This time his mind is on the lightly-tanned girl waiting for his arrival on the beach. He can hardly recognise her from this distance, but he doesn't have to, because her traits are burned into his mind; her pearly, full-teethed, laughing mouth, her lovely nose with the slightly slanting, almond-coloured eyes above, her delicate hands, one of them now shading her high forehead from the sun, occasionally brushing windblown wisps of raven-black hair back behind her ears. And he specifically remembers her petite but very feminine frame, which his large hands had pressed against his excited body only 12 hours before. He has memorised her small, firm breasts, reflecting the moonlight from their perfect creamy skin, and the delicious rounding of her naked buttocks when she walked ahead of him into the sparkling sea after their lovemaking on the powdery beach. He had always been attracted to Elena, but after yesterday he had fallen head over heels in love. He has tried to resist the temptation of course. He had not come to the Philippines to be strung along by another woman – on the contrary! And Elena is specifically off limits, being the only daughter of old Mr. Lee, his superior and owner of the resort where Robert is General Manager. She seems a lovely mixture of her father's Chinese genes and her mother's hot Spanish blood and is preordained to marry into the exclusive club of the Filipino aristocracy of Spanish decent. But the young woman always radiates so much happiness, so much uncomplicated love for life that he, in the end, just hadn't been able to resist. And of course he had been flattered by the attention of this girl, more than 15 years his junior, who had been flirting and teasing him almost from the first day they had met.

Robert William Delsey-Cauloyne had arrived in the Philippines almost two decades before with little money to spare, a shameful past and no apparent future at all. Disgraced back home, he had, like so many young British men before him, tried to find a new life in the Orient. His degree from Cambridge was quite useless in the Philippines; Robert quickly found out that the hard-nosed Chinese, who dominated business life on the islands, had no need for any of the Sumerian languages he mastered, so he had to work for his living, and he had to work hard! Old Mr. Lee, a Chinese

3

immigrant to the Philippines and father of his roommate at Cromwell College, had given him an opportunity as an administrative clerk in his merchant empire on the island of Negros. Hours were long and the offices cramped and stuffy. Not exactly what he had aspired to, but he made some money and was reasonably content; the cost of living was low, the drizzle back home had been displaced by eternal sunshine and the girls were, at least for a 'long-nose' like him who was willing to depart with a bit of money for their services, far more lovely and accommodating than the girls back home. But something was lacking in his life. On the rare occasions he had consciously thought about his future, he had often pondered what it actually was he was lacking. What did he really want out of life? Wealth? A family? Success? Appreciation? Well, probably a bit of everything, but he just couldn't seem to get his act together to work consistently on any of these goals. He was happily floating along the river of life, hoping one day to stand on an inviting beach he might really like. And surprisingly, after many wasted years of idle hope, he finally got his opportunity to make sense of his life.

Lee Jr., his former roommate in Cambridge, had contacted him with an offer. Lee Jr.'s father, Zhiheng Lee, had recently acquired a 10-acre, run-down mango and coconut plantation on Siquijor from an impoverished Spanish-Filipino family unable to pay their outstanding bills to him. Old Mr. Lee had evicted the family from the grounds and now planned to convert the former colonial home into a tourist resort for wealthy foreigners. Like many wealthy Filipinos, Zhiheng Lee felt slightly xenophobic towards foreigners, but he simultaneously craved their attention and confirmation of equality. This feeling was probably born from a century-old inferiority complex. An inferiority which the Spanish Grandes, who had ruled the country with a hard hand for more than 300 years, had promoted with help of the Catholic priests; it was God-ordained that the Spanish should rule and the Filipinos should serve! Zhiheng Lee, although being a first generation Chinese immigrant, strangely enough reacted in the same way as his Filipino peers. Did he only try to conform to his peers, or were there other reasons? For those who know Chinese history a bit, things are not as strange as they look at first sight. After all, these Chinese immigrants had experienced similar conditions at home, when arrogant European powers had humiliated China during the Boxer War at the beginning of the 20th century; their small but modern armies had defeated anything the Chinese had thrown against them and thereby broke the might and spirit of the huge Chinese empire. Europeans became the virtual masters of this proud country and in the course of it reduced all Chinese to second-rate citizens of this planet. No wonder the Chinese resented all Westerners. But equally no wonder they felt inadequate and craved to become as powerful and influential as their Western conquerors....

No matter what reasons Zhiheng Lee had to build this particular resort, he still had no firm idea how to do it. After all, his business was buying and selling goods and he had to admit to himself that this was a far cry from attracting wealthy foreigners to spend their holidays in a resort. But his oldest son, Lee Jr., whom he had sent at great expense to England in order to learn the ways in which Europeans live and do business, knew a lot more about foreigners. After his son's return, Zhiheng had had great hopes that the new skills his son had acquired would propel the family business to new heights. But his hopes had been shattered when it showed that his son had not only acquired new skills but also new values. Lee Sr. had initially worried that he might have lost his son to the foreigners for good, such was the behaviour of his son upon return, imitating his former English hosts like a trained parrot. But in the end, Lee Jr., as any obedient Chinese son, had to acknowledge Zhiheng's authority as head of the family and accept the fact that he, although thoroughly ingrained with new virtues and skills, was still only the son of a wealthy Chinese merchant. From that point onward, Lee Jr. became useful again and proved to be a shrewd hard-working member of the family.

So it was with a heavy heart that Zhiheng now had to call on the special acquired skills of his son. He asked Lee Jr. to find a foreign manager to set up the resort and put it on the tourist map. Lee Jr. had met Robert many times in the early seventies in the offices in Dumaguete, the capital city of Negros Oriental, and had enjoyed reliving Robert's cynical English quaintness during the occasional dinners they had together. Robert, from his side, was surprised by the changed lifestyle of his former roommate. Gone was the affable behaviour of a loose-living playboy, replaced by the tough manners of a hard-working Chinese with the airs of a Spanish Grande. But to Robert's relief, he noticed that Lee Jr. had not completely forgotten his experiences from England; he had picked up some new values during his stint abroad and no matter how hard he tried, he could not ignore them. So, like many wealthy Filipinos with foreign experience, he now disdained the local Filipino managers who, in his eyes, were useless and lazy scoundrels, just like all other native Filipinos. He therefore knew that he had to look elsewhere for a manager suited for the particular job of manager of his father's new resort. In Lee Jr.'s opinion, only a civilised Englishman like his former roommate Robert could recreate the colonial atmosphere the place had once possessed and which the potential Western guests apparently seemed to like so much.

So Robert was offered the job, took over the management of the would-be resort and had made a jolly good job of it. He designed and managed the complete construction, working like a slave to bring Bayun Bay resort to life. After several years of hard work, he could look down at his creation from the top of the hill where he, as manager of the resort, was allowed to occupy the former main house that had a free view of the valley and the ocean beyond. Below him, a scattering of semi-open, hardwood buildings with classical Nippa roofs occupied the lower section of the small valley all the way to the beach. Here were the two restaurants, the dive shop, three lounges, offices and other utility buildings of the resort, while the hillsides were lined on two sides with a variety of private bungalows for the guests, all with a breathtaking view over the ocean. Over the years, the garden had grown into a tropical haven and the guests could immerse themselves in this artificial jungle and forget about the stressful jobs they had in the outside world. But the active guests were also catered for; behind the biggest lounge, which doubled as club house, was a large gravel tennis court, only used by the hardiest players who could withstand the heat and high humidity, and a bit further on a small 9-hole golf course. Next to the snack bar was a huge kidney-shaped pool with an in-water bar, separated from the Olympic-sized swimming pool by a small channel cutting through an artificial rock formation.

Robert was a methodical man; even before the resort was finished, he had produced sales material containing colourful high-gloss pictures with artists' impressions of the future resort, and had started to market the resort amongst high-end agencies in Europe and America. Thanks to the assistance of some of his old college friends, the resort quickly became popular as a quiet holiday refuge for well-to-do foreign businessmen and celebrities, craving luxurious relaxation in a tropical haven by the sea. The resort had taken all of Robert's time and energy for more than four years; it had become his life, his baby. He had brought it to life, nurtured it during its infancy and now proudly looked upon his child growing into maturity. The Chinese owners gave him all the freedom he needed and a share in the profits as well. No wonder Robert saw Bayun Bay Resort as his own, and thought nobody was going to take that away from him.

Now this proud man, who had achieved success and appreciation and a little bit of wealth, thought he had found the woman with whom he could to share his achievements with. First, he had to sort out a small thing that had bugged him all afternoon… But as it happened, he would never manage to sort out that small thing, because the gods of fate move in mysterious ways, especially on the Island of Siquijor.

TWO

With a hissing sound, the sharp bow of the *banca* slides onto the sandy beach. Immediately the crew comes to life and jumps overboard, pulling and heaving to secure the little vessel high on the beach. Robert guides them with loud instructions in a rough version of the local Visayan tongue. It is an odd sight; the tall bare-chested European, coloured beautifully by the tropical sun, surrounded by the much smaller Filipinos, who desperately try to protect their swarthy skins from the tanning effects of the sun. Old T-shirts are wrapped around their heads, leaving only a small slit for the eyes, and old coats are worn backwards, leaving their T-shirted backs free for the cooling breeze but protecting their forearms against the sun. Satisfied with their work, Robert grabs his waterproof bag from the *banca* and, beaming with happiness, approaches the woman he loves.

Elena seems equally happy to see him; her eyes shine brightly and her delicate body tenses with excitement: "Robert; I have been waiting for you all day! I am sooo exited! I've got such wonderful news!"

Elena speaks quickly and, as always, her voice is full of promises of sensual delight. All sentences are put forward in her warm local accent and each sentence seems to end with an exclamation mark; a fact he has come to love over the years he has known her.

He laughs at her: "And *I* have a present for you to celebrate our new-born friendship."

"Really, a present? How nice of you, Robert!" she replies coquettishly in a husky voice, which turns all business-like the moment after: "But first let me tell you about *my* news!"

She puts her hand on Robert's arm and, while she continues talking to the man who towers over her by almost two heads, guides him towards the main buildings of the resort. The *Amacan* walls of the restaurant glow in the last rays of the descending sun, while the guard salutes and opens the gate to the restaurant.

"Thank you Nonoy! How are you today?" Robert inquires perfunctorily.

"Fine Sir, thank you!" A large grin of white teeth splits the broad, tanned face of the guard almost in two.

"Good man!" Robert exclaims while passing the guard into the shady coolness of the restaurant. Robert pulls out the chair for Elena before sitting down himself, while waving at the waitress to come and take their drink order.

The waitress approaches nervously: "So sorry, Sir Robert. I was sick this morning so I was late to make your coffee before you left."

"Oh, don't worry Teresa, I managed. Nonoy made me a strong pot of coffee which lasted me all the way to Negros," Robert replies while nodding pleasantly to the grinning guard in the background. "And in Dumaguete, the office people had prepared a good breakfast, so I was OK!"

Visibly relieved, the girl takes their orders – rum and coke for Robert and white wine for Elena – and disappears behind the bar to prepare the drinks.

When she is out of sight, Robert turns to Elena and takes a deep breath to ask his question, but Elena is quicker: "You know Daddy was here this week, don't you?"

Of course Robert knows of the visit of the old man; he had had a drink with him the day before he left home again.

"But of course you know, Robert; you know everything that happens in the resort, don't you?" She continues, while her lovely face throws a beaming smile up to him. "So you probably can also guess what we discussed, don't you?"

Robert had initially thought the old man had just wanted to visit his favourite child, but apparently there had been more to the visit than he had thought. "No love, I haven't the foggiest what you and the old man have discussed." he replies, not quite honestly.

Elena giggles and her pretty eyes slant into small slits: "He's not that old, Robert; he's just a bit over 60, but he wants to make sure all his children can take care of themselves once he is gone."

Robert must look puzzled, because she continues: "Sometimes he is so Chinese and can only see true happiness through fruitful and successful business. And he thinks his children must be just like him! He thinks I can only become truly happy if I get into business myself!" She pauses and looks at Robert with sparkling eyes before continuing: "Of course I am privileged and don't have to start from scratch, just like Daddy had to do. He offered me a flying start; he wants me to take over the resort, Robert! He just called today on the telephone and confirmed I should do it; he wants me to start leading the resort! Isn't that great?"

While she continues to beam with happiness towards a dumbstruck Robert, she continues: "He has so much respect and admiration for you, Robert! He wants you to stay until he is sure I can do it all by myself!"

Elena is totally unreceptive to the apparent distressful emotions that flit through Robert. "Isn't it great? We can work together and you can teach me all you know! Oh, I am so looking forward to it!"

She slings her arms around his neck and places a soft wet kiss on his cheek, while her firm, pointy breasts press against his chest. He almost forgets his distress when hot shivers of delight poke through his body. But alas; only almost. His confusion and distress soon take the upper hand. He must have misheard or misunderstood; had she really said that she would take over? So was the rumour true? Had she really said that *she* would become the manager of the resort, implying that *he* eventually had to leave Bayun Bay Resort? That can't be true; that isn't right! He loves Elena dearly, but she is far too young and inexperienced to run the resort. And besides, it is *his* home, *his* life, *his* baby! A wave of confusing emotions starts to engulf Robert's mind, while he mentally sees his life unravelling.

From a distance he hears Elena's' voice: "Robert? Robert, are you OK?" Slowly his mind focuses again on the present situation. He is confused and has apparently risen abruptly from his chair without knowing it. He isn't feeling well. He has actually felt pretty washed out all day and this news really takes the last strength out of him. Now Elena is looking at him with worried eyes, her small hands cupping his face: "Thank God, I thought you were going to faint! Are you OK, Robert?"

"Yes, ahh… Yes, I'm OK," he manages to mumble. "The news is just a bit… overpowering."

"Yes, isn't it just?" Elena beams at him, all excited again: "It is great news! This will change my life! And I will not, not ever, disappoint my father; he will be so proud of me!"

Suddenly, in a brief flash, Robert can distinguish the inherited iron will underneath the bubbly, sensual surface of this apparently superficial young woman. She is truly the daughter of her father, and of her business-like Spanish mother; tough, ruthless and determined to get what she wants, whether in love or in business. And all of a sudden he starts to feel the first stings of uncertainty that the night before possibly hadn't been a coincidental meeting of soul partners after all…

"Say something Robert! What do you think? Isn't it great?" Elena pats the chair next to her: "Sit, please!" She looks around. The restaurant is empty; too early for dinner guests, too late for afternoon snacks. So they can talk undisturbed. She takes his face in her hands again and turns it towards her. Her dark shimmering eyes are very close when she lets out a low husky: "Sooo?"

Involuntarily he has to smile.

"What does Robert, my potent lover of the night, think?"

"So you finally remember we were lovers last night, Elena?" Robert complains.

"Oh Robert; please don't sulk now. This is such a wonderful moment. And yesterday was also a wonderful moment! But now we have to talk about the future; how we will manage the resort from now on!"

Robert doesn't know how to handle this situation. He thought he was in love with her… No, he definitely *had* fallen in love with Elena and his body and soul are aching for her closeness. Yet this lovely creature, who he only wants to smother with his love and tenderness, is now tearing at the most important thing in his life and seems, ignorant of his strong feelings, willing to take Bayun Bay Resort away from him. Again, dark emotions start to overpower him – emotions he has held at bay for so many years. But the walls he had built around him to save him from being hurt again slowly start to crumble under the joint attack of rejected and misunderstood love and loss of fulfilment. His fuses blow out one by one when he, all of a sudden, realises with utter clarity that he had fallen in love with a woman who does not deserve him; a woman who obviously is unworthy to receive his devoted attention and trust. A woman who has broken the bond of trust, by using her body so viciously to soften him up for the final blow, and will now take his life work and the only achievement he can be really proud of away from him!

Rage flushes through his system like an untamed river, barely checked by the natural emotional control he normally is so proud of: "I know what you are trying to achieve!" he hisses into her surprised face. "You and your family have abused me; used my strength and my abilities to build all this up!" He gestures in a wide encompassing movement: "But you will never, ever truly own this! *I* have made it into what it is, and *I* am the true heart of this resort! You cannot take it over; it will crumble in your hands and again fall to dust, just like it did before!" By now Robert is standing again, trembling with rage.

Elena cowers frightened in her chair and whines: "Robert, please Robert, control yourself! You are forgetting yourself! Please, please Robert!" Tears start to flow freely out of the corners of her beautiful eyes.

Robert has never been able to withstand female tears and he definitely can't withstand them coming from the most beautiful eyes he has ever seen, despite the fact that they are the eyes of the woman who had, just a second ago, inflicted more pain on him than he has ever felt before. He instantly calms down and falls to his knees beside her: "I'm so sorry! Sorry Elena; I don't know what came over me. It's just such a big shock to know that I will have to give up Bayun Bay."

"But you don't have to give it up, silly; it will take time until I can handle it by myself and I need you until then." Elena sniffs: "And besides, you can always visit me, you know."

"Well..." Robert replies more calmly and thoughtfully: "After last night I had thought that I would not occasionally visit you, but would have a more permanent place by your side!"

Elena sighs. "Oh Robert; yesterday was lovely, and I will remember it the rest of my life. But you know that you and I would be totally unsuitable partners, don't you? I mean, we are ages apart and besides… you are English!"

"What do you mean. I am English? Of course I am English! What's wrong with that?" Robert replies indignantly.

"Nothing, Robert, apart from the fact that you are not Filipino. You know, my parents would never consider a foreigner to be suitable as a son-in-law.

You know how proud they are. It just has to be a Filipino, preferably a Spanish Filipino..."

So there it is; the plain truth. It had been a one-night-stand, an experiment. She had tried to soften him up before taking the resort away and now she adds insult to injury by implying he is not good enough as a partner, but good enough for some liberal, sexual romping; try a real good English cock, before she gets married to a degenerated Spanish Filipino. A Filipino with good bloodline, land and culture obviously. But degenerated none the less.

All of a sudden, hatred against all Filipinos claws its way into Robert's soul and must be seeping out through his eyes, because Elena involuntarily leans back again. "Why are you so upset, Robert? You knew we could never have anything seriously. Really Robert, you must have known..."

Yes, he should have known, but has probably suppressed it after that wonderful experience last night. How could he have been so stupid? But there is nothing he can do to change now, is there? But Robert does not intend to give up so easily. He stays with Elena briefly, forcing himself to calm down and finish his drink. He then excuses himself with the explanation that he wants to freshen up after the long trip. He does not go to his house right away but first goes into the office, which is deserted at this late hour. He calls the operator and asks for a connection with the Lee offices in Dumaguete. Robert thinks that old Lee will surely still be there, and he is not disappointed. The telephone on the other side only rings twice before a faint Chinese voice answers: "Yes?"

"Mr. Lee?" Robert asks into the telephone.

"Yes, speaking; who is this?"

"It's Robert, Sir."

"Ah, Robert, my boy; how are you?"

"Thank you for asking Sir, but not too well after the news your daughter dropped on me today."

"Ah, yes, Robert. My daughter... I told her to wait, but she is young and... impatient. You know that, Robert. Yes?"

"I know that, Sir. It's just... I had expected to stay involved in Bayun Bay Resort. I mean; I built it up. I made it into what it is. I had expected –"

Old Lee interrupts: "Yes, Robert; I understand. But my daughter... she's

13

family, you know. I have to make sure she is… OK. This is how things have to be; you understand, Robert?"

Robert recognises that the conversation is leading nowhere, so he replies resentfully: "Yes Sir, I understand." Then he sighs: "I am sorry to have disturbed you unnecessarily, Sir. Of course you do what is right for you and your family and I obviously respect your decision."

Lee Sr. sounds audibly relieved: "Good, good, Robert… You are a good man, Robert. And that will be rewarded. You have been with us long and served us well. I will not forget. You did well. When all is over on Siquijor, you come back to Negros, yes? Come back to Dumaguete; I have a good job for you here in the office."

"Yes Sir, I will. Thank you . Goodbye."

"Goodbye, Robert. Come and see me in a few weeks, yes? Goodbye!"

Robert ends the connection. No way he is going back to Negros. He does not want another job in an office. He has a life-fulfilling job here and he intends to keep it…

THREE

"Juan, don't!" Elena says laughingly, while the dive guide, who holds her in his arms, pretends to be prepared to throw her overboard into the clear waters of the reef. Elena, Juan, Robert and a group of American scuba divers are on a large dive boat mooring at the dive site Paliton Wall, just a few hundred metres off the coast. Of course, Juan wouldn't throw her; even in a game he knows that he has to obey the wishes of his mistress, so he puts her down on her feet again. Still giggling, she approaches the group of divers that is gathered around Robert. All but one had laughed while the spectacle took place and it is obvious to even the most unreceptive spectator that the tall Englishman, whose eyebrows had formed a menacing straight line above his icy-blue eyes while he was observing the little incident, has not enjoyed seeing Juan's eager arms enclosing the trim waist of Elena at all.

"Oh Robert, don't be such a bore; it's just fun. Isn't it, Juan?" she says while inviting the young guide to acknowledge the truth in her statement. Juan eagerly nods his head. It is great to get the attention of his beautiful mistress and his fantasies go even further than just a hand around the waist.

Robert is jealous of the guide; jealous of his age, which is at least 15 years below his; jealous of his body, which was at least 20 kilos lighter; and jealous of his ability to jest lightly with Elena, while he can only brood and thereby push her away from him, while he actually still aches to be close to her. He will and can never admit it, of course. She obviously thinks he can be replaced by any man; her little flirt with Juan has only confirmed this, and he does not want to humiliate himself any further by grovelling for her attention. But the thought that he is expendable, not only as a man but also as a manager, is hurting him deeply.

They have been working side by side now for a couple of weeks. In a remote and cordial way, Robert has taught her all he knows. She has slowly taken over the daily chores from him and during this period has only asked his advice when it has concerned contacts with agents and clients from abroad. But he is sure that also in this area, he will soon become superfluous… He has to admit, albeit grudgingly, that she does a good job. But then, how could she not? He had organised everything so minutely that everything can run nothing less but smoothly. *But wait till she will hit the first unexpected waves; then we will see whether she is up to the job*, Robert thinks.

Robert, who has been briefly distracted by these unsettling thoughts, turns his attention to the group again and looks at the pathetic bunch in front of him. The group – six heavy-weight executives on an incentive trip – are eager to get into the water. Robert observes them in unspoken disgust. *How can people let themselves go that much?* he asks himself silently. Looking at them; all, except one, were heavily overweight, so they had to dive in t-shirts and shorts, because no wetsuit is big enough to fit them. The good food, beer and wine has ballooned their stomachs, which are now pressing against their tight t-shirts. Their faces are bright red from too much sun and too much booze. Still, these guys have got all they wanted; they have responsible jobs, grand houses, snazzy cars and probably even a respectable-looking wife, who knows nothing about their extramarital exploits during their trip to the Philippines.

Still he manages to put a small smile in his voice when he addresses them: "So, if it's OK with you, we will now ask Juan to do the pre-dive briefing, before you all jump into the water for your first dive in paradise!" The men laugh and put down their beer cans in order to concentrate on the briefing.

Elena stands close behind him and whispers in his ear: "Isn't it supposed to be dangerous to drink before diving?"

The sensation of her moist lips just next to his ear make him shiver, but he replies briskly: "If you think it is wrong, *you* can say something to your guests. They probably will obey you, just like every other man would!" He brusquely turns around to sit down demonstratively with locked arms on the sideboard. He knows he is being childish, but she brings out the worst in him at the moment. Elena clearly does not know how to react to Robert's behaviour and looks helplessly at the group before turning on her heels and disappearing behind the pilothouse. It is a small, insignificant and pitiful victory for Robert. In the end, he thinks grimly, she is going to be the winner and he will lose big time.

The group makes two consecutive dives along the wall, only interrupted by a 60-minute surface interval, which the group uses to down a few more beers. Even Elena, who normally rarely drinks beer, has joined in, laughing, giggling and clearly enjoying the attention the men give her. After a few beers she doesn't seem to mind the lewd looks the intoxicated men give her breasts that are barely covered by a tiny bikini. She even provokes some coarse remarks when she wriggles her slim hips in between two men as she passes them to get some more beers and laughs loudly when one of the younger Americans fondly slaps her half-covered buttocks. Robert has not joined the dive, even though he is a proficient enough scuba diver. He has settled down behind the pilothouse with a paperback and stayed there, well away from the group, as well as during the surface interval, although by then he has difficulties concentrating on the book. He seems unperturbed by all the commotion but inside he is fuming and simultaneously he is annoyed that he gets so riled by the improper behaviour of the girl. He knows she only does it to irritate him.

Not surprisingly, the dive trip is a success and after they return to the resort the Americans noisily disappear into one of the lounges to continue their drinking. In the fading light, Juan and the crew empty the boat and drag the equipment and empty tanks to the storage room. Normally Robert would inspect the proceedings, but after he has spotted Elena mingling with the crew, he decides otherwise. He also withdraws to the lounge, well away from the raucous Americans, and finds a good spot to observe the entrance of the storage room. While he slowly sips his ice-cold rum and coke, he spots Juan approaching and addressing Elena. He wishes he could hear what they are saying. It is obviously an animated discussion, in the course of which Juan sits down next to Elena, far too close to be considered decent. But she is probably still half intoxicated by the beers and they are laughing and fooling around. Robert feels his blood surging to his head and pounding in his temples. Juan touches Elena's shoulder ever so slightly. She puts her hand on Juan's leg, only so briefly. Something is going on there that is not proper, and it is no big secret what it is.

"Oh, Juan, you really make me laugh!" Elena exclaims, slurring slightly.

"I am glad; you seemed unhappy long time, yes?" Juan replies in his broken English. Although Elena is born and bred in the Philippines, she has never learned the local language properly and prefers to speak English, just like most Filipinos of the higher classes. In order to please her, Juan tries his best to be charming in his cumbersome English. Something that never had been a problem to the female tourists, who apparently thought that Juan had other and better qualities than linguistic ones.

"So you want to see me happy, is that it, Juan?" Elena says while she inconspicuously looks over Juan's shoulder at the quiet figure sitting in the shady lounge.

Juan nods eagerly: "Yes Ma'am; I like to make you happy, yes?"

"Very well." Elena seems to have come to a conclusion, nods briefly and business-like before she squeezes Juan's muscular thigh. She bends over to him, breathes briefly in his ear and whispers huskily: "Meet me at the cabana on the cliff tonight at 11."

Juan almost keels over in surprised shock. "Ma'am?" He knows girls are attracted to him and that a little bit of persuasive urging normally makes him successful in achieving the ultimate goal. But he would never have expected that Miss Elena, the daughter of the almighty Mr. Lee, would fall for his tricks; it surprises and simultaneously frightens him.

"You heard me; meet me at the cabana on the cliff at 11!"

Juan swallows and nods.

"And Juan..."

"Yes Ma'am?" comes the suppressed answer.

"Please wash!" Then she smiles drunkenly at him, gets up too swiftly, places a balancing hand on his shoulder and finally manages to walk without tripping, her head high and dark hair flying behind her, towards one of the bungalows, and finally disappears in the fading light of the day.

Robert does not know exactly what had been discussed, but knowing Juan's reputation with the weaker sex and knowing that a drunken Elena was a distinctive, and in her state probably very receptive, representative of exactly that sex, makes him put two and two together and come to the conclusion that what he had been observing had been the foreplay to a more intimate encounter. He decides to continue observing and see what will happen. He is puzzled by his own behaviour; after all he has neither right nor wish to be jealous, but somehow he just can't resist…

This is foolishness; why has she invited Juan to meet her tonight at that remote spot on the cliffs? Elena is laying flat on the king-size bed of the bungalow she has occupied since her arrival at the resort. It is one of the more spacious bungalows, with a living room downstairs and a huge bedroom with veranda upstairs. A large air-con unit is silently blowing cool air into the room. The standard outfit of bamboo furniture has been complemented by various knick-knacks that young women seem to think are indispensable in their rooms; some romantic posters, a few statuettes of swans in various poses, bright pillows, piles of clothes carelessly discarded in the corners and on the chairs during the previous days, and the inevitable array of perfumes, creams and bottles of nail polish. But in her present state, the interior decoration has a nauseating effect on her and her head is spinning. She thinks she has to vomit, but suppresses the urge since she doesn't have the strength to get up and go to the bathroom. She swallows down the bile and tries not to move so that the room will finally come to a standstill. She tries to keep her eyes closed, but has to open them once in a while because her eyelids are irritating her sensitive eyeballs. Subconsciously she wonders how the Americans can keep on downing can after can, while she is thoroughly pissed after only four cans of that horrific brew.

And what has she done with Juan? She could have flirted with anybody, so why did she pick the stud with the biggest libido on the whole island and why in heaven's name did she invite him to meet her at night? What had she been thinking of? But it had just come over her when she had seen Robert observing them from his hiding place; it had made her feel so… rebellious, so she just had to. She tries to recall what she had actually intended, but is unable to remember. Oh, with hindsight she could have handled it better, more maturely. She should just have confronted Robert with his behaviour and put an end to it. He has to go, anyway; she has a pretty good idea how to run the business, all is well arranged and she can do well without that love-sick, over-aged puppy running after her. Not that he is unattractive – far from it! But he is just so… serious in this affair! He had been a great and thoughtful, mature lover and she would have loved to spend more time with him. But not if she can see the wedding bells chiming in his eyes. It is bad enough that her father and mother insist on her meeting 'suitable candidates' every time she is in Dumaguete or goes to their city house in Cebu. She is young and wants to enjoy life before joining the group of old wedded matrons who crowd their homes every weekend! And besides, he is English: nice, ever so polite and with a great sense of humour, but not at all suitable as a husband for a decent Filipino girl. She smiles when she thinks of this last bit, because isn't she actually a very indecent girl, who is going to meet a boy later tonight with the only purpose of having sex? She doesn't feel guilty though. After all, her future husband will surely be happy when she uses her extensive experience to please him between the sheets.

FOUR

The dark sky envelops the small cabana on top of the cliffs almost completely. A storm is approaching, but for the moment all is still as if preparing for the inevitable onslaught. The soothing sound of the crickets in the rustling trees is broken by a sharp snap of a breaking twig that frightens her out of her thoughts: "Juan?"

"Yes Ma'am!"

The moon keeps disappearing at shorter and shorter intervals behind the heavy clouds that race by, but she can still distinguish his lithe body and broad grin. "Stop calling me Ma'am and come here." She drags him into the little cabana, a small bamboo contraption, open on all sides but with a solid *Nippa* roof, and playfully pushes him back onto one of the benches on the side. He lets himself be pushed down and drags her with him. Seemingly helpless, she is now half lying on top of him when he plants a big kiss on her smiling mouth. She parts her lips and he eagerly pokes his agile tongue into her mouth while rubbing his trim body against hers.

Hmmm... Easy to excite him, she thinks before his hand disappears into her loose blouse and squeezes her left breast. Involuntarily her body reacts and her nipples stiffen. Juan notices the distinctive hardening and smiles. He takes her reaction as an invitation and his other hand starts squeezing her buttocks, then creeps to the front and find its way between her legs, where he ferociously starts rubbing her mound.

This is going too fast, way too fast, she thinks while she wrestles to get some air and space. She is more or less sober by now and can finally think clearer about her actions and their consequences. Still angry with Robert, she had been looking forward to this rendezvous, but the possible consequences of

21

sexual intercourse with an employee, and for all matters a very common one, make her recoil now: "Please, Juan, stop it!" she pants.

But it is difficult to stop a hot-blooded Latino once he gets going. Juan's eyes are glowing with lust, the naked skin of his breast shining with sweat and he keeps touching her while pressing her forcefully against the backrest of the bench. She has to distract him and quickly finds a way: "Juan, please look there; the lights on the sea. What is that?"

Juan is rather unwilling to look now that he is rapidly approaching his goal, but her body language tells him he will not achieve anything right now, so he grudgingly turns around to search for the lights. From the cabana, perched precariously on top of the cliffs, they have a wide, unimpeded view of the ocean below. In the distance he can see impenetrable darkness approaching quickly, pushing huge foaming frothy waves in front of it; these are the forerunners of the typhoon that had already pounded Mindanao, the second largest island of the Philippines, leaving destroyed livestock and property in its wake. It had lost some of its destructive might when it travelled over land, but when it reached open water and hit the Sulu Sea it picked up force again and wind speeds increase to almost 140 kph! Fortunately for the inhabitants of Siquijor, the typhoon will veer slightly to the east before reaching their island, and they will therefore be spared the massive destructions the typhoon had created on Mindanao. But the two observers on the cliff do not know that yet. They worriedly eye the wall of utter darkness that approaches their position and an unnerving unease creeps into their minds.

Juan, whose forefathers had been struck many times by similar storms since they had crossed the oceans from present-day Malaysia more than 1500 years earlier, has an instilled respect for the forces of nature. Right now, he has to suppress his instinctive urge to run into the mountains to avoid the full onslaught of the storm. Only the presence of the woman beside him makes him hold his position, lest she would call him a coward. And besides, his curiosity is aroused, because she is right; there are lights out there! Or more correct, there is one strong irregularly blinking light sticking out clearly against the black wall approaching it. But it is not an ordinary light from a passing vessel or the permanently illuminated lights with which the small fishing boats attract their prey. Anyway, it is far too stormy for the fishermen to be outside. And this light is blinking! Juan doesn't know Morse code, but he does notice that this light is blinking with irregular intervals and repeats the same 'code' on and on. "That is strange Ma'am," he reluctantly admits, feeling his unease dwindle to be replaced by some kind of unexplainable curiosity.

"Yes," she whispers. "It looks like Morse!"

"Ma'am?" comes the reply from the dark.

"It doesn't matter," she replies curtly. "Look, there! What's that?" She points at a small light below them on the beach that seems to reply to the Morse code from the sea.

"I don't know Ma'am!" comes the worried reply from the dark. Juan is not an educated man, but with the instincts of an animal he smells when there is trouble lurching ahead of him; better to leave things that need to be left alone, alone.

Unfortunately his partner that night does not have the same instincts and whispers excitedly: "Come on Juan, let's go and have a look!"

Now it is clear to Juan that the only excitement he will find tonight will be on the beach below him, so he reluctantly puts on his shirt again and grudgingly follows Elena down the cliffs.

Robert had followed the whole occurrence, hidden in the darkness behind the cabana, and been a reluctant observer of the brief sexual foreplay, main incident and the whispered conversation afterwards. Several times he had been tempted to jump up and drag the boy away from Elena and stomp him in the face and any other body part he could reach with his large fists, but had decided otherwise in the end. Now he intends to follow them and see what will happen.

The shadowy figure on the beach flashes his light one last time and then waits patiently. While the storm gathers its forces, the figure thinks that this is a perfect night for his purposes; quite stormy, with many clouds and hardly any light. That should prevent any unwanted observers observing what should not be observed. Finally he hears the high-pitched whine of a small outboard engine and a small black shape is lifted out of the water by the surf and smacks down onto the beach while the big wave retracts. The engine is cut and four shadows hastily jump into the shallow water to drag the dinghy out of reach of the waves that try to drag the small vessel backwards into the sea again. The four shadows form a protective cordon in front of the fifth shadowy shape, obviously their leader, who nimbly jumps out of the small vessel. The leader approaches the lonely shadow on the beach and briefly flashes his light into the face of his opposite. "Elder brother!" he exclaims in Chinese, while he respectfully embraces Lee Sr.

"My younger brother Yunlin; welcome!" Lee Sr. breathes back in the same language, while he squeezes his younger brother tightly in his frail arms: "So good to see you after all this time!" He puts his arm around the shoulders of the younger man and leads him towards the rocks. "Speak English please; there's no need for your peasant crew to understand us. I am sorry to be so curt, but a typhoon is approaching and soon you must return to your ship. Do you have the merchandise? Is it safe?"

The younger man nods proudly and shouts a short command in Chinese. One of his men quickly approaches with a large bundle under his arm. He flops it down unceremoniously in front of the two waiting men and, in the small beam of light from the torch of his master, cuts open the bundle to present a square package to his master's older brother.

The latter takes the package eagerly, switches open a pocket knife and makes a short incision through the brown oil paper. He extracts a small morsel of whitish substance, rubs it between his fingers and licks it. A large smile slowly appears on his wrinkly face: "Excellent quality, younger brother!" He then pats his brother on the shoulder and exclaims loudly to make himself heard above the increasing howl of the storm: "You brought your older brother excellent heroin!"

"You hear Ma'am Elena? Heroin!" Juan whispers: "That package is heroin! That is illegal. Is bad!" After they had descended down to the beach, they had approached the small group of men, carefully avoiding open spaces and staying in the shadows of the stunted trees all the time. They are now crouching behind some bushes not even five meters away from the group of Chinese men.

Elena is dumbstruck. Maybe Juan has not noticed who these people were, but she had clearly seen the face of her father when it was illuminated by the torch. And the other man apparently is her uncle, who supposedly had died many years ago in Hong Kong! This does not make sense! What does her father have to do with heroin? He is a trader in copra, corn and other commodities! And why is her supposedly dead uncle suddenly standing on the beach, chirpily alive and delivering heroin to her father? Confused thoughts are swirling in her mind and she can't think straight any more; not here, not now, not with this jabbering Filipino by her side. So she whispers: "Juan, let's go. Let's go home." And she briskly turns around and climbs the steep path up to the cabana again.

Out of respect for his mistress, Juan holds his tongue, but all the way to the top she can feel his accusing eyes burning into her back. When they arrive at the cabana again Juan can no longer hold his silence: "Ma'am Elena. These men are bad men. Heroin, Ma'am Elena... Heroin killed my older brother. Is no good. We have to go for the police!"

"No Juan," she hastily replies: "No police!" Why did he have to be so stubborn? And why is he heading back to the village now? He is not going to the police, is he? No matter how confused Elena is feeling right now, she knows one thing for sure; she cannot allow Juan to go to the police. Not now. Maybe later, after she has talked to her father. It must be a misunderstanding. Yes, that's it; a misunderstanding. But first she has to prevent that fool from notifying the police. She starts to run and quickly gains on the dark figure walking along the cliffs in front of her. "Juan; you must wait!" she pants while she grabs his shirt.

Robert is probably as dumbstruck as Elena when he identifies the dark figure on the beach as his employer Zhiheng Lee, but in contrast to Elena he keeps a clear head. He has observed something that might be useful for his future... And when Elena and Juan climb the hill again, he decides to follow them; he has seen enough on the beach. But just before he leaves his hideout, he hears small sounds of careful feet being placed on the dry leaves covering the sloppy ascent; there are more people following Juan and Elena!

"Did you hear that, older brother?" Apparently Yunlin has picked up an odd sound and now also Lee Sr. is straining his hearing to pick up the sounds his younger brother had heard. But the sea is crashing heavily on the beach and the wind is picking up too, so his older ears are unable to hear the low whispers from Elena and Juan, which the younger ears of Yunlin Lee

25

apparently had picked up. Yunlin does not wait for his brother's reaction and a short command is enough to send one of the obedient shadows on its way. The younger brother waits impatiently for the return of his spider. He does not have to wait long before the shadow returns. It bows before his master and reports in Cantonese: "Master! Two people scaled the cliffs and discussed what they had seen. They know about the heroin!"

"Were you able to identify them?" Younger brother asks brusquely.

"Master! It was dark, but the boy was clearly Filipino and the girl seemed mixed breed. She called him Juan. Her name was Elena."

"My daughter!" Lee Sr. whispers while all colour drains from his face.

"We must act before it is too late!" Younger brother exclaims grimly and with a curt nod sends his man back up the cliffs again. The older brother does, for once, not know what to do and indecisively sees the dark shadow of his brother's minion disappear into the howling darkness of the night...

FIVE

Another day in paradise... Slowly the sky turns from the deepest, tropical night blue into blood red, before the sun finally peeks above the low hills of Siquijor, illuminating the crystal-clear waters of the sea and almost immediately thereafter throwing its blinding light over the shimmering, white sand. The sea is perfectly calm again and nothing indicates to the uninformed observer the stormy events of last night. There is however something disturbing the apparent peace; a dark, longish object is bobbing on the waves, drifting slowly towards the island, and gets stuck behind a low rock on the beach. A couple of children, all of them between six and ten, approach from the distance, running, screaming and once in a while kicking at objects half buried in the sand. The eldest child, the leader of the pack, suddenly stops when he sees a pretty foot with a cute sandal attached to it peeking from behind a large boulder. He sniggers and silently motions his friends to follow him. When they get closer they recognise a shapely caramel coloured leg and naked thighs covered in sand. The sniggering increases; as yet, the children do not realise what they have just discovered and their childlike innocence is still undisturbed. But that changes quickly when they take a quick peek around the rock and the whole scene is majestically spread out for them; a pair of prim young breasts hardly covered by a torn blouse, raven black hair still floating in the sea, creating an aura of innocence around a pretty face with wide open almond eyes that stare lifelessly at the frightened children. The sniggering stops abruptly and a small girl starts to cry while the others stare at the lifeless body in obvious horror. The children's leader, a small compact boy around eleven years of age, keeps his cool and sends one of his friends rushing off to the village for help, while he guides his gang into the shade of the bushes

27

bordering on the beach, where they wait for the grown-ups to take over. The Barangay officials arrive within minutes. They drag the body higher up the beach and easily identify the remains; it is without a shadow of a doubt the daughter of old Mr. Lee, Ma'am Elena Lee, 22 years of age, who, judging from the strange angle between head and torso, apparently died of a broken neck.

One day later, a sweating and panting, well-dressed, youngish gentleman balances across the boarding plank towards the safety of the massive concrete mole that protects the small harbour of Siquijor against the unpredictable forces of the ocean. Since the day before, the wind has increased in strength again and churns up the previously tranquil sea into an unnerving mixture of smaller and larger waves, which with irregular intervals sprays the lingering stevedores on the quay. Following a porter carrying his valise, the man, who is of Chinese origin, is mumbling to himself. He is probably unaware of this fact, since he is fully concentrated on ignoring the churning wet substance below the moving plank, which is his only way to safety now. With a few more rapid steps, he finally, and with obvious relief, reaches the irregular but secure surface of the mole. He urges his porter to greater speed towards the main quay in order to avoid the spraying mist in which the sea is trying to envelop him.

No, Mr. Jonathan Sy is not a friend of the wet elements. Although his grandfather had been a squid fisher from the Chinese island of Penghu, he himself had never been taught the skills of swimming. A fact he has never regretted, since his father, whom he had always admired for his calm, cultured manners, had regularly exclaimed that a true gentleman needs not be able to swim.

In his early youth, Mr. Sy had assumed that his father, who had acquired a scholarship at Cambridge, had picked up this morsel of erudite wisdom during his college years, but later his mother had confided in him and whispered that his father was just plain frightened of water and that he did not even dare to dip his head under the surface of his bath water to rinse his head! This was, of course, after his father had died, since otherwise his mother would never have considered such a faux pas. But Mr. Sy did not mind. He could even, to some extent, understand his father's phobia, although he himself, a mature man 36 years of age, is not afraid to submerge himself totally in his bath water. He does however have some qualms about entering the deeper waters of a pool, not to speak of the unimaginative horrors of a deep hostile sea. So normally Mr. Sy refrains from approaching deep natural waters and therefore naturally also resents travelling by sea. But alas, in the course of his duties as a special criminal investigator in the force of the Philippine National Police, he once in a while has to leave the safety of the large island of Luzon, where the capital city of Manila is to be found, and hence where the national headquarters for his division are placed. When his duties force him off the mainland, he prefers to fly, but unfortunately in this case the murder has taken place on Siquijor, an island without a proper airfield. Irritatingly enough, the commissioner had, hinting at budget restrictions, declined his request for a private plane, which could have comfortably dropped Mr. Sy off on one of the wide beaches. So he was resigned to the fact that he had to make the trip by sea.

Mr. Sy is hugely relieved when he finally reaches the end of the quay, where an officious-looking person is questioningly peering at the unfamiliar faces from under his peaked cap. Penetrating black eyes look at Mr. Sy from above a flat, wide nose set in a broad dark face. When the person sees Mr. Sy appear from behind his porter, he drags up his Sam Brown belt, bellows to the porter to hand him the valise and identifies himself: "Chief of Police Daniel Arozo, a great honour to meet you, Sir!" So his reputation as one of the sharpest minds in criminal investigation had already preceded him, Mr. Sy ponders. He graciously bows slightly towards the huge man with his considerable potbelly and formally introduces himself: "Inspector Jonathan Sy, special investigator; it is a pleasure to meet you!"

"You must be tired after the voyage," the older man bellows while he turns on the heels of his shining boots and heads towards a rampaged old Buick Riviera, which is steaming in the sun. He opens the creaking passenger door for Mr. Sy, unceremoniously throws the valise on the back seat and places his formidable bulk behind the steering wheel. With some effort he manages to get the vehicle started and while they swerve out of the harbour compound onto the dusty road, he shouts over the hammering noises penetrating the passenger compartment from below the hood: "I suggest I bring you to 'Uncle Joes'; it's the most comfortable inn in town, so we have chosen this for you. I am staying there myself most of the time. You can first freshen up and then we will have a drink on the veranda."

"How far is it?" Mr. Sy asks loudly, while swallowing down the bile that had spontaneously erupted into his mouth when Chief Arozo had started on the shaking, stomach-churning trip, which so much reminds Mr. Sy of the movements of the sea vessel he had just left.

"Not so far," comes the equally loud answer; "maybe two miles up the hill." Arozo points vaguely to the left while absentmindedly turning the steering wheel into the same direction as his pointing finger, thereby almost causing a head-on collision with a lorry approaching on the opposite lane. At the last moment, however, the chief gives a firm tug at the wheel and the heavy car is tossed back into its own lane while the lorry with its petrified driver disappears behind them in the dusty distance. Mr. Sy is used to the reckless traffic in Manila, but it seems the islanders here are a class above that. The trip ends abruptly when the chief slams on the brakes and the car comes to a wiggly standstill in front of a pretty wooden colonial house with a large porch. The chief kills the engine and Mr. Sy stumbles out of the car to be enveloped by bellowing dust clouds created by the now slowly ticking Buick.

"Please follow," the chief bellows while he tugs Mr. Sy's valise under his arm and scales the steps onto the porch. "Uncle Joe!" He loudly repeats the question again into the shady darkness of the house: "UNCLE JOEEE!"

"Yes, yes, yes…" comes the frail answer from a bent person, who waggles, supported by a stout walking stick, towards the two men. "What makes you think I didn't hear you the first time? I could hear your car from miles away! When will you finally get yourself a proper car, Danny?" It is obvious that the old man is an American since he is pale white and his words are voiced in a drawly Texas accent.

The chief embraces the thin American and turns him proudly towards Mr. Sy: "This is Uncle Joe, my godfather. His countrymen somehow forgot to take him along when they left in '45!" Despite his bantering tone, it is obvious that the chief adores the old man, and vice versa. He can't be stopped from telling Uncle Joes' life story, or at least the part since '45, when he had been a liaison officer to the Philippine resistance and was honourably discharged from the army. Unwilling to return back to Texas, Joe had decided to use his inheritance to start a home, in the very house they were standing in now, for orphaned war children in order to repay his debt to the kind

Philippine people, who had, more than once, saved his life during the four years he spent fighting the Japanese army on various islands of the Philippine archipelago. The chiefs' parents, who both had been fighting the Japs from the jungle and were permanently detached to Uncle Joe's unit in '44, had had their eldest son Daniel along, and when the parents got killed in a shoot-out, it was unavoidable that 'Uncle Joe' become the godfather to the young boy.

But the orphanage had been closed down almost twenty years ago, when the last boy left the place to move to Dumaguete to study. Uncle Joe was alone again, and since he had used his last cent on his orphans, he now had to choose whether to return to remote Texas, a place he hardly remembered, or to stay and try to make a living somehow. His orphans eventually made the choice for him, and in a concerted effort they started to transform the dilapidated orphanage into a new form of livelihood for their Uncle Joe. They had cajoled and bribed the local citizens and businesses into donating timber, paint, nails, plumbing, furniture, mattresses and pillows and turned the building into a comfortable inn. Some children of the original orphans now patrolled the harbour to catch any innocent tourist who needed a comfortable place to stay and guided them to Uncle Joe's place. So after a short while, 'Uncle Joe's' became one of the most popular places to stay on Siquijor.

"A wonderful story; so life confirming, isn't it?" Mr. Sy exclaims.

The chief nods vigorously while he beams at his godfather: "Yes, Uncle Joe has done good and has been rewarded amply; everybody loves him!"

A small blush colours the parched cheeks of the old man. *Charming!*, Mr. Sy thinks. Then the chief excuses them and drags Mr. Sy onto the veranda, where he invites him to sit down in one of the comfortable rattan chairs. With a sigh, he sits down himself and reaches towards the small fridge standing next to his chair. The chair groans frighteningly when he bends forward to drag out a chilled bottle of old Tanduay rum from the humming cubicle.

"Let's drink to life…" he exclaims, while he fills the two glasses with some ice cubes and a liberal shot of local rum, "… and talk about death!"

So no short freshening up in my room and a relaxed nap, but immediately to business! Mr. Sy thinks. *Ah well, let's get this over with then!*

"Yes, let's drink!" he replies, while he lifts his glass towards the big policeman, observing him over the rim of his glass thinking: *Can this man be of any use in my investigation, or will he be a nuisance, like most local policemen?*

"So, Chief Arozo; please tell me about the case. Don't leave out any details!"

The huge man sighs, takes a large swig and places his empty glass on the table. "Another shot? No? Ah well, then I can just as well begin, I suppose." But before he starts to report his findings, he quickly refills his own glass. "The girl's called Elena Lee. Really a lovely girl; a bit flippant, but nice. Her father is old Mr. Lee; you heard about him?"

Mr. Sy shakes his head in denial. "Only from the report, Chief Arozo."

"No? Well, he is a first generation Chinese immigrant from the province of Hunan. He came here all alone in, oh it must have been 1949, and started a small trading firm. Now he owns plantations, shipping companies, shops, pawn houses and trading companies all over the Visayas. He is mainly residing in Dumaguete or Cebu, but often comes back here. He built his first house here, you know. Over there, behind the cliffs."

The chief vaguely points southward. "Nice house; extended several times, with a huge private garden." He opens the fridge again for a refill: "Another shot? Oh, come on, just a little one!"

He forces another glass of rum on Mr. Sy, who patiently reclines in his chair while absorbing every little detail of what the chief tells him. This is one of Mr. Sy's strengths; being a patient listener, he absorbs all information in his formidable mind, moving and shifting it, like pieces of a gigantic puzzle, until he can finally identify the full picture that, more often than not, leads him to solving yet another murder case.

Mr. Sy hardly ever drinks in public, afraid to lose his composure and turn into a happily smiling babbling idiot, like most Filipinos do once they have a few glasses too many. Not that Mr. Sy dislikes alcohol, but he prefers to drink it alone in the intimate privacy of his apartment in Manila, where he, undisturbed by onlookers, can enjoy the relaxing effects of the alcohol. But today he does not wish to enjoy that effect, since he knows he has to keep his mind clear. He feels like a lonely hunter who has picked up a faintly lingering smell of a track, and now has to sharpen his senses to utter clarity in order to pursue his prey to the inevitable end. And for that reason, the second glass of excellent rum ends where the first one had preceded it; unnoticed by the chief, slowly trickling through the floorboards of the veranda.

The chief has by now cleared the third glass and opens the fridge for the next refill, not bothering anymore to return the bottle to its chilled hideout. Even though one would think the bulk of the man should have been able to absorb huge quantities of alcohol, without visible effects on the receiver, the chief is in this respect typically Filipino. He, as all Asians, lacks the specific enzymes that enable Caucasians to break down alcohol quickly into more innocent ingredients, and he therefore quite soon becomes victim of the debilitating effects of the liquid. So the further he progresses in his report, the more slurring his speech and the more honest the words become.

"He's a bit of a mystery for us policemen; looks kind and is very courteous, loves his daughter… Sorry; I must say *loved* his daughter very much, but there are many indications that he is involved in illegal activities."

There is a long pause. The chief stares towards the panorama of the purple and brown rolling hills while he absentmindedly refills his glass again.

"Like what?" Mr. Sy says, trying to get the story rolling again.

"Uh? Oh, like smuggling, blackmail, extortion and, worst of all, drugs. No proof as yet, but you develop a feeling after twenty five years on the force; you know what I mean?"

Mr. Sy knows exactly what the chief means; this feeling, this unerring instinct that good policemen all over the world seemed to possess, very often makes these men follow a track, which initially seemed less than likely to lead to solving the case, but actually makes them hit bullseye in the end. So Mr. Sy patiently urges the chief to continue.

"For example; how come a seemingly penniless immigrant can amass a fortune and build up an empire within less than ten years? How come, when we pick up little criminals and middlemen involved in these crimes, they are also Chinese and more often than not from the same town or province like old Lee? They are a secretive lot, these Chinese. Oh sorry, Inspector; no offence intended!" The chief blushes slightly in embarrassment when he remembers the race of his visitor, but Mr. Sy waves the excuse away and asks the chief to continue.

"Well, it's almost impossible to crack these guys; they'd rather die than give up their patrons. But we manage to crack the occasional hood, and you know what? Every time, the name of old Lee pops up!"

The chief takes a big swig. "No proof or evidence of course, and every time the hood is finally willing to testify, he meets with an 'accident' in jail;

slips in the showers or falls into a machine. So..." he takes another swig that empties his 5th glass, "... officially Lee is still clean as a whistle, but we all know that something dark is hidden behind that polite smiling face!"

The chief refills his glass again, almost toppling off his chair in the process. "And you know what? Now, all of a sudden, since yesterday, his brother is here! His *brother*! The guy always claimed his brother was dead! And now he's here, alive and well! And you know who the guy is?"

Mr. Sy does not know.

"It's little Yunlin; one of the head men of the Hong Kong triads, and their specialist in the drugs trade!"

That *is* a surprise to Mr. Sy, who knows of Yunlin Lee, also called Little Yunlin. But he did not know the man was on Siquijor and apparently related to old Mr. Lee. "How do you know of this fact, Chief?"

The chief clears his throat: "Yunlin was briefly incarcerated in Hong Kong, but was soon released because the witnesses refused to confirm their previous accusations against him. While he was in jail, he shared his cell with a young Filipino who was accused of money trafficking. As fate wanted, this man, Tata, was one of our orphans and he begged me to help him out. I was only a young and much slimmer policeman back then..." The chief pauses to pat his considerable belly: "... But somehow I managed to convince my colleagues in Hong Kong that taking a few dollars into the Crown colony was not a matter of organised crime, and they let him go." The chief pauses again and probably recollects the times he had been young, slim and virile. "Anyway, when I visited Tata in his cell, I noticed this small, well-groomed Chinese man, so obvious out of place in the overcrowded cell, and Tata confirmed it was the famous drug lord Little Yunlin. The very same man I met when I visited old Lee on his estate yesterday to interrogate possible witnesses!"

"And?"

The chief has paused again, apparently falling into a state of semi-unconsciousness, and Mr. Sy has to get him going again.

"Uh? What? Oh, he didn't recognise me today, obviously. I mean; it was a long time ago. I have changed, and anyway, I am just another Filipino, right? But he hadn't changed! OK, a few slight wrinkles in his immobile, tight face, but still the same sharkey smile with these little teeth – a man to dislike on first sight!" The chief visibly shudders. "For me, this only confirms my suspicion; old Lee is a hood, no matter how much good he does for the community and how friendly he is to our people; once a hood, always a hood!" With a big burp, he slumps back in his chair and mumbles: "But we can't get hold of him; slippery eel!" Another pause is made, while the chief refills his glass yet again: "Anyway, that's just a bit of background on the girl's family." The chief suddenly jerks up while he brightly exclaims: "But I have completely forgotten the girl's mother, Cornelia! Such a lovely lady; very classy and charming! Spanish, you know! I know her from before; her family supported the orphanage and I met her several times then; beautiful girl! How could a girl like that marry a scoundrel like Lee?" By now the chief is whispering and no longer seems to notice the presence of his visitor. He turns uncomfortably in his chair: "Money, I suppose. Cornelia's family lost their fortune when her daddy lost big in the stock market. After that he couldn't support their lifestyle anymore, so he married Cornelia to this nouveau riche Chinese hood, just so they could stay in their palace in Bacolod, pah!"

The chief almost spits out the words. Mr. Sy wonders whether his lively interest in Cornelia is more than just professional.

The chief reclines in his chair, closes his eyes and sighs: "Well, that's how life goes once in a while. Now she's stuck with the guy and her daughter is dead." For a while, the laborious breathing of the chief and the chirping of the crickets are the only sounds to break the humid silence of the afternoon. Then he slowly opens his eyes and tries to focus on his guest: "Hmmm… must have dozed off a bit. I am a bad host!"

Mr. Sy tries to protest, but the chief shakes his head vigorously; most probably to expel the hazy heaviness that has enveloped his mind. "I am, really I am. Here we are, drinking rum in the afternoon, and you haven't had a chance to freshen up yet!"

The chief heaves his heavy body out of the creaking chair and motions Mr. Sy with an uncertain movement to follow him inside. He almost bumps into Uncle Joe, who is sitting on a stool just inside, unsteadily passes him and rushes toward the stairs leading to the first floor.

"Come, come; Uncle Joe has prepared his best room. It's the Presidential Suite!" He chuckles briefly: "A private joke of his, since the president of the local rotary club once used it to spend the night with his mistress. And when the man stole the towels, Uncle Joe decided to immortalise the guy! He loves to tell anyone who cares to listen how the room got its name."

Mr. Sy smiles politely while the chief finds his way down the dim corridor, once in a while finding support against the walls. He leads him to the last room on the right and with a grand movement opens the door. "Here we are; the Presidential Suite!"

It is a nice, airy room with a great view over the Sulu Sea that is glistening in the distance.

"If you need me, I'll be right next door." And off he stumbles.

A door slams, water is rushing and after a few minutes Mr. Sy can hear heavy rumbling snoring sounds escape from the room next to him. Mr. Sy smiles before opening the tap over the washbasin to wash his hands. After drying them, he silently opens his door and nimbly walks down the stairs. In the shady hallway he meets Uncle Joe.

"So you heard everything we talked about, Uncle Joe?"

"You can't sleep? Too exited about the case?" comes the answer from the old man.

Mr. Sy smiles. "Let's go outside and drink the last dregs of the rum."

The old man lowers himself in the chair the chief so recently has maltreated and sighs: "No need to waste precious rum; I don't drink it and you really don't seem to have a taste for it either!" he says, while nodding towards the dark stain discolouring the floorboards.

Mr. Sy blushes; it was rare that he was caught out: "I am sorry; I didn't want to insult the kindness of the chief, but I need to keep a clear head during my investigations!"

"Quite so, my boy; right you are! And a clear head you will need; this whole matter is complicated, believe me!"

Mr. Sy looks questioningly at the old man. "How so?"

"Well," the old man pauses and sighs, while he tries to make himself comfortable in the creaking chair, "it seems like a simple case, doesn't it? A dead girl washes up on the shore. Her boyfriend, a local dive master working in the very same resort the girl is managing, already told the police *before* the girl was found that something was amiss with her, and vehemently denies that he had pushed her off the cliff. Odd, isn't it? How did he know the girl was dead? And how did he know the girl was pushed off the cliff? The police found that out only several hours later, when they found small bits of textile hanging on the brushes lining the cliffs. And it was only much later that they managed to identify these bits as being identical to the textiles of the girl's blouse. How could the boy have known? So the police question the boy, who immediately breaks down and goes into an emotional fit; crying, shouting that he had loved the girl; that he hadn't meant to hurt her, but that he had to report what he had seen on the beach."

"Oh?" Mr. Sy utters a small questioning sound.

"Yes; Juan, that's the dive master I was talking about, pretended that he saw smugglers, drug smugglers in fact, on the beach and that the girl tried to stop him to report it. But he felt obliged to do so. Seems his brother died of an overdose and Juan is therefore very much against drugs. So when she held on to him, he pushed her away and ran off."

"And what do the police say?" Mr. Sy asked.

"Well, they don't say a lot, but our friend upstairs has an imaginative mind and considers various options. He actually seems to think the boy is innocent, although evidence and the coroner's statement say the opposite!"

"What's in the coroner's statement then?"

Uncle Joe smiles knowingly. "That's still confidential material, but Daniel left the provisional report lying around in the parlour and I had a peek at it!"

"Well?" Mr. Sy asks impatiently.

"It says the girl died of a broken neck. No water in the lungs. Many abrasions on legs, arms and torso. But the most remarkable fact; there were some remnants of skin tissue under her nails!"

Mr. Sy bends forward: "And do the police know where this skin tissue stems from?"

"Not definitely, but the blood group coincides with the blood group of Juan: O negative! Not a very common blood group in this area!"

"But not totally uncommon either?"

"No," Uncle Joe admits. "The evidence is therefore still circumstantial and there are no eye witnesses that he pushed her, although there are several witnesses who saw them together before the incident."

"You are well informed, Uncle Joe! So, who are these witnesses?"

"Let me see: her father, her uncle, Robert Delsey – that's the manager of the resort – Nonoy, the resort guard, and some members of the Torosa family;

37

they have a lot next to the path leading to the cliffs."

"Well, well; an open and shut case then? What do *you* think, Uncle Joe?"

Uncle Joe winks back at him. "It doesn't matter what I think, as long as *your* mind is as sharp as they tell me it is. So get going, young man; unearth the truth and make the guilty pay for their sins!"

Mr. Sy smiles a knowing smile and counters: "I think your mind would not have been amiss in our department, Uncle Joe. Thank you for your help!"

"What help, my boy? You will uncover the truth even without my help. Not that I am unwilling to take my share, but maybe you should first get some other opinionated impressions. Then we can talk again later."

"I will, Uncle Joe. I will." With these words, Mr. Sy rises and takes his leave. He puts on his hat and walks down the hot and dusty road towards the small village, where, yet still unknown to him, further unfortunate incidents await him.

SIX

Mr. Sy stops in front of a ramshackle bamboo hut surrounded by a rotting fence of the same material. In Manila, you could knock on a door to seek entrance. Here you have to shout to attract the attention of the inhabitants. Mr. Sy does not like to shout, so he calmly waits until a small, grubby face appears at the fence.

"Where's your father?" Mr. Sy asks softly in Tagalog. As a reply, the boy turns around and shouts, "PAPA, a towney is here for you!"

An undernourished small figure appears from the darkness of a shed, rubbing fish scales from his fingers. "Yes Sir? What can I do for you?"

"You are Mr. Torosa?"

"Yes Sir!" The figure nods vigorously and opens his mouth in a wide grin, revealing a few stained teeth left in his dark gums: "Antonio Torosa. And this is my son, Rolly!" he pats the grubby child on his naked back: "Open the gate and let Sir in!"

The kid does as he is told and then runs off to spread the news of the arrival of a 'towney' to the rest of the village.

"Sit, please sit, Sir!" The fisherman beckons Mr. Sy to sit down on the bench in the shade of an acacia tree. "How can I be of service, Sir?"

"My name is Inspector Jonathan Sy. I am a special investigator from Manila, here to look into the untimely death of Ms. Elena Lee. I understand you knew the lady?"

"Yes Sir." Again the fisherman bobs his head, so strong one almost gets the impression it might soon fall off. "I have been selling my fish to the resort for many years now and also had the honour to meet Ma'am Elena many times, especially since she took over from Sir Robert."

"Oh, I thought Sir Robert is the manager?"

"Oh yes, he was." Again, vigorous nodding: "But old Mr. Lee told her some months ago to take over the management and Sir Robert has to leave soon." Then suddenly the eyes of the skinny fishermen go moist: "Oh, but that is maybe not so any longer, now that Ma'am Elena is dead." And then, more cheerfully: "So maybe Sir Robert will stay now! Sir Robert is a good man; hard but just!"

"Right so, well, well…" Mr. Sy ponders. "So, Mr. Torosa, please tell me about the last time you saw Ms. Lee."

The face of the fisherman clouds over: "It was so sad… Juan Aldones, you know; a real womaniser. No honour… Well, Juan was trying to charm Ma'am Elena. And Ma'am Elena… well, after her fall-out with Sir Robert, she was very upset and maybe lonely. I don't know. Well, at least she didn't tell Juan off openly and maybe… well, maybe he saw a chance. Ridiculous, of course; Ma'am Elena is a real lady. Her mother is Ma'am Cornelia. She is the daughter of Don Pedro and his family is from Madrid!" the fisherman proclaims proudly, as if some of the nobility of this family had rubbed off on him during the years he has supplied his fish to them.

"I am sure he tried to seduce her up there at the cabana. And when she refused, he must have attacked her to get his ways. And she would never let herself be dishonoured, of course. So she must have tried to fight him. Well… the path is narrow up there and in the dark you hardly see the edge. And it was very dark and stormy last night, Sir. So maybe she fell, but more likely he pushed her; yes, he probably pushed her! But anyway, she dropped down the cliff. You know it's a fall of more than 30 metres! Of course poor Ma'am Elena died!"

Mr. Sy has let the man jabber on to make him feel relaxed and comfortable, but now it was time to explore the hard facts. "Yes, very sad indeed! She was a beautiful girl, wasn't she?"

The thin figure nods with tears in his eyes.

"And there was no mistaking it was her who passed by your house two days ago?"

"Oh no, Sir; I recognised her!"

"Even though it was dark and stormy, as you say?"

"Ah, I know what you mean, Sir! But we have a light opposite the gate;

Mr. Lee had it mounted some time ago, so he could see the turn-off to his cabana even at night!"

And indeed, now Mr. Sy can see a bare light bulb hanging in a coconut tree on the other side of the path. "So no mistaking her for somebody else?"

"Oh no, Sir! And I also recognised Juan! He came by on his way to the cabana shortly after; no mistake about that! Although it was late, very late."

"So why were you up then?"

"My cow, Sir. It was restless because of the storm and we expect it to calve soon, so I kept my eyes on her. And at night she is always tied to the fence over there." The fisherman nods to a small dusty part of hard earth in the corner of his property. "So when I lie here on the bench, I have a good view of her *and* the path!"

He smiles triumphantly. "Ma'am Elena was whistling; maybe she was afraid of the *wog wog*! So I recognised her at once! *And* I recognised Juan. Also when he rushed back to the village, alone, maybe half an hour later. He was running, panting, speaking to himself."

"What did he say?"

"Oh, that I don't know, Sir. But he was upset; *that* was clear!"

"How do you know?"

The fisherman just shrugged in reply.

"And Ma'am Elena?"

The fishermen casts his eyes down in apparent shame and answered in a little voice: "I don't know, Sir. I mean, how could I know something had happened to Ma'am Elena?"

"So what *did* you do?"

"I followed Juan, Sir. I thought he was up to something important, so I didn't want to miss it!"

"And…"

"Well Sir, he went to his uncle. That's Roberto Aldones; he's the Barangay secretary. They talked a long time and then his father and some more family members came. And they talked more."

"And what did you do all this time?"

"Oh, I was in the house of my auntie, opposite the Aldones compound, so I could see it all. I couldn't hear what they said, but they were all very upset and discussed all the time!"

41

"And then?"

The fisherman gets more and more excited: "Then they called Ricky, our Barangay captain, and they discussed very loudly. And then one of the boys left and came back with Chief Arozo. You know; he is a second degree uncle of Juan."

"Is that right?" Mr. Sy replies pensively. "How interesting this all is… But back to Ms. Lee and Juan going up to the cabana; were there any people, before or after they went up, who followed the same path?"

"I am not sure, but I don't think so Sir; I am a light sleeper, so I would have noticed."

By that time more and more spectators, called in by the exited Torosa Jr., had gathered in front of the fence and are curiously observing the well-clad man from Manila. Mr. Sy rises, confident in his knowledge that he would not get any more useful information out of the fisherman.

"Thank you, Mr. Torosa. This has been an enlightening conversation; you have been a great help!"

The skinny fisherman beams proudly: "Glad to help the Manila police! If you need more information, you know where to find me!"

"Yes, Mr. Torosa. Thanks again for your time." Mr. Sy passes though the throng of curious on-lookers on his way to his next witness. He has the premonition that this is going to be a very different case in a very different setting.

SEVEN

Mr. Sy is glad to be out of the glaring sun, because, even though it has almost disappeared behind the extinguished volcanoes of Negros Island, it still has a lot of strength at this time of the year. So after the long walk to the Lee estate, Mr. Sy is sweating profusely under his lightweight linen suit. A tall, white-chalked wall, here and there covered by masses of bougainvillea, surrounds the perimeter. The main entrance is shaded by a few large mango trees, with paper envelopes protecting the vulnerable fruits against bats, shimmering in the setting sun. Mr. Sy rings the old-fashioned handle-bell next to the gate house and can faintly hear its chiming through the great house, the roof of which is just visible above the waving palm trees in the garden. After a moment, a small door in the main gate is opened by a gardener, who smilingly invites the officer to come in. Mr. Sy marches to the main house, a large pile with a design vaguely resembling a French country retreat, and stops at the wide stairs leading to the French windows that apparently make out the entrance to the house. Here a housemaid in uniform donning a stiff white apron awaits him. When he asks for Mr. Lee, his credentials are taken and he is shown into the library, a large high-vaulted room next to the entrance hall with a few bookshelves, several tables piled high with popular magazines and many vases with tall, yellow canna flowers. The pictures and mirrors in the room are covered with plain white sheets. The large doors lead to a terrace and the windows are all open to allow a light breeze to enter. It would still have been oppressively hot in the room were it not for several fans rotating lazily under the ceiling. Their air movement is sufficient to make the temperatures bearable.

Mr. Sy does not have to wait long before he hears small and hasty footsteps in the hallway, and a middle-aged, delicately built lady enters the room and stops in surprise when she sees Mr. Sy. Even though middle-aged, she is still a remarkably attractive woman with bright, almond-shaped dark eyes in a finely chiselled face. Her black dress cannot hide the shapely curves she still seems to possess.

When she steps forward and smiles uncertainly, small wrinkles appear around her eyes: "Oh, I am sorry. I did not know we had guests. I am Mrs. Lee!"

Mr. Sy takes her outstretched hand and holds it briefly. "My condolences for your loss, Mrs. Lee. I am Special Investigator Sy. If it is not too inconvenient, I would like to have a few words with your husband."

"Ah, you are a colleague of Daniel then?"

"Chief Arozo? In a way, Madam. I have been sent by Manila headquarters to look into the sad death of your daughter Elena."

Upon hearing her daughter's name, the elegant lady visibly slumps and Mr. Sy can feel that behind this composed surface is a mother ravaged by the loss of her only daughter. A mother who, because of her upbringing and standing, is unable to show her grief too obviously. But grieving she obviously does, albeit not in public. Mrs. Lee straightens her back again and quietly answers, "I will call for him then." And she leaves the room in a swift stride.

Yes, Mr. Sy thought, *I can well imagine why the chief is attracted to Cornelia Lee.*

Mr. Lee's arrival is less swift; the person who approaches Mr. Sy is completely clad in white and uses a walking cane to support himself. His entrance is slow and ponderous, but his presence immediately fills the room. He is not a tall man, nor is his attire very prepossessing, but he exudes the air of a kind gentleman, with a pure radiation of power and confidence. And, as opposed to Mrs. Lee, the investigator cannot observe any traces of grief in the immobile and unreadable face of the old man. Without greeting, Lee Sr. lowers himself into a large comfortable chair next to the reading table, while beckoning Mr. Sy to sit opposite him on a far less comfortable, straight-backed chair. "So you are the investigator from Manila. They sent you to catch the murderer of my daughter."

It seems to be a statement and not a question. Involuntarily, Mr. Sy is impressed by the natural authority of the older man. But then, any man in his position needs authority to keep his empire intact and expanding.

"Yes Sir, I am Special Investigator Sy and I have been ordered to investigate the untimely death of your daughter. I would hereby like to express my honest condolences for your loss."

Lee Sr. grumbles in reply and says: "She was my only daughter; beautiful, just like her mother, and bright. A bit lively, but youngsters are like that, aren't they?"

So the old man has some feelings after all, Mr. Sy thinks. "I am afraid I have no children of my own, Sir."

"Hmm..." comes the answer. "I wanted her to take up some responsibility; all my children hold responsible positions in the firm and I wanted her to start by taking over the management of Bayun Resort; an easy beginning, don't you think?"

"If you say so, Sir. Can we please start with the happenings on the day your daughter died?"

"Was murdered, you mean!" the old man erupts. "My daughter was murdered by this good-for-nothing beach-boy Aldones, who is now hiding behind the back of the Barangay captain and that oaf Chief Arozo. But *I* will get to him, if you don't do your duty!"

"Sir, with all respect for your loss, we do not know for certain that Juan Aldones was the perpetrator. It is for me to ascertain, after having heard all witnesses and investigated all proof, how your daughter died and, in the case that her death was not accidental, who the possible murderer of your daughter is when I present my final report."

This does not seem to be a satisfactory answer for Lee Sr.: "Listen, it is obvious that she was killed by this Aldones fellow. Just ask around; everybody knows he's a useless individual. He's got no background, no morals, no scruples! And now he's killed my daughter!"

"Let's look at this in a rational way Sir, and I am sure we will find the perpetrator together."

This answer seems to calm the older man a bit. "Rational? OK, I can be rational. Get on with it then, Inspector."

"So Mr. Lee, on what facts do you base your assumption that Juan Aldones killed your daughter?"

Mr. Lee rises from his chair, bends down towards Mr. Sy and whispers: "Have you met the boy, Mr. Sy?"

Mr. Sy had to deny that he had.

"Well, if you had, you would have known the boy is good for nothing. Diving and womanising is all that's on his mind. His mother left him when he was a toddler, so maybe that's the reason he doesn't respect women. Use them; yes. But respect? None whatsoever! He only approached my girl to further his so-called 'status', his ego; something to brag about when he is with the boys. The daughter of the boss; isn't that a great trophy? So of course he was chasing her! And in a weak moment, Elena encouraged him. Nothing serious, obviously, but he thought he had a chance. And when she, for obvious reasons, rejected him, he must have blown his fuse and killed her. You know how hot-blooded these Filipino boys can be, Inspector. Latino temperament and all?"

Mr. Sy nods to encourage the old man to continue.

"Besides, I personally saw him hiding in the bushes down at the beach and chasing after my daughter when she left."

"So you personally saw him that night?" the inspector asks, surprised.

"Yes indeed! I was having a stroll along the beach with my younger brother, who had just arrived from Hong Kong, when we heard them whispering in the bushes. We were still some distance away, but could distinctly hear them. Elena was plainly rejecting him and he seemed to urge her to stay so he could have his way with her. She then ran away and he chased after her. If only I had been younger and could have run after them, I could have prevented this catastrophe. But alas, Inspector, as you can see I am an old man and even scaling the path towards the cabana is a tedious task for me nowadays." The old man briefly falls silent before continuing: "I asked my brother to go after them, but he just laughed. He doesn't know Juan and what he is capable of, so he didn't take the situation seriously. And I... I almost believed him; I wanted to believe that nothing would happen to my little girl. I felt so helpless, powerless... A strange emotion for a man in my position."

Mr. Sy nods: "I understand, Sir. I have a question, though; it seems that Juan claims he saw drug smugglers on the beach. Do you happen to know anything about that?"

Lee Sr. laughed bitterly. "Inspector, a man who has killed a girl in cold blood will invent any story to point the attention of the authorities in another direction, don't you think?"

"Well, that is not uncommon, Sir. As I said, I have not yet had the chance to interrogate the young man personally. I was just curious to hear your opinion."

"And now you have it, Inspector; the plain and simple truth."

"Yes Sir. I will make a note of that and mention it in my report."

"You do that, Inspector, and please put that boy behind bars before something worse will happen to him."

With that, the old man rises and, without any further words, leaves Inspector Sy alone in the room.

Mr. Sy leaves the mansion in a pensive mood and lets the conversation go through his head while he walks the long way back to the Uncle Joe's inn. The throng of youngsters that has accompanied him for a while falls back when they see that nothing more exiting is happening and Mr. Sy is finally left alone with his thoughts. Old Mr. Lee felt sincere in his emotions, but the words were not convincing. It would take another meeting to establish a better truth.

EIGHT

Shortly after nightfall, Mr. Sy is back in the inn and finds the chief in the kitchen, fervently chopping up onions, peppers and sayote at the large table that dominates the room, while Uncle Joe is cleaning a chicken.

"You like chicken, Inspector?" Uncle Joe asks and, without waiting for an answer, he continues: "Grab a glass and pour yourself a drink. You must be thirsty after your long walk back from the mansion."

"So you already know I was there?" Mr. Sy asks, surprised.

"Uncle Joe knows everything," the chief replies, "he has an army of young spies that reports everything of importance to him."

"Is that so?"

Uncle Joe smiles: "It's a small community, Inspector; difficult to keep anything secret. It's not like Manila, you know!"

"So do you also know what was discussed?"

"No, but I am sure you will tell us now!"

Mr. Sy can not help himself but laugh at this cheeky reply. "Uncle Joe, this is an official police investigation and not some sort of social visit I can discuss amongst friends, no matter how dear they are to me! But I can tell you this much; Mr. Lee points his finger in the direction of Juan Aldones. He has no doubts whatsoever."

"Pah…" Uncle Joe replies. "The man might be bright in other fields, but he must be a fool to think so. Juan might consider himself to be the Philippine version of Casanova, but he has a head and a heart like this little animal." He slams his cleaver down to severe the head from the body of the chicken: "He just isn't up to things like that. *And* he is honest."

"What makes you think that?" Mr. Sy asks.

48

The chief is quick to answer: "He has never lied to his family, ever. No matter what he did, he never lied about it. He'd rather face the consequences than lie to his family."

"A noble trait, so unusual for a Filipino!" Mr. Sy murmurs.

The chief does not appear to have heard the comment and continues, "So if Juan says he did not kill the girl, not even by accident, I think I can believe him!"

Uncle Joe nods his consent.

"And since you are related to him, he must speak the truth to you too, is that right, Chief?" Mr. Sy asks.

The chief is slightly taken aback, but recovers quickly: "Yes, it's true that Juan is remotely related to me, so I know the boy, and therefore know he wouldn't lie. He knows that the consequences of a lie discovered are worse than telling an uncomfortable truth straight away."

"A truly bright boy, Chief. So let's, for argument's sake assume the boy is indeed innocent; who then killed the girl?"

The ensuing silence becomes longer and longer, while the chief and Uncle Joe look at each other and a silent communication takes place between the old man and his godchild. The chief finally gives in: "Look Inspector, at this stage we are all speculating and there is no hard evidence; none. So I prefer to keep all options open until we turn each and every stone to uncover the truth."

"Sustained, Chief. But surely you must have some idea who might have done it?"

The chief is mentally bending backwards to avoid having to make a statement he would later regret.

"Oh come on, Daniel; if you don't say it, I will," Uncle Joe says forcefully. "There are several suspects."

"Oh, several? Indeed!" Mr. Sy exclaims.

"Yes, several!" Uncle Joe is annoyed and stares hard at the inspector from below his bushy eyebrows before he continues: "And they all have better motives than Juan."

"Elaborate, if you please," Mr. Sy says with a smile, while he sits down on one of the kitchen chairs.

Uncle Joe seems uncomfortable to have been caught in this situation: "OK. So let's first look at Robert Delsey –"

"The resort manager?" Mr. Sy asks.

"Yes, the *ex*-resort manager – since Mr. Lee took the resort away from him and asked Elena to run it."

"So you think that is sufficient reason to kill the girl? Surely he must have known for months that he had to leave, so why this sudden murderous attack?"

"Yes, Inspector; fair enough. But you know, he also had a crush on Elena. Rumour goes that they even had a brief affair, which Elena apparently ended quite recently. And Robert has a strange relationship with women."

"Just like Juan has, I heard."

"No, Inspector," the chief answers, "Juan likes women, likes being with them and charming the pants off them and he is bloody good at that. But he holds no grudge against them, not like Robert does."

Uncle Joe takes over: "Robert Delsey cannot sustain a normal relationship with women; he either treats them indifferently, as if they are just not there, or runs after them like a love-sick puppy, like with Elena. Maybe you should investigate why Robert had to leave England. Rumour goes it was because he had done some dreadful things to a woman!"

"I see…" Mr. Sy replies slowly. "So when he saw his beloved Elena with Juan –"

"He lost his mind and, in a bout of jealousy, killed Elena!" Uncle Joe enthusiastically finishes the inspector's sentence.

"A neat theory, Uncle Joe; any evidence to support it?"

Uncle Joe's enthusiasm puffs immediately into thin air. "None!" he replies gruffly. "All circumstantial."

"Right. But you mentioned *several* suspects, did you not?"

"That's right!" Uncle Joe takes up his thread again, "Then there is Mr. Lee and his younger brother Yunlin!"

Mr. Sy laughs incredulously: "Surely you don't suspect old Mr. Lee to kill his own daughter?"

Uncle Joe seems insulted: "You met the man, Inspector; cold as ice."

"Yes, but –"

"*And* involved in illegal activities. Now let's assume that the drug deal on the beach and the sudden appearance of a drug lord, the very brother of Mr. Lee, on our island are not coincidental; it becomes evident that old Mr. Lee must in some way be involved."

Mr. Sy must look somewhat baffled, because Uncle Joe continues hastily: "I am not saying he killed her personally, and maybe not even intentionally, but if Elena and Juan indeed saw him being involved in the drug deal, she must have become a potential threat to his business and to his brother."

Uncle Joe let the words hang in the air for a while and, when the silence continues, adds: "Don't you think so? Mr. Sy? Daniel?"

The chief had stopped chopping long ago and now slowly puts the knife aside: "There is no evidence, Uncle Joe. It's all circumstantial. It's a neat theory, but I am sure the inspector could come up with just as nice theories pointing at, well, at the butler, or with lack of a butler, to Teresa, she's the head waitress, or poor retarded Nonoy, the resort guard."

Uncle Joe huffs and Mr. Sy smiles. "I am grateful to you both for having taken me into your confidence. I can see that there are many aspects in this case and many suspects. Now, tomorrow is Monday and I will go and see the coroner. Maybe it has been an accidental death after all. Then the investigation will obviously be of another character. And if not…" Mr. Sy shrugs, "Well, then we will have to investigate all other leads that guide us towards the true perpetrator. I wish you a good night, gentlemen!" With a short nod, he disappears upstairs.

"No dinner?" the chief mutters. "Strange fellow!"

NINE

Mr. Sy had retreated quickly to his room in order to avoid embarrassing his hosts by not joining them for dinner. It is not that Mr. Sy is not hungry or does not enjoy the company of other men, but it is a sad fact that Mr. Sy's stomach is still upset from the rough boat journey he had experienced last night. This is how it always was: for 24 hours after each sea journey, his stomach rebels against most foods. Yet another reason why Mr. Sy loathes travelling by sea. Over the years, Mr. Sy had experimented with various combinations of light fare, and had discovered that his stomach accepted simple dry biscuits washed down with plain water – the latter not too cold. So with a sigh, Mr. Sy sits down on his bed, opens his valise and retrieves a can with English biscuits, no sugar, low on fat, and a thermos flask with fresh water. He blankly stares out of the window into the dark night while munching his biscuits. The crickets and other creatures of the night have started a true inferno of cacophonic noises, but this does not in the least disturb the pensive mood of Mr. Sy, who lets the happenings of the day pass through his mind. Useful bits of information are stored, half-facts and lies are evaluated and dissected in order to retrieve yet another morsel of useful input, and slowly the faint outline of an image starts to appear in the mind of the inspector. But something keeps nagging in the back of his mind. Sure, he still lacks the input of the coroner and the remaining witnesses-cum-suspects, but he also expects that their input would not alter the present image substantially. And yet there is something or someone else playing an all-important role from out of the murky darkness of the yet unknown. Mr. Sy of course does not yet know what or who this is, but, contrary to his normal instinctive understanding, he is, on this occasion, quite unsure whether he will be able to solve this case. He does not know why, but his gut feeling rarely leads him astray. With a sigh, he starts to undo his jacket, by now moist with perspiration, and hangs it on a coat hanger in front of the open window. Maybe it will be dry tomorrow. He opens his shirt and hangs it on a hanger next to the jacket. Then he lowers his pants and folds them neatly under the mattress. With a feeling of great relief, he now slides between the cool starched sheets of the old fashioned bed. Mr. Sy normally forces himself to go through the actual case before he goes to sleep; he is convinced that his mind, when the body is finally asleep and can no longer be distracted with physical futilities and discomforts, will then continue its analytical process and that this could bring a successful conclusion nearer. So as always, Mr. Sy closes his eyes and lets the events of the day pass through his mind. Shortly after, his body relaxes and twists slightly, and finally he falls asleep. Only the occasional fluttering of his eyelids indicates that Mr. Sy's brain is indeed still active and that it is not unthinkable that his sharp mind is going over every little detail of that day once again.

Mr. Sy surfaces slowly from his restless sleep the next morning. Although he thinks he is awake, disquieting dark, bodiless images keep swirling in and out of focus in his semi-conscious mind and he is still unable to force his unwilling body into action. A slamming door is the catalyst needed and Mr. Sy wakes up with a jolt; all unclear memories fade for good and he is now wide awake. He is already standing next to his bed when a quick rap on his door and a loud and cheerful *"Maayong buntag!"* indicates that the chief is already awake, apparently without any detrimental effects from his nightly bout of heavy drinking.

Mr. Sy opens the door and the smiling face of the chief appears in front of him. "6 o'clock, Mr. Sy; the bathroom is free and breakfast will be ready in 15 minutes. Our appointment at the coroner's is at seven; Dr. Gonzales prefers to start and finish work early!"

And off he stumps down the stairs. A faint whiff of fried bacon swirls into Mr Sy's nostrils and activates the starving sensory system of his stomach; it starts rumbling right away and Mr. Sy suddenly noticed how hungry he is. Ten minutes in the bathroom suffice for a quick cold shower and cleaning of his pearly white, straight teeth that have no cavities; they are one of the few bodily features Mr. Sy is rightly proud of. He then quickly changes his underwear and shirt and dons the suit of the previous day; Mr. Sy is ready for another exciting day. But first, breakfast!

Uncle Joe has not forgotten how to prepare a properly cooked American breakfast. Mr. Sy normally disdains Americans and all they stand for, but their breakfast is superb; thick sweet pancakes with maple syrup, bacon, waffles, scrambled eggs, muffins, cheese bagels, fried toast and lots of locally grown strong Baracco coffee! The three men attack the food with obvious gusto and the silence is only broken by an occasional satisfied grunt when an especially nice morsel of food is discovered and devoured. When the plates are finally empty, the chief lets out a heavy bellowing burp, followed by a more discreet burp by Mr. Sy.

Uncle Joe smiles with obvious relish: "So you liked my food, eh? Well, that should keep you boys going until tonight. Glad to see your appetite has returned, Mr. Sy!"

Mr Sy blushes and thanks Uncle Joe for the opulent breakfast. By then, the chief is already on his legs and bellows, "Thanks, Uncle. We're off to see Dr. Gonzales and then we'll visit young Juan in his cell. Right, Mr. Sy?

Mr. Sy nods, excuses himself to the old man and follows the chief towards the decrepit Buick. The chief lets the car roll down the hill, slams it into 2nd gear and releases the clutch. With a jerky lurch, the heavy straight-eight engine comes to life and the chief powers it up to 40 miles an hour, which seems to be all the engine is still capable of. Mr. Sy is thankful for that, because the dusty road leading to the small town is cluttered with tricycles, Jeepneys, belching old Japanese surplus lorries, peasant carts pulled by docile water buffaloes and ignorant pedestrians and dogs, who obviously still have not comprehended that their small country track has become a major fairway across the island; they are crossing the road without consideration of the heavy stream of traffic. Dead carcasses of dogs on the side of the road remind Mr. Sy that this cannot always be done without impunity. The chief seems to be unaware of the dangers on the road and is weaving in and out of traffic, often using his horn to chase a hesitating pedestrian or dog off the road. The two miles to the mortuary of the small town therefore only takes five minutes. The mortuary is a simple, white-washed, hollow-block building with a corrugated steel roof leaning against the local health clinic. The walls are covered by tropical creepers and bougainvillea that interrupt the simple lines of the building. Inside are two rooms; the first room is used as an office and reception room and the second is the actual mortuary. The chief crosses the empty office with big steps and opens the door to the mortuary. A slightly nauseating whiff of cool formaldehyde-drenched air welcomes them into the brightly-lit, windowless room. One wall is lined with a battery of stainless steel doors, while the other three walls are barren, except for one, where a small rack, holding various containers of chemicals, fluids and unidentifiable body parts in murky glass jars, forms the only colourful accent on an otherwise naked white wall. In the middle of the room, a large man of about sixty years of age, dressed in a green surgical coat, is bending over a bloody torso displayed on a marble slab that has been mounted on a simple cement pedestal. A strong lamp hanging from the ceiling illuminates the body. Without turning towards the visitors, the man begins to speak calmly: "Look at this, chief. Your boys brought it in this morning."

He turns the body on its side so both spectators can take in the details, which the coroner obviously wants to share with them. The torso seems to be intact, but one arm is twisted in an awkward position, while the underarm of the other has been torn off and is lying next to the body. The skull is squashed on the left side and lacks the eye, while both legs, still covered in jeans, are unnaturally flat.

"Drunk!" the coroner mentions calmly. "Too much *Tuba* and then just ran onto the road. Pity for him a Jeepney just passed. Driving too fast, of course. The driver tried to brake, but his tyres had no traction whatsoever, so he hit the poor guy on the head, dragged him under the wheels, tore off his left arm and squashed his legs. He was a strong guy; it took him 20 minutes to die… Unbelievable!"

He drops the torso back down again and wipes his bloody gloves on his apron. "But you are here for the Lee girl, aren't you? You must be Inspector Sy. Sorry I can't shake hands; as you can see…" The coroner apologetically holds up his soiled gloved hands. "Manila already sent a telex to announce your arrival. We are bound to give you all the support you require; isn't that right, Chief?"

The chief looks slightly nauseous but bravely confirms this with a nod. Mr. Sy, who has seen many mangled bodies during his career, seems unperturbed.

Using a rag to clean his gloves, the coroner pulls a gurney over and pushes it to the back wall. "So let's have a look at her. A real pity. I knew her father, you know; a prominent member of the society and a generous supporter of the community."

Mr. Sy is not sure whether there is a sarcastic undertone or not.

The coroner now opens one of the lockers and heaves a sheeted body onto the gurney. "There she is; Elena Lee, 23 years of age. Time of death: approximately between 11 and 12 midnight, two days ago. Cause of death: broken neck." With the elegancy of an experienced conjurer, he removes the sheet from the body in one fluid movement.

The girl is pale and her eyes are closed, but otherwise she does not look dead at all; her hair is lying clean and shining on the left side of her head. Her pert naked body seems quite intact apart from a few abrasions on her shoulders and legs and some bluish impressions on her upper arms.

"Please lead us through your findings, Doctor." Mr. Sy speaks for the first time, while observing the body closely from all angles.

The coroner clears his throat: "Hmm, well; when she was brought here by the Barangay officials, she still had the remnants of a blouse and a slip on. That was all. I took them off and they are both over there." He nods vaguely in the direction of some plain boxes standing below the rack. "She must have had a skirt too, but that got lost somehow." He then continues, "Ah, and of course there is a small golden ring, two golden earrings and four golden bangles. They're also in the box." The coroner looks Mr. Sy in the eye. "I'm not a police officer, but I would therefore assume it was not robbery with a fatal outcome."

The chief adds: "We didn't find a bag or any cash on her, but her parents confirmed that she never used that. So I tend to agree with the conclusion of the coroner."

The coroner bends graciously towards the chief before continuing: "The blouse is of good quality, obviously imported goods, but some chunks are missing."

Again the chief interrupts: "We found some of the missing parts stuck onto some hardy shrubs on the slopes down the cliffs. We assume that they were torn off during her fall."

The coroner adds: "Yes, and during this fall she presumably attracted the abrasions and small wounds. I retracted a thorn from one of the wounds and it matches the thorns of the mentioned bushes. I have no idea what these prickly things are called officially; a botanist might be able to help you there, but I can confirm they are absolutely identical!" He walks around the body and points at the girl's pubic area: "I investigated her vagina; there's no sign of forceful entry. The lips were slightly swollen, but that is not unusual after recent sexual contact. And Inspector..." The coroner answered the unspoken question of Mr. Sy: "She indeed *did* have recent sexual contact. We found traces of semen inside the vagina."

"Any idea when she had intercourse?"

The coroner looks pensively at the ceiling: "It is difficult to say. Such cases are not so common here, and she has been lying in sea water for some hours... But an educated guess: slightly before the actual point of death, give or take an hour."

"So, you mean the semen could also be inseminated *after* death?" Mr. Sy asks.

The obvious look of disgust on the face of the coroner changes into a look of puzzlement: "That's... well... Yes, that cannot be ruled out, Inspector. But surely –"

Mr. Sy smiles. "Just a thing I once experienced in Manila. Please continue, Doctor!"

The coroner returns to the body, but is obviously confused by the new perspective Mr. Sy had just presented. "Right... Well... The lungs... I had a quick look at the lungs; they seemed OK. They were clear with some small damages I haven't been able to identify. But otherwise, there are no fluids there, so we can assume that she was already dead before she entered the water."

The coroner slowly gets back into his stride: "What I think did kill her, however, was a heavy impact on the back of her neck exactly between the cranium and the top vertebrae." The coroner carefully turns the girl around so both men can see the discolouring on the girl's neck.

"Look here." The coroner points closely to the affected area: "There's no doubt about it; the tissue was stretched beyond capacity and invalidated the nerves. The girl must have died instantly." He continues: "I have removed some particles stuck in the hair and had them investigated; it was soil. The same soil that sticks to the rocks on the slope of the cliff."

"So we now assume the girl fell down the slope and hit her head on a muddy rock," the chief adds.

Mr. Sy slowly turns towards him: "Or was struck in the back of her neck by a person swinging a blunt object caked with mud, Chief."

The chief stares back hard and finally replies: "That is of course also a possibility, Mr. Sy."

Mr. Sy turns his attention back to the corpse again: "What are these blue impressions on the upper arms, Doctor?"

"Yes, them. These seem to be the impressions of thumbs and fingers, as if a person held her in a very tight grip."

"Any idea when they were caused, Doctor?"

"Hmm, I would say also shortly before her death, but certainly not more than a maximum of one to two hours."

"Male or female, Doctor?"

"What?"

"Do you think they were caused by a male or a female person, Doctor? A female usually leaves impressions that are interspaced more narrowly than those of a male," Mr. Sy lectures patiently.

"Oh, that's correct of course. Hmmm; it's difficult to say. Possibly female or maybe from a small man, maybe Filipino, but definitely not from a large Caucasian man."

"Any fingerprints, Doctor?"

"Only smudges on the bangles, Inspector. But too little to serve for identification purposes. We did manage to identify the blood type of the skin tissue buried under the nails of her right hand though! It is O negative. Not very common, but not uncommon either."

"And do any of our suspects have this rare blood type?"

The chief cringes visibly, and answers defiantly: "Of course we tested Juan's blood type and he does have O negative, just like eighteen percent of the population."

"Hmmm…" Mr. Sy says quietly, while the others look at him expectantly. And then again: "Hmmm… So, we think we have the probable cause and time of death, are unsure about the method of death and know precious little about the person or persons that obviously were with her shortly before or during her death… Except that he or she had small fingers and has blood type O negative, just like our only incarcerated suspect, Juan."

The chief tries to protest, but is stopped by Mr. Sy's raised finger: "I am only referring to the findings of our doctor, Chief; nothing else."

The chief breathes out again and keeps his silence.

"Do you have anything to add, Doctor?"

"Nothing that's not in my report, which I already presented to the chief."

"Well, then I bid you farewell, and thank you for spending some of your time with us, Doctor." Mr. Sy politely bends slightly towards the coroner and takes his leave, the chief in his wake.

"You really think the coroner's results are inconclusive?" The chief asks while opening the front door for Mr. Sy.

"Dear Chief..." Mr. Sy replied calmly: "The dead rarely speak and can therefore not deny nor confirm the things that have happened to them. It is the living who interpret, twist and distort objective information; they remove, hide and mislay the bricks and thereby bring the puzzle into disorder. But the bricks are still there somewhere and both you and the coroner have just now been so gracious to hand me some additional bricks, for which I am grateful. I don't yet know where to place them, but they will come in useful at some stage. Now, let's talk to some living persons who can contribute with *their* bricks and once I have all the bricks put together, I will at some stage finally be able to see the pattern and finish the puzzle. So let's go and visit Juan!"

TEN

"Juan! Special Investigator Sy is here to speak to you!" The chief opens one of the four cells in the back of the police station and beckons Juan to come out.

"No handcuffs, Chief?" Mr. Sy asks.

"Pah! Juan won't run. He's innocent, and besides, where could he go?"

"A contradictory statement, Chief!"

The chief looks puzzled.

"Never mind, Chief. Hello Juan, I am Special Investigator Sy. Let's sit down, Juan. I can call you Juan, can't I?"

Juan nods nervously.

"Thank you. I am here to hear your side of the story. So can you tell me in your own words what happened two nights ago?"

Juan swallows nervously. He looks pale and grey after spending two days as a presumed killer in a cell, but it is still obvious why the girls like Juan, especially when he smiles his slow smile. He is not too tall, but well-built. It is warm in his cell, so he has taken off his T-shirt and his flat muscular belly is annoyingly visible to Mr. Sy, whose stomach already protrudes a bit over his belt. Juan has straight half-long hair, which constantly falls over one eye and is then thrown back with a little arrogant flop. His skin is blemish-free. He must have Spanish blood in his veins, because his nose is not the usual flat and broad Filipino item, but straight and aquiline, as carried by the old Spanish Conquistadores depicted in the naïve murals at the local church. His shoulders and arms are powerful, probably from dragging heavy tanks and equipment to the boats, and his legs are muscular from the many hours of diving he does every day. He radiates a purely male aura, but with a hint of

60

vulnerability and innocence. The most attractive trait is however his obvious and apologetic boyish charm, which evokes their maternal, protective tendencies. A powerful combination that has worked well with nearly all girls Juan has been interested in, but, unfortunately for him, did not work at all on men! On the contrary; men feel an uncomfortable urge to strike that charming smear of a smile from his face, exactly because they can see what it could do to girls. To all girls – also their own! So he is considered as the natural enemy of the combined male sex; one of the reasons Juan's own gender is not especially fond of him.

Mr. Sy feels uncomfortable to admit that also he experiences a certain revulsion when he looks at Juan. He consciously represses this emotion and smiles: "I understand Ma'am Elena was quite fond of you?"

A broad smile appears on Juan's face: "Oh yes, Sir! She liked me very much; I made her laugh when she was sad."

"And had she been sad the last days before her death?"

Juan's smile disappears, as if a cloud has just covered the sun: "Well, first she was very happy, but then later really sad."

"Why was that Juan, do you know?"

"I think, Sir, happy because she was now manager of the resort and that was good. And unhappy because Sir Robert was angry with her."

"Oh? Can you elaborate on that, Juan?"

It is obvious that Juan has problems explaining complex emotional occurrences; not only because his English is less than perfect, but also because deeper emotions are unknown to him, as he usually happily floats above them. "I don't know, Sir. Maybe Sir Robert was jealous."

"Of whom, Juan?"

Juan's face brightens: "Of me! Ma'am Elena liked me more!"

"I heard she liked you so much that she invited you for a rendezvous?"

Juan looks puzzled. Mr. Sy explains impatiently: "She wanted to meet you alone in the cabana, is that right?"

"Yes, yes!" Juan replies eagerly. "She wanted me and we met at eleven at the cabana."

"So what happened? Please, right from the beginning."

But Juan is too eager, too excited and too disturbed to tell a coherent story in English. Mr. Sy's Visayan is virtually non-existent and since Juan has never been taught proper Tagalog, which, although it had been the official Philippine national language for some time, was mainly spoken in Luzon, the discussion becomes exceedingly difficult and Mr. Sy becomes exceedingly exasperated. So in the end he fumes: "Chief, please calm the young man down and tell him, in his mother tongue if you please, that I will ask him some straightforward questions, *he* can answer in Visayan and *you* will translate it into English!"

Juan seems to understand the principle and eagerly looks at Mr. Sy, waiting for the first answer.

"When did you agree to meet Ma'am Elena that night?"

The chief quickly translates and Juan starts on a lengthy story, only to be stopped again by Mr. Sy: "Chief, please tell him to be brief and focus on the facts. Otherwise we will still be sitting here all night!"

Juan obeys and starts to relay: "I had talked to Ma'am Elena right after the diving trip and she asked me to meet her at eleven that night at the cabana on the cliffs."

"Why did she invite you?"

Juan smiles: "She was in love with me and wanted me to make her happy. You know, touch her and make her body tingle. She also liked touching me and I didn't mind; she was a pretty girl."

Mr. Sy understands the gist of it. "So what then?"

"I first went back home, ate some rice and *bangus* with my father and uncles, then had a nap and later washed myself at the pump. It was already dark and I was all alone. I used some of this nice soap from America, you know –"

"Yes, yes," Mr. Sy replies, irritated, "continue with the moment you left home that night."

"OK. I went up the path towards the cliffs."

"Did you pass the house of the Torosa family?"

"Oh yes; it is the only proper way from the village to the cabana. There is another way, of course, but this one is the best and passes by the Tarosa compound."

"So did you meet anybody there?"

"No," comes the proud answer: "I did not want to be seen, and besides it was late and dark, so who could have seen me?"

"And what happened then?"

"Well, when I arrived, Ma'am Elena was already there. She was frightened in the dark. So I tried to comfort her. But she was resisting, you know; just like girls do when they really like you, but pretend not to, so you get even more excited and in the end just have to –"

"I understand, Juan," Mr. Sy sighs. "What happened then?"

"Well, I tried to kiss her, and she played a bit. You know, saying: *No, no, no, Juan* but meaning: *Yes, yes, yes Juan*! She is a real lady, so of course she has to pretend to defend her honour. But I knew better, because why did she want to meet me there, alone? I am a man and she knows that. I did not come there to look at the stars with her!"

"So what happened then, Juan?"

"Well she kept playing around and it was difficult to kiss her, so I was getting impatient. Then she says: *Look there, a light!* First I think it is another game. But then I see it too; there was a flickering light at sea. Not a boat or a fisherman; the weather was too bad for that. But a light that went on and off in a rhythm. Ma'am Elena called it 'Morso' I think."

"You mean 'Morse', like a code?"

"Yes, that she said too! And then there was a light on the beach doing the same! She wanted to go and look. But I didn't want to. I preferred to stay and make her happy. And besides, who could be blinking with lights in the middle of a stormy night? It could be pirates, or worse; Muslim terrorists from Mindanao! So I told her to stay with me. But she is a hard-headed woman and she just started to climb down the slope alone. So I had to go along. She is just a woman, so I had to take care of her, yes? Maybe she fall, or worse…"

"So you followed her?"

"Yes. It wasn't easy in the dark, but at the foot of the slope it got easier; it is flat with hard soil and also there are big bushes to hide behind. There I found her again and we saw some men, I think Chinese, talking and hugging."

"You remember some details, maybe? How many? How old? Their clothes? Their faces and posture? Or anything else that was special?"

"Yes!" Juan exclaims brightly. "They had heroin!"

"Let's leave the heroin till later, Juan. Let's first have a look at the men."

Juan stares hard at the wall above Mr. Sy's head in order to retrieve the dark images from two nights before: "I think there were six men. Two were important men; they talked. The other four were just standing around; I think they were helpers."

"What did they look like?"

Juan hesitates: "I think all the same, just like all Chinese. But it was very dark; it was night, so difficult to see. But wait! One shone a torch onto the other, who was standing with his back turned towards me. But I think that one was old. Yes, he *was* old; he talked old and had a stick!"

Mr. Sy groans inside; this boy was not the brightest! "And the others?"

"Well, the other important one was smaller and younger. Yes, definitely younger; he did not have a stick and jumped off the boat easily!"

Mr. Sy decides to ignore another bout of irritation. "So there was a boat?"

"Yes, of course!" Juan is surprised the inspector did not know that. "The young leader and the four helpers came with a small dinghy. I think it was a Poseidon, or maybe a Zodiac, about 15 feet and with a four-stroke Evinrude, I think 50 H.P."

"You lost me there, Juan; a what?"

"Not important Mr. Sy," the chief grumbles: "That's just boat-talk; I've got it all on file anyway. Let him continue. What about the four others, Juan?"

"They were just small men. But one came with a package and opened it for the two leaders. The older man looked at it and then shouted that it was heroin. I could clearly hear it; *heroin*! So I told Ma–"

Mr. Sy interrupts quickly: "What *exactly* did he say? What were his exact words, Juan?"

Juan starts to think deeply and a large furrow appeared on his smooth forehead: "He said *heroin* and what else? He did say something else!" Juan keeps mumbling the same words over and over again, but seems unable to recall the rest of the conversation.

"No problem, Juan. Continue; what happened then?"

Juan is visibly relieved to be off the hook. "I don't like heroin. I am not a criminal! So I say to Ma'am Elena, we have to go to the police! Heroin kills people! But I don't understand her; why doesn't she want to go? I don't know why. Maybe she wanted to go back to the cabana so I could make her happy. But I didn't feel like that any more, Inspector. So I leave her and run to the village to the police outpost. But she runs after me and grabs my shirt. I think she is hot, yes, maybe? *Now* she wants to make love! But I can't, Inspector; I think of my brother who died of heroin. How can a man make love when his dead brother is watching?"

In a weird way, Mr. Sy does understand the twisted logic of the young man. "I understand, Juan. Please tell me what happened next."

"So I pull myself free, but she grabs me again! Now I have to tell her honestly that I have to go, so I grab her…"

"How did you grab her, Juan?"

"Well, like this." And he grabs his left bicep tightly with his right hand. "Then she gets *really* angry and wants to hit me, so I have to use lots of strength to keep her on a distance, but she is a wild cat! So suddenly she scratches me, right here!" And he pushes the left side of his face forward and points with his finger.

And indeed, now the inspector can see some faint stripes on his otherwise flawless skin. "So did it hurt?"

"Oh yes, Inspector. Very much so. And I thought; now I am bleeding! At least I thought so first, but fortunately there was no blood; just my tears because of the tremendous pain. It really hurt very much! So I had to push her away, you see? So she could not scratch me anymore! I didn't want to lose my eyes or have scars!" Juan exclaims while he lightly brushes his damaged cheek. "But it was just a little push; no more! She was still standing there, screaming at me while I ran away!"

"What was it she was screaming about, Juan?"

"Oh, she screamed something like: *Don't go. Don't tell the police!*"

"What should you not tell the police, Juan? That you had been together or that you supposedly saw a drug deal?"

That makes Juan look up: "Maybe that was it! Of course, she was also against drugs, but she did not want people to know we were lovers! That's OK then, I can be discreet!" But then he slumps again and groans, "Oooh, but she is dead and everybody now thinks *I* did it! But my family knows I didn't do it. And you, Inspector; you also believe me, yes? Now that you know the truth." His moist dark eyes beg Mr. Sy to believe him.

Had Mr. Sy been a woman, he would have taken the adorable head of the youngster against his bosom and would have comforted him with small soothing sounds. But Mr. Sy is a man, *and* a special investigator with cool, clinical judgement; at least most of the time. But as much as he emotionally wants this Casanova with his inflated ego and utter disrespect for women to be guilty, and despite the overwhelming circumstantial evidence presently available, the professional policeman inside finally convinces him to keep an emotional distance and let all evidence be heard before passing final judgement. So he only nods neutrally to the boy and says, "God passes final judgement and the innocent will be heard." Whereupon he rises and, with a curt nod, bids the young man goodbye.

The chief runs after Mr. Sy and when he finally reaches him halfway across the plaza asks him, out of breath, "What did you mean, Mr. Sy; 'God passes judgement'? You think the boy is guilty and God will punish him, or what?"

"No, Chief," comes the irritated answer, "I just did not want to encourage a young man still under suspicion of committing a grave criminal act, nor did I want to discourage him. At this stage I only wanted him to look into his own conscience and establish for himself whether he has been honest to himself and his environment. If he can answer this question with a clear 'yes', he can face all accusations with a clear conscience and God will surely not see him punished for acts he did not commit. Or do you think otherwise, Chief Arozo?"

The chief is too baffled to give a reply and Mr. Sy leaves him standing in the middle of the square while he marches off towards the Jeepney terminal on the other side. Mr. Sy has decided to pay the Bayun Beach Resort and its former manager a visit and this time he decides to skip the long walk and be transported in the relative comfort of a true Philippine Jeepney.

ELEVEN

In the end, Mr Sy regrets taking the Jeepney; the incessant stopping and starting to pick up or drop off passengers, and the all-enveloping dust cloud that penetrates the bus every time it comes to a halt, becomes increasingly irritating. So after the longest thirty minutes of his life, Mr. Sy is finally let off at a shady alley made of ancient Talisay trees. When the pottering diesel sound of the old Jeepney finally fades into the distance, the soothing sounds of the country side take over; chirping crickets, the rushing of water in the brook, the rustling of the leaves in the trees and, in the distance, the nervous crowing of a fighting cock. Laughing voices come closer and Mr. Sy notices some young women appear from under the shady protection of the trees. Their hair is wet and their sarongs are nearly translucent after a dip in the refreshing waters of the nearby brook. They stop in embarrassment when they see the gentleman in front of them.

Mr. Sy addresses them in English: "Is this the road to Bayun Beach Resort?"

The girls giggle, trying to hide behind each other, and utter some unintelligible words in their local language.

Mr. Sy gets a bit embarrassed. A Filipino unable to communicate with his fellow countrymen; what has become of this world? But what embarrasses him even more is that he cannot refrain from staring at their young bodies and the hard, protruding dark circles that almost perforate the top part of their flimsy, nearly translucent cotton sarongs stuck to their still moist skin. The girls seem quite coy, so why are they pressing their small bosoms forward, stretching the thin fabric even more? Mr. Sy feels an awkward excitement develop in his body. And the girls are laughing! Surely not at him, or are they? Have they noticed his excitement? Or do they laugh because he is different? Pedantic? Too fat? Or too old to look at young women?

Mr. Sy starts to blush until one girl finally takes pity on him and kindly points behind her, along the road: "Sir, the resort is there!"

Mr. Sy bows as politely as he can and marches off, the giggling voices of the girls lingering in his head for a long time.

When he comes around the bend, a breathtaking view overwhelms him; below him, a broad panorama of waving tall grasses, interspersed with occasional tall trees, roll down towards the sea, stopping shortly before by an enchanting garden with several smaller buildings placed in a setting of lush, blossoming vegetation. Further down stand some larger buildings bordering on the powder-white beach of the bay. Furthest away, several small, white *bancas* bob on the swell of the calm, azure-blue sea, which becomes almost emerald closer to the beach. This must be Bayun Bay Resort!

Mr. Sy increases his pace and after a few minutes reaches an impressive Spanish-style gatehouse. The gate itself is missing, but a guard in a sparkling white uniform, sporting a large pump gun, is roaming the premises behind and rushes towards him when he passes through the gate. The dark, broad, smiling face stands in stark contrast to his glaringly white uniform. Oddly enough, the guard has rolled up the trousers of his uniform and is walking around in blue plastic slippers! The pump gun he is toting is rusty but real and Mr. Sy decides it wise to identify himself and his errand. When the guard hears his title, he becomes extremely servile and leads the way in a rapid trot. He disappears between the larger buildings and stops in front of one of them and his voice echoes in the empty office: "Sir Robert? Sir? Inspector Sy from the Manila Police is here to see you!"

There is no reply, so the guard trots towards the restaurant and discusses his errand with a waitress, gesticulating wildly and pointing at Inspector Sy. After many words and gestures, he returns to Mr. Sy and says: "Sir Robert is on the large *banca* over there to check the engine. But he has his PMR radio along and I can call him with the personal unit he has entrusted to me!"

With a proud flick of his hand, he detaches a walkie-talkie from his belt, presses the call button and pompously whispers: "Sir Robert? Head guard Nonoy here! I have apprehended a visitor while roaming the resort. He is now in safe care, standing beside me, waiting discreetly for your arrival. Over!"

The screeching answer comes promptly: "Say again, Nonoy; what's that about apprehending a visitor at the safe? He surely didn't want to take it; that thing weighs a ton! Or is it stuck again? I *told* you to have it fixed several times; *I can't* do anything about it from here, man! Tell the office to call a technician and apologise to the guest for the inconvenience!"

The guard smiles nervously and a light shade of embarrassment colours his dark cheeks: "Yes Sir; I will. But Inspector Sy from Manila is here waiting for you! Over."

The walkie-talkie scratches again: "Why didn't you say so in the first place man, instead of mumbling about guests and broken safes! Tell him I'm on my way! Over and out!"

The guard barely dares to look into the smiling face of Mr. Sy, but Mr. Sy spares him further embarrassment and looks out over the sea. When he turns around, the guard has disappeared into the garden. *No doubt trying to 'apprehend' the next needy guest*, Mr. Sy thinks with a smile.

It takes Robert Delsey less than 5 minutes to bring his dingy to the beach. He kills the small engine, jumps overboard and drags the small craft onto the beach. Mr. Sy remains in the cooling shade from the overhanging Nippa roof and extends his hand to the larger man approaching him. *A very manly man, Mr Sy thinks; so much in contrast with Juan.* This mature man is tall, with wide bulky shoulders, a broad neck and powerful legs. However, the fashionable pink Lacoste polo shirt cannot hide the fact that some fat is beginning to develop around his waist. His eyes are piercingly blue, in strange contrast with his olive-coloured skin. And he is loud and definitely present; there is nothing soft or effeminate about him. Mr. Sy would not have been surprised if Robert Delsey had admitted that his forefathers had been swashbuckling buccaneers in the Mediterranean; he definitely looks the part!

"Delsey is the name. So you must be Inspector Sy; your colleague had already mentioned that you would pay me a visit." Robert grabs Mr. Sy's outstretched hand. "I must apologize for the behaviour of our guard." Robert Delsey leads his visitor to the open restaurant and continues talking while walking, "The man's a fool and has recently acquired some odd airs that are totally out of line. But it's not easy to get good guards down here, so we are

afraid that we only get the same crap back when we throw him out! Drink?"
Robert Delsey places himself on a bar stool and invitingly drags out another
for Mr. Sy.

"Thank you! Yes, a *Calamansi* juice, please!"

"Oh, take anything you like Inspector; it's on the house! I'll have a San
Miguel Pilsen myself."

"Calamansi juice will be just fine, thank you Mr. Delsey."

"Please call me Robert. And your first name was again…?"

Mr. Sy replies uncomfortably: "Sy; Jonathan Sy."

"Ah, Jonathan; a good British name! Your family are from Hong Kong?"

"Kowloon, actually, so I suppose you can call it Hong Kong."

"Yes, I suppose one could. Educated in England?"

"No, I'm afraid not, but my father studied in Cambridge."

"Really? What college was he in then? I myself am a Cromwellian!"

"Oh, I really don't know. I'm sorry, Mr. Delsey… Sorry; *Robert*… But my
father died when I was still a school boy, so I am afraid I never listened
properly when he talked about his studies in England."

"Well, no matter. It's good to meet a person with some affiliation to
British culture down here. It's such a godforsaken cultural wasteland, don't
you think, Jonathan?"

"I really wouldn't know, Robert; I am not from here, you know. Anyway;
to the purpose of my visit –"

"I apologise, Inspector; I know it is not a social visit. Yes, Elena; a dreadful
matter. She was such a nice girl; I was quite fond of her. You see, I have been
working with her father for a long time and have become quite close to the
family over the years. I saw her growing up; she almost saw me as her big
brother, you know. She does have an older brother, he's an old pal of mine
actually, but he was hardly ever there; he's mostly abroad. So I think she got
attached to me… and I to her. Dreadful, dreadful! I still can't comprehend
that she is no longer amongst us; I still think she might come through that
door any moment!"

Mr. Sy nods understandingly and lets the man talk.

"But she won't, will she? Because some ignorant bastard, who was only
thinking with his dick, decided to snuff her out, just because she rejected his
slimy advances!"

"So you know who killed her, Robert?"

"You don't? But you must have heard what has happened, haven't you? Who else could have done it? Everybody knows he has been crawling around her, looking at her, undressing her with his eyes, just like he does with all the girls!"

"I assume you are referring to Juan Aldones."

Their drinks have, in the meantime, been served by a pretty waitress. Robert Delsey nods grimly in reply while he swigs down a large gulp of the locally brewed San Miguel Pilsen.

"But surely he has not killed all the girls he has been interested in?" Mr. Sy laughs and carefully sips at his sourly refreshing Calamansi juice.

Robert Delsey throws an angry look at the inspector. "Of course not! But other girls don't resist his advances. Most of the girls *want* him to look at them and touch them; they are looking for an affair!"

"And Elena was different?" Mr Sy asks with a slightly raised eyebrow.

"Yes, of course! I mean, she is from a good family; a very good family. She has been raised properly and her parents are good Catholics."

"Meaning she is not?"

Robert Delsey laughs shortly: "Touché, Inspector; touché. No, she is a good girl… maybe not the keenest church-goer, but she knows what is proper and what is not. I mean, she is, sorry *was*, a kind person, so if Juan approached her, she probably didn't reject him straight out. That would have been embarrassing for him, and we can't afford to lose Juan; no matter what his moral deficits are, he *is* a good dive master and the guests love him for that!"

"So you think that, since she didn't reject him straight out, he assumed he had a chance?"

"Obviously! Why otherwise would he have persisted?"

"Hmmm…" Mr. Sy seems to ponder over that statement. "There is a small thing I don't understand. If she wasn't interested in Juan, why did she meet him at the cabana in the middle of the night?"

"Oh, I don't know, Inspector! Maybe she went there alone and he followed her, maybe she asked him to meet her there in order to tell him in private that she wasn't interested; there could have been so many reasons –"

"At 11 o' clock at night?"

"Yes, why not? In the daytime there are always too many curious ears

71

listening in." Robert Delsey makes an annoyed movement: "Oh, I really don't know. But fact is that he assaulted her there, she resisted and then he went amok, you know how hot-blooded these young Filipinos are, and pushed her over the cliffs. Oh, he probably regretted it afterwards, crying big crocodile tears in front of his family and his uncle Daniel, but that doesn't change the fact that he killed her!"

"But how can you be so sure that this is how it happened?" Mr. Sy asks, exasperated.

"Firstly," Robert Delsey lifts his forefinger, "he was seen going to the cabana by that fisherman living there –"

"Mr. Toroso?"

"Correct! Mr. Toroso. Secondly," he lifts his middle finger, "he was observed down on the beach below the cabana by Mr. Lee; he told me himself!"

"Old Mr. Lee or his younger brother?"

"What? Oh, yes; Yunlin Lee… No, no; I mean Lee Sr., of course! He saw them together in the bushes when Juan chased Elena."

"Juan chased Elena?" Mr. Sy asks, surprised. "First they were at the cabana together and then in the bushes below? How odd… So what else did Mr. Lee say about what happened?"

"Oh, not too much; he is grieving a lot, you know. He had high hopes for Elena –"

Mr. Sy quickly interrupts: "Like running the resort?"

Robert Delsey lowers his head in embarrassment. "Well, yes; eventually she was going to take over the resort, after I had trained her properly." He looks the inspector straight in the eyes and continues: "I mean, I didn't want to stay here forever; I've got a good education and Mr. Lee really wants me back at headquarters in Dumaguete –"

"Yes, you told me: Cambridge! What exactly did you study there, Robert?" Again Robert Delsey seems a bit embarrassed. He briefly looks outside before answering the question, "Oh, of course I had a formal education; classical languages, actually. But most importantly, of course, one gathers broad social and cultural experience during one's contact with peers and tutors, acquiring leadership skills while one goes along."

"So you did have good contacts with all your… hmm, peers and tutors?"

Robert Delsey squirms a little and answers rather gruffly: "Of course one cannot have good relationships with everybody; that's just not how things work between people of diverse background and culture… But yes, in general I had good contacts."

Mr. Sy decides to drop the subject for now.

But Robert Delsey apparently feels compelled to elaborate on the subject: "Quite useful contacts, actually. Of course I lost touch with some, but several of my friends are now in influential positions around the world and I have been using this network, to mutual advantage, mind you, to develop Mr. Lee's trading business and especially this resort!" He looks around proudly, obviously again more at ease. "Yes, the resort has done extremely well; much better than Mr. Lee initially expected!"

"It must be hard to be forced to leave it all behind?"

"Yes," Robert Delsey answers quietly, "but on the other hand; life must go on! And besides; this place now reminds me too much of the horrible thing that happened to Elena."

"Yes, let's return to the case; you were mentioning the reasons why you thought Juan was guilty?"

"Ah, yes…" Robert Delsey quickly repeats his arguments: "He was seen by Toroso, then by Mr. Lee who saw him chasing Elena, and," He lifts his ring finger, "thirdly, Toroso saw him running back to the village alone, where he presented a flimsy tearful story that he was more or less assaulted by Elena. I mean, honestly, Inspector; he claimed that he was *assaulted* by a girl, because she was desperate for him!? Then he comes up with an even less plausible extension of his rubbish tale and claims that he was no longer interested in some hanky-panky with her, because he had to report a drugs deal!? *Come on!* So poor Juan had to 'defend' himself, push her away, but didn't push her off the cliffs? At least he admitted pushing her! And let's be honest, Inspector; how did the girl land at the bottom of the cliffs only moments later?"

"Yes…" Mr. Sy says pensively. "How indeed…"

TWELVE

"It seems as if the whole island knows all the so-called 'facts' of the case," Mr. Sy ponders absentmindedly as he strolls back to Uncle Joe's place at a leisurely pace. He hardly notices the lush countryside around him, or the curious peasants who are standing knee-deep in the muck of the rice fields, briefly interrupting the planting of young saplings to watch this stranger from Manila passing by.

Uncle Joe is right; nothing remains a secret on this island very long, least of all juicy unsubstantiated gossip. But something has been eluding him. He is sure that all the witnesses – Mr. Lee, the coroner, Juan and now Robert Delsey – have given him some facts. But unfortunately he also suspects to have received plenty of misleading information, intended to divert his attention away from the real issue. But what is the real issue? Mr. Sy suspects that it is not only the murder of a young girl. No, something else is going on. He is convinced that some witnesses are trying to set up a smokescreen to hide other uncomfortable truths.

Did Juan kill Elena? It's a possibility. Most evidence and most witnesses seem to point in that direction, but Mr. Sy doesn't have a good feeling about it. Maybe because some witnesses are so desperate to frame Juan? And maybe because he's got the impression they do so to hide other uncomfortable facts?

And why has old Mr. Lee told everybody his brother was dead, while he is obviously still alive? Or is he? The only 'proof' is the statement of Chief Arozo, later confirmed by Mr. Lee himself. Had the chief identified the famous drug lord as being Mr. Lee's brother to give Juan's story credibility? And could it be that Mr. Lee had confirmed the fact that the stranger was his brother in order to explain the presence of a stranger, whom he met on the beach that night? Is the Chinese visitor indeed Mr. Lee's younger brother Yunlin, or is he somebody completely different? Was Mr. Lee's presence on the beach completely innocent, or was there something going on? And then there is Robert Delsey. Why did he hide the fact that he had been besotted with Elena? On the other hand, was that correct at all? He seemed sincere when he talked about his brotherly feelings for the girl, but the chief had said there had been more to it. Why? To bring a new suspect on the scene? It was also the chief and Uncle Joe who had brought up the subject of his dark past in Cambridge! On the other hand, had Robert Delsey not squirmed visibly when Mr. Sy had started prying into his past relations in Cambridge? But then, it could have been a completely innocent reaction. After all, everybody, even Mr. Sy, has something from the past they don't want to reveal. Questions, questions, questions… And preciously few good answers. Maybe he should not try to evaluate the available information yet and just concentrate on gathering what was available; he still has plenty of witnesses to check – Yunlin Lee, for instance! And possibly some character witnesses from the resort, who could establish some background information. And he wants to question old Mr. Lee, Juan and Robert Delsey again – but not today. Mr. Sy's head is spinning and he decides to call it a day. He returns to the village the same way he arrived. This time there is no meeting with the local beauties, so Mr. Sy swiftly reaches the road and, after a short wait, a Jeepney picks him up and brings him back to town with hardly any stops. He decides to walk to Uncle Joe's Inn, just to clear his mind a bit before his next confrontation with a well-informed player of the game. Mr. Sy has decided to tackle Uncle Joe again, but this time he will pry him wide open!

Mr. Sy is in luck and finds the old man alone in his house.

"Ah, Inspector; back so soon?" the old man inquires.

"Yes, Uncle Joe; I have had so much new information that I decided to call off the hunt in order to digest the available information."

The old man chuckles: "You're a hunter then, eh? Yes, I suppose you must see it like that! Can I offer you a drink? I'll have a beer myself."

"Thanks, a glass of cold water will do just fine, thank you!"

Uncle Joe gets a glass and puts it in front of the inspector before sitting down expectantly: "Well?"

Mr. Sy takes a sip and sighs. "It is exasperating; there are so many contradictory statements."

"Like what, Inspector?"

"Mmm…" After a good swig, Mr. Sy puts down his glass. "Like, why is the chief so sure that Juan is innocent, while objectively all facts are against Juan?"

"Yes, I understand your puzzlement, Inspector. But then, you have not lived on this island for thirty years and do not know the locals like I do. You see, the locals have a very liberal attitude towards the truth and will lie through their teeth if they have to protect their kin against outsiders."

"Outsiders like me?" Mr. Sy asks.

"Yes, correct. Daniel is from here and has known the boy since birth. So he will probably cover up some misdoings of the boy and have a quiet talk with the boy and his father afterwards. That's the way things are done here. But on the other hand, Daniel is a very honourable and honest man. And he was educated properly. He had his police training in Massachusetts, did you know that?"

Mr. Sy shakes his head.

"Yes, and there he was, ingrained with some good police virtues, which sometimes are at odds with his cultural background. Now, I know Daniel, probably better than he knows himself. And I know that Daniel would never cover up a murder. Some hanky-panky with a minor; OK, or a small theft from the resort; that can all be settled discreetly. But not murder! No, that goes too far for Daniel. So now his training and conscience have taken over; he has forced himself to look objectively at the case. He has given Juan the benefit of the doubt and is grateful he can do so, because he knows there is something bigger going on in the background."

"And what is that, Uncle Joe?"

"You think that Yunlin's sudden appearance right at the moment of the murder is a mere coincidence, Inspector?"

Involuntarily, Mr. Sy shakes his head.

"I thought as much! And so does Daniel! That's why he thinks Juan got involved into something bigger when he reported the drug deal. He is more or less convinced that Juan had a fight with the girl, I give you that. But it is too much of a coincidence that of the two only witnesses of a possible drugs deal, one is now dead and the other in prison; far too coincidental for me, Inspector! So I suppose that's why Daniel thinks that Yunlin and his older brother are indeed involved in a drug deal, that Juan and Elena stumbled over it by accident, and that the brothers, by accident or on purpose, have killed Elena and are now after Juan. So actually, Daniel is grateful having to arrest Juan, because now he can keep him safe from those people who would like to take him out!"

Of course Mr. Sy has thought along the same lines, but he did not want to let Uncle Joe off the hook so easily. So he decides to play another pawn: "Don't you think Chief Arozo's judgment is clouded by other… mmm… how shall I say… More amorous considerations?"

Uncle Joe obviously doesn't understand what the inspector is pointing at and he raises a bushy eyebrow.

"I mean, isn't Daniel still in love with the beautiful Cornelia Lee?"

"How did you know that?" the old man utters in surprise.

"Well, I wasn't sure, but you just confirmed the fact!" Mr. Sy replies, a tiny glint of a victorious smile in his eyes.

"You are a very perceptive man, Inspector!" the old man grudgingly admits. "Nevertheless, you're on the wrong track there. Daniel might still be somewhat infatuated with the lovely Cornelia, but if you think he would use such a cheap trick to incriminate her husband in order to win her back, you are dearly mistaken!"

"It was just a thought," Mr. Sy mumbles. And that was all it was, he has to admit to himself. He hasn't really been convinced either that the chief would use this opportunity to take out his opponent in order to win back his childhood love Cornelia. And anyway, it doesn't explain the murder itself. Nevertheless, he had been obliged to evaluate the possibility.

The inspector directs himself to the old man again: "Let's talk about Robert Delsey; you said yesterday that he had a colourful history, and possibly a better motive than Juan to kill the girl."

"Yes," Uncle Joe replies, "I said that, didn't I? That was very indiscreet of me; it must have been the booze! Anyway, I still think he is a suitable candidate for the crime." Uncle Joe adjusts his position in his chair to make himself more comfortable and starts to explain: "You know, Robert has been here in the Philippines for a long time. He came here as a young man; good education, good manners, but somehow… How should I explain it? He's a bit, well, shifty and, hmmm... unsure of himself. As if he is on the run from something – or someone. After some time, rumours started to flow when some of his pals visited the resort and dropped some barely hidden hints about Robert's dark past. Never anything direct, mind you; only insinuations. But what I gathered from these rumours was that Robert had had some kind of affair with a young girl and, because of that, had to leave the country. And by young, Inspector, I mean *young*; apparently the girl was only fifteen or sixteen, and sex with minors is still illegal in England. To avoid incarceration, he fled to the Philippines and just got stuck here; he hasn't been back to England in nearly two decades!"

Mr. Sy decides to provoke the old man a bit: "But surely that is no reason to suspect him of murder? A girl and a boy falling in love, crossing the division of age and crowning their love with the most intimate act between a man and a woman… It happens every day! Just in this case, the girl was a bit younger than law permits."

Uncle Joe takes the bait and carefully says, "But isn't that just the indication that Robert has different, how shall I define it, *standards* than most of us?"

"Can you explain his standards then, Uncle Joe?"

Uncle Joe moves uncomfortably in his chair. "It is not easy for me to talk about these subjects, and anyway, most of the information is from stories I heard; you know rumours."

"Please continue."

"Well, Robert is normally quite aloof towards women. Not that he is impolite, but, you know, he keeps a distance. I think he gets along better with men." After seeing Mr. Sy's questioning look, Uncle Joe adds hastily: "Well, not in a sexual way, but he is a guy who enjoys drinking bouts with his buddies – the competitions, the brawling and boasting. With his buddies, he relaxes and seems to be himself. In front of women, he is awkward, as if he doesn't know what to do. Of course, the women notice this and mostly keep their distance, although he is not a bad-looking fellow – certainly better looking than most guys, and at times he can be quite charming and entertaining. However, women rarely swoon over him – not even the Filipinas. Odd, isn't it?"

Mr. Sy doesn't completely understand, but nods anyway.

"But I think he misses it. I mean, the contact with women." The old man stares dreamily into the distance, possibly recalling his last encounter with the opposite sex. Then he is back again and continues: "But there has been the odd occasion where Robert has shown his emotions!"

"Oh yes?" Mr. Sy encourages the old man to continue.

"Yes; normally it has been the woman who took the initiative and started to flirt. A few years ago it was an American tourist, and two years ago it was a waitress who should have known better. They were both real cock-teasers and led him unto the garden path a long, long way."

Uncle Joe pauses, gets out of his chair and starts rummaging in a drawer. He returns and places a picture with several girls in waitress uniforms on the table; they all have dark straight hair and pretty faces, but the one in the middle, with lighter skin and faint Caucasian traits, bears a distinct resemblance with the deceased Elena. Uncle Joe notices the look on Mr. Sy's face and says: "So you see the resemblance too, don't you?" He stabs his bony finger several times at the picture: "That's Jessica; one of my 'children'. She became a waitress in the resort. And her predecessor, the American, looked exactly like her, albeit a bit older!"

"Yes, I agree; there is a resemblance. The man likes a specific type of girl; so what?"

Uncle Joe smiles knowingly: "Well, apparently the English girl also looked like this!" "Yes," Mr. Sy replies a bit impatiently, "as I said, the man falls for the same type of woman."

"Ahh," Uncle Joe says with a devious smile, "but did you know he also *treats* them the same way?"

"Please explain."

Uncle Joe sits down again and the piercing eyes, under his bushy eyebrows, try to get hold of Mr. Sy as if to pin him down. "Once Robert falls for the advances of the girl, it is difficult to stop him. The girl becomes an icon for him and he smothers her with his love, overloading her with gifts and clinging obsessive attention. His behaviour would suit a sixteen-year-old teenager with a simple mind, but not a grown-up educated man!"

"So what does he do?" Mr. Sy asks, his curiosity aroused.

"Well, he gets totally possessive and wants the full attention of the girl. Won't accept her doing anything or going anywhere without him. Wants her to keel over when he proclaims his love and demands full obedience to his wishes. He becomes a tyrannical romantic. Inspector; the man turns into a virtual monster, a nightmare for any girl who has just a sprinkle of independence left in her! The girl is no longer a human being to him, but an idealised image of how he sees his Perfect Woman. Initially, he tries to ignore the parts of the personalities he does not like and coerces them in the 'right' direction by rewarding suitable behaviour with gifts and attention. Then he forcibly tries to erase their traits and replace them with ones that suit his ideals better, so that in the end they will become an obedient doll with open adoration for their master; the man their universe rotates around!"

Mr. Sy is surprised and appalled and it obviously shows.

"Yes, Inspector; who would have thought this of that man? He is a psychopath, Inspector; a *psychopath!*" He sits down again and continues more calmly: "Of course, the girls don't like it and eventually try to end the relationship."

"But Robert doesn't like that," Mr. Sy guesses.

"Correct, Inspector. He has gone too far, opened himself too much to the outside world and shown too much of his true self as to be able to retract. No, he can't give up and he clings to the girl even more. First he begs and then he threatens; whatever it takes to keep her."

"But the girl doesn't want to?"

"No, the girl doesn't want to. They can't comprehend how this person they initially liked could change so much. They probably encouraged him in the beginning, maybe even liked his obsessive attention initially. It must have been quite endearing for some, especially simple girls like our waitresses; he overwhelms them with loads of gifts, mountains of flowers and uncountable poems. But, as I said, he always goes too far and then they get frightened. And once he notices that, something snaps in him."

"And what happens then?"

"He…" Uncle Joe hesitates briefly, "he gets violent. In both cases, he attacked the woman and tried to strangle her. Fortunately, in both cases there were other people around and they managed to pull him away. Nothing serious happened then, but I can't imagine what would have happened if he had been alone with these women."

"Well, we will never know, will we?" Mr. Sy sighs. This is quite a story and he is curious to find out how much of it is true. "So, how did the story end, Uncle Joe?" Mr. Sy asks.

The old man coughs. "Nothing really happened after the attacks; Robert seemed completely dazed, regretting his behaviour and apologising profusely.

The American lady never pressed charges; too embarrassed, I suppose. Jessica was transferred to Dumaguete, apparently with a fat wad of dollar bills in her purse!"

He then continues: "So you see, Inspector; Robert can be violent when he feels rebuked and maltreated. And don't you think the situation between him and Elena shows some uncanny similarities?"

Yes, Mr. Sy can see some similarities. There is the possibility of a motive, but he is still unable to place Robert at the site of the crime. He must look into that! And then there is Uncle Joe's mentioning the Lee brothers as possible perpetrators. It cannot be denied that, in case Juan and Elena had indeed observed a drug deal, there is a good motive for the Lee brothers to remove any witnesses. But then; eliminating kin? Maybe Yunlin could be so scrupulous; after all, he hardly knew the girl and he must have eliminated many people on his way to the top of the drug cartel. But old Mr. Lee? He too is a hard man, but eliminating his own daughter? No, Mr. Sy did not think so. And he probably wouldn't allow his younger brother to snuff out his daughter either. Unless, of course, he had known nothing of it... Mr. Sy has instinctively removed old Mr. Lee from the list of possible suspects, but then his professional mind took over; he just could not allow his subjective feelings to cloud his judgement. He needs to keep all options open until they have carefully been investigated and evaluated. Until then, both old Mr. Lee and his brother Yunlin stay on his list of possible suspects.

Mr. Sy expects Uncle Joe to know more about the Lee family, and he is not mistaken. He changes the subject and slowly guides the old man towards this new set of possible suspects: "Fair enough, Uncle Joe; we cannot exclude Robert Delsey from our list of possible suspects, although we still do not know whether he was in the vicinity of the crime scene at all. I have to check his alibi before I can say more. So let's put him aside for the moment, shall we?"

Uncle Joe nods in acknowledgement.

"So maybe we can talk a bit about the Lee brothers. You mentioned that they too had a reason to kill the girl!"

Uncle Joe squirms slightly when Mr. Sy brought up his previous statement so bluntly. "Maybe I was a bit overhasty when I accused old Lee. Sure enough, he probably is a criminal and a ruthless one at that, but then, he has always doted on his children – Elena in particular. So when I think of it, I am no longer so sure that he would allow her to be killed. Sure, he wants to protect his empire, but he could have prevented Elena from blowing the whistle in different ways!"

"And what about his brother, Yunlin?"

Uncle Joe is quiet for a moment before he carefully addressed Mr. Sy again. "Look, I don't know the guy personally. Never saw him in my life and the first time I heard about him was two days ago when Daniel mentioned him after his visit at the Lee estate. According to Daniel, he is definitely bad news. But I make a very unreliable witness here; it's all hearsay, although I tend to believe Daniel when he says the guy is a crook and capable of anything to protect his business."

Mr. Sy is a bit surprised to hear Uncle Joe admit his ignorance regarding Yunlin; he had expected the old man to support the chief all the way, and he says so straightforwardly. The old man blushes: "Thank you, Inspector. I am an old man with my own peculiarities and some have developed into bad habits over the years. But no one can accuse old Joe of being stupid and closing his eyes to the truth!"

"That thought was far from my mind, Uncle Joe. So let's unearth the truth, shall we? I have been thinking, there is something odd about this case. It seems quite simple and straightforward, doesn't it: boy tries to seduce girl, girl resists, boy pushes girl and girl falls and dies."

Uncle Joe nods and wants to say something, but Mr. Sy is faster: "But there is something else, isn't there? You suspect something and so does the chief. I wonder whether the Lee brothers are indeed involved? They have a motive, but probably also have an excellent alibi."

Uncle Joe interrupts, "And probably also a good reason *not* to kill the girl!"

"Yes," Mr. Sy ponders, "old Lee was fond of his daughter. So maybe we should have a closer look at Robert Delsey; he might have had a motive. Let's see whether he has an alibi."

"That a good starting point, for sure," Uncle Joe admits. "So have you dropped your suspicion against Juan then, Inspector?"

"I can't, yet... There are just too many damning facts that indicate the boy is involved, so I can't ignore that, although my gut feeling tells me that there are other forces at work. But there is still nothing substantial to support the alternative theory of another murderer. Of course I will look into that, but I have to have a closer look at the boy's case, too; both my conscience and my superiors require me to do so!"

Mr. Sy sighs deeply and reluctantly pushes himself out of the comfort of his chair. "I suppose I should have another talk with the boy. Don't stay up for me, Uncle Joe; I'll let myself in with my own key." And with these words, the inspector bids farewell to the old man and wanders off into the disappearing light of the day.

When Mr. Sy enters the police station, he runs into the chief, who is quietly talking to three men. They look like field workers; barefooted, with black impenetrable eyes in immobile weathered faces, wearing tattered t-shirts and the superficial subservient behaviour of ordinary Filipinos in company of their betters. Once the men spot Mr. Sy, they quickly rise, mumble some unintelligible words to the chief and, while clearly trying to avoid eye contact with the man from Manila, leave the room.

"Mr. Sy; good to see you!" The chief closes the door behind the departing men and smiles at the inspector.

"Good evening to you too, Chief. Who were those men? They seemed to be eager to leave once they saw me!"

"Oh, they are just some workers from the resort. They told me some disquieting stories about Robert Delsey. Unfortunately they also made some insinuations about Juan, but I suppose that's unavoidable in this situation."

"Oh? What did they tell you then, Chief?"

"The usual; nothing I did not know yet. That Delsey has a weird attitude towards women. That he was besotted with Elena, but was rejected by her. That he was going bonkers because she had pushed him out of his position. They made it evident that he had lots of motives to hurt the girl; the usual stuff. I wonder where they get these ideas from? He's not considered to be a bad boss, you know! And it's not just one or two people who talk about it – the whole village seems to be buzzing with the same rumours!"

Mr. Sy smiles slightly. "Yes, that's odd, isn't it? But then, the villagers have ample time for gossip and precious little work to distract them from that, don't they?"

The chief smiles back: "Yes, they are a lazy lot. Not bad people per se, just lazy; that's all."

"And they love a good gossip, I would say! So, what do they say about Juan?"

The chief lets out a deep sigh. "As I said, nothing I haven't heard before; he had a fling with Elena, was rejected and pushed her. But most damning is his statement when he arrived at his uncle's – that he didn't kill her! It is indeed a strange thing to say if you are innocent. But he did say it, I even heard it myself!"

"Well Chief, let's try to shed some light on this case, shall we? Can we talk to the boy now?"

"Certainly; he's just finished his dinner and a bit of distraction will do him good."

The chief leads the way towards the back of the building and instructs the guard to open the cellblock. There are two rows of four cells, each with only two of them occupied; a snoring tramp is in the first cell and Juan is in the relative privacy of a cell at the back. They are like most cells in the Philippines, with simple concrete floors and walls with sturdy bars at the windows and towards the hallway. No luxuries, just a sleeping mat on the floor and a smelly bucket in the corner. The chief nods vaguely toward the empty cells. "On the weekend we sometimes have four to five guys in one cell, all high on *Tuba* and *Shabu*! Some broken noses and bruises, but rarely anything serious. By Monday, the cells are empty again."

Mr. Sy nods and waits until the guard has opened Juan's cell. "Good evening, Juan; how are you today?" he inquires politely.

The boy is crouching against the wall and actually doesn't look good at all; his healthy skin has become pasty and sweat is pearling down his body. Prison does clearly not become him.

In a desperate tone, the boy asks Mr. Sy: "When can I get out, Inspector?"

Mr. Sy sits down on the chair the guard has put in for him, while the chief is leaning against the bars. Mr. Sy almost feels sorry for the boy. "Difficult to say, Juan; it depends on the fact whether or not you killed the girl."

"But I didn't kill her, Inspector!" The boy starts on a lengthy story in Visayan.

With a curt movement of his hand, Mr. Sy stops the boy in his tracks and looks at him hard. "Please, wait! *I* will ask questions and *you* will answer, clearly and briefly. OK?"

The boy nods miserably.

"And the chief will translate – right Chief?"

The chief nods too.

"Right!" Mr. Sy straightens up again and asks: "You claim to be innocent. And you also said so, right after your fall-out with Elena on the cliffs – remember?"

The boy nods eagerly. "Yes, I am innocent and told everybody at my uncle's!"

"But why did you tell them that?"

The boy looks surprised. "Because I am innocent; what else could I say?"

Mr Sy sighs; apparently the boy doesn't understand what he is after. "I mean, why did you say that right *then*? After all, the main reason, as you claim, for going to the village, was to report the drug deal, right?"

The boy looks questioningly at Mr. Sy. He definitely doesn't understand what the question is leading to.

"Look, Juan; if you indeed are innocent and Elena was alive when you left her, I would assume that you ran into the village, excited to tell everyone about the drug deal. But apparently you ran into the village and told everybody that you didn't kill Elena! Odd, isn't it? Why did you say that?"

Juan is reacting even slower than normally when faced with this intellectual challenge; Mr. Sy can almost hear his brain crunching behind his sweaty brow. A deep furrow appears in his shining forehead. Mr. Sy waits patiently and his patience is rewarded, because after a few seconds some thoughts have apparently crystallised in Juan's brain as he exclaims, "I didn't tell them!"

Now it's Mr. Sy's turn to be confused, but fortunately Juan continues on his own account. "I mean, I did run into the village and told my uncle and some other relatives what had happened. I told them the whole story – about me and Elena being alone together and about the drug deal, and that I ran back and Elena tried to stop me, about her attacking me and that I managed to escape."

The boy stops and looks expectantly at the inspector.

"Go on Juan, what then?"

Unhealthy red spots of excitement appear on the pale cheeks of the boy as he continues excitedly: "Yes, now I remember better; I repeated my story several times because more and more people came in who hadn't heard my story yet."

"It must have been exciting to have such a big audience," Mr. Sy states, matter of factly.

The boy nods sagely and replies solemnly: "I was proud to have uncovered this crime. You know that my brother died from drugs, Inspector? So now I could take revenge for his death."

"So you repeated your story several times. What then?"

Juan has lost track of his story and has to think briefly before continuing. "Yes, I told my story many times. And then they asked me whether I had killed Elena."

"Just like that?"

"Oh no, Inspector; I was just saying I had pushed Elena when somebody asked whether I had killed her."

Suddenly the chief pushes himself off the bars and interrupts excitedly: "Damn, that's right; I also heard that! How could I have forgotten that?"

Mr. Sy ignores the outburst of the chief and asks: "Who is 'somebody', Juan? Who asked you that question?"

The boy leans back against the wall again and closes his eyes. He seems exhausted from the interrogation and the hard thinking process he has been forced into. It takes some time before he answers again: "There were so many people. I think…" It is obvious Juan is thinking very hard now; his body is tense, his jaws are clenched and his teeth move back and forth as if trying to crush the resistance in his head. But then his body goes slack again. "No, I am not sure, Inspector. There were so many and in the end, several people asked me. You also did, Uncle; you remember?"

The chief lowers his head when he remembers that he had also asked that insinuating question. But Mr. Sy does not notice the embarrassment of the chief, nor the helpless expression on the face of the boy who can't remember the name of the questioner. Mr. Sy is deeply in thought, trying to make sense of this new bit of information. So apparently the boy had not spontaneously blurted out his statement, but someone had asked the question and thereby prompted Juan's reply. Was it an innocent question, born innocently in the heat of the discussion? Or, was there someone who posed the question to incriminate Juan? And if that person tried to incriminate Juan, this person must have known more about the matter. Had this person seen Juan push Elena over the cliffs? Or had that person possibly seen Juan and Elena fight, and when Juan ran away, saw someone else kill the girl? But why then would he then try to incriminate Juan? Was he in the service of the killer, or did he maybe blackmail the killer? *That is unlikely,* Mr. Sy thinks; *there had just been too little time between the murder and Juan's tale at his uncle's.* Not enough time to observe the crime, talk to the killer, convince him to pay whatever the observer wanted and then run to Juan's uncle's house to pose the question. No, that is a very unlikely option. Far more likely the observer himself had used the occasion to settle an old score; he had seen Juan push the girl, waited till he was out of sight, killed the girl himself and then ran to the house to pose his incriminating question. *Yes,* Mr. Sy thinks; *this is a far more likely scenario.* But that person couldn't have been Robert Delsey; his tall bulky frame would have stuck out from the crowd like a sore thumb. Everybody would have remembered it if he had been around and had posed the question. No, it must have been a Filipino or Filipina, for whom it was quite natural to be at Juan's uncle's house. Mr. Sy is puzzled.

For quite a while, both the chief and Juan are observing the inspector who sits, deep in thought and with closed eyes, slumped in his chair. Juan soon loses his concentration and slips down the wall, his limbs going slack. He too has closed his eyes and his breath is coming in rapid short puffs from between his bloodless lips.

With a short jolt, Mr. Sy comes back into this world and looks at Juan; the boy must be exhausted and prison life does not seem to become him. Well, Juan *is* an outdoor man, not used to staying in enclosed areas for prolonged periods at a time. He reminds Mr. Sy of a colourful wild bird who is locked away in a small cage and wilts away while his ruffled feathers lose their colour. Mr. Sy rises from his chair and, as a farewell, says a few kind words to the boy. The boy nods briefly and then stretches out on his sleeping mat. *Yes,* Mr. Sy thinks, *it is time to go to sleep and let the night bring us some answers to the questions that painfully rack our minds in daytime.*

THIRTEEN

With a jolt, Mr. Sy sits up in his bed. It is still dark outside, but insistent hammering on his door has awakened him. "Yes, yes, yes; I'm coming!"

Mr. Sy stumbles to the door, sleep still heavy in his limbs. He opens it and looks straight into the upset face of the chief, who blurts out: "Juan is dead!"

"What?" Mr. Sy hears the words, but does not completely comprehend the meaning. "Sorry Chief, what did you say?"

"Juan is dead! Sergeant Ramos, my duty officer, just telephoned from the station; he found him dead in his cell! We have to get over there before the rumour spreads and people start spoiling a possible crime scene."

"Crime scene?" Mr. Sy mumbles, still half asleep, while he turns around to fetch his clothes. "You think it is a crime scene?"

"Juan was a healthy boy, Inspector; boys like that don't die suddenly!" the chief replies angrily.

Mr. Sy hurriedly puts on his clothes. "Of course, Chief. I'm sorry; I think my brain is still asleep."

The chief is already on his way down when Inspector Sy says: "Let's treat it as a crime scene until the opposite is proven. Please instruct the sergeant accordingly."

"Already done," the chief answers grimly while he drops his considerable frame into his car. He hardly gives Mr. Sy time to get in before he rockets the old Buick down the hill.

At the station, they have to fight their way through a throng of curious onlookers who, despite the early hour, have already gathered in front of the police station. A worried-looking guard opens the door and lets them in,

88

preventing several others from slipping in together with the chief and his guest. The chief goes through to the back straight away and is welcomed by Sergeant Ramos, a heavy-set, efficient-looking man in his early forties who quickly briefs them. Dr. Gonzales is already squatting in front of the distorted corpse lying in a puddle of vomit and other bodily substances. The coroner briefly looks up and, when he recognises the visitors, returns to his observations. "Well Chief, he certainly is dead. Doesn't look too good. I need to do an autopsy, of course, but if you want my first-hand opinion, I would say that he's been poisoned."

"Poisoned?" the chief exclaims, surprised.

"Yes. Well, look at his strange pallor, the distorted position of the body, the hardened intestines and all this vomit. Here; smell." The coroner dips a gloved finger in the disgusting substance and holds it in front of the chief, who visibly retracts. "You can actually smell the poison. It smells faintly of almonds – it's arsenic!"

Mr. Sy had observed the brief exchange of words from the entrance of the cell. His brain is already working full speed. The boy had not looked well the evening before. Could it be that he had already been ill then? He addresses the coroner: "Doctor, how much time normally passes between the administration of a lethal dose of arsenic and the ensuing death?"

Dr. Gonzales rises and steps away from the body and strips off his gloves before thoughtfully answering: "Hmm, let me see… It depends on the quantity of course and what quantities of liquid and food the victim had taken in before the arsenic was administered. And of course on the victim's general health."

"I understand, Doctor. But any guess how long it could have been in this case?"

The doctor thinks again before answering. "Oh, I suppose eight to twelve hours."

Mr. Sy adresses the chief: "When was the body found, Chief?"

"That must have been around 4 AM." He turns towards the sergeant, shouts a brief question in Visayan and says, after he gets his reply, "Sergeant Ramos says the boy died exactly at 4.05 AM. He had heard some moaning all through the night, but had ignored it."

"Probably tried to get some sleep," Mr. Sy interrupts laconically.

"Well… maybe. Anyway, around 3.30 AM he heard piercing screams from the cell and he found Juan rolling over the floor, vomiting blood. He immediately telephoned Dr. Gonzales."

"He called you?" Mr. Sy asks in surprise.

The coroner lifts his shoulders apologetically: "Twice a week I am also the physician on call. I arrived maybe half an hour later, but it was too late; he had already died."

Mr. Sy thanks him and the coroner collects his instruments and, with a short nod, leaves the cellblock. Mr. Sy and the chief follow him out.

"I will have the body moved to the mortuary by some of my men," the coroner confirms. "You will have a preliminary autopsy report by noon." He leaves the building to return to his other duties.

The chief sits down on the old swivel chair behind his desk, motioning his guest to take one of the rickety chairs in front of it. He is obviously shocked by the death of the boy and emotions drench his words. "I still can't believe someone poisoned the boy! This is no coincidence; it has be connected to the drug deal Juan observed. I suggest we immediately go to the Lee estate and –"

"Hold your horses, Chief. Let's not get entangled in suspicions about who has done it right away, but let's first systematically work out who had access to the boy. And, more importantly, who had an opportunity to lace his food and drinks with the poison; I doubt that the boy voluntarily would have drunk a bottle of arsenic!"

The chief apparently agrees because he falls down in his chair again and bellows a hoarse command towards the cellblock. A short discussion in Visayan is followed by the appearance of a hefty logbook the sergeant has dug out of a shabby filing cabinet.

"They jot down the names of all visitors to the cellblock in this book. They are very conscientious with this task," the chief explains. "Let's see who visited Juan yesterday afternoon and evening. Hmmm… Rolly, that's the officer of the day, twice… Jerry and Willy; they're first grade cousins of Juan. Several years younger, but they seem pretty close to him." The chief follows the lines further down: "And… yes, then Teresa, the resort waitress. I suppose to bring some food. And Alejandro, that's the night officer… and… Oh, that's odd! Mrs. Lee!" The chief looks at Mr. Sy in clear surprise: "Why would Cornelia visit Juan?"

That name also surprises Mr. Sy. "Well Chief, I think we should pay the lady a visit as soon as we have reached a decent time to do so. So maybe we could first talk to the cousins – I suppose they are up by now?"

"Yes they are, I actually saw them in the crowd outside."

"Well, get them in. By all means, get them in!"

The chief beckons the guard at the door to call the two brothers in. A few seconds later, two grubby, sheepishly grinning youths are standing in front of the chief. They cast short nervous glances towards the man from Manila, but don't dare to look him in the eyes. The chief, although sitting below them on his chair, seems to tower over them. He starts his interrogation in brusque Visayan and the brothers answer back timidly. Mr. Sy does not interrupt; his initial suspicions do not include the two boys, but duty requires him to go through the motions. Apparently the chief thinks likewise, because after a few short minutes he sends the boys away with a short dismissive wave of his hand and the two boys scuttle for the door.

"Just as I thought; they know nothing and have seen nothing. They only came to visit Juan out of curiosity, because they never had seen the cells from the inside. Daft buggers!"

"Well, let's as a precaution ask one of your men to take their statements to protocol, if you please, Chief."

The chief sighs, but gives the order anyway.

"So can we now interrogate the two guards, Rolly and Alejandro?"

"Alejandro is still in the cell, cleaning up the mess. I'll call him." The chief bellows a command into the direction of the cellblock again. "Rolly is probably still asleep, but I'll have him fetched; he doesn't live too far away."

In the meantime, Alejandro, the night guard, appears. He is a slim, good-looking man in his late twenties; his good looks are however marred by a gaping black hole in his front teeth. *Apparently dental health is too expensive for prison guards*, Mr. Sy thinks. The man is visibly nervous, but eager to tell his story; he tells Mr. Sy that he had started his shift, as usual, at 7 PM and had checked on the prisoners first thing. Since there was only one prisoner left, the inspection round didn't take long. "How was Juan's condition?" Mr. Sy asked.

Alejandro laughs. "Well, not too well, after 3 days in a cell."

The guard could see that Mr. Sy did not appreciate the joke and hastily continues in a more sober tone: "Juan didn't look good, to be honest. But I wasn't concerned; after all, he is an outdoor boy not used to confined spaces. So, since there are no visitors allowed after 7 PM, I locked up the cellblock for the night."

"And he didn't complain during the night?"

The guard scratches his head. "Well, he did moan a bit all through the night, but he had also moaned the night before too, so that wasn't so strange."

"Was it the same kind of moaning?" Mr. Sy queries.

The guard looks puzzled. "Well, moaning is moaning, but Juan *was* complaining of an upset stomach and requested water several times." His face lights up, "Ah, I did open up the cell block again to get him some water!"

"And who gave you the water?"

"Nobody, Sir; I got it from the water dispenser in the office."

"Anybody else use that water?"

Alejandro head bobs happily. "Uh huh; I also drank it."

"And you are OK? No complaints?"

"Yes Sir, no complaints!" The guard smiles and pats his stomach.

"Hmm," Mr. Sy mumbles pensively, "so that can't have killed the boy either."

After the questions have dried up, the chief looks questioningly at Mr. Sy. The inspector sighs and nods; there are no further questions from his side. The chief dismisses the guard and mentions Rolly, the day guard, who has meanwhile arrived, to approach. Rolly, an overweight officer in his late fifties, doesn't have his uniform on and now looks exactly like the labourers in the fields, albeit with a cleaner t-shirt. His tale is pretty straightforward: he had allowed several visitors in. Two of Juan's cousins and Teresa; they had arrived shortly after each other.

"So tell me exactly what happened," Mr. Sy demands.

"What happened?" Rolly scratches his balding dome. "Not much, Sir; the two boys came first, somewhere around 4 PM, and they were just horsing around a bit. You know, to cheer him up. But it didn't work."

"Did they give Juan anything?"

"I don't think so. Anyway, they were in there only for a few minutes and then got bored."

"So when did Teresa arrive?"

"Oh, that was just after the boys left. She came with the food from the resort."

"And what happened then? Please do not leave out any detail!"

"Yes, Sir; I saw exactly what happened." The guard lowers his voice and looks around him, "I was on my post outside the cell and could observe exactly what was going on!"

Mr. Sy expectantly bends forward, "Yes, continue!"

"She brought him a basket."

"Yes?"

"With rice."

"And?"

"Dried fish."

"And what else?" Mr. Sy is getting slightly impatient.

"Bananas."

"Come on, man; what else!"

The guard gets even closer to Mr. Sy and whispered, "Whether you believe it or not," he pauses briefly, "a thermos with coffee!" He straightens up again, smiling contently.

"Coffee?"

"Uh huh; a whole thermos with *real* coffee!"

Mr. Sy groans. "That's it? That's what you saw?"

"Confirmative, Sir." The guard beams: "Real coffee, yes Sir!"

Mr. Sy slumps back in his chair: "So since you know exactly what was in the basket, maybe you also know why Teresa brought it to him?"

Again, the guard scratches his head: "That's the odd thing, Sir. Teresa doesn't even like Juan. I mean; he didn't treat her nice. And she hardly spoke to him, either – she was very brief, yes she was."

"So why did she bring him some food, then? I mean, you normally don't do that, give somebody you don't like a present."

"Yes Sir, that's right. But I think she was ordered to bring the food."

"Ordered? By whom?"

The guard's balance moves from one leg to the other. "I don't know, Sir. It's not my job to ask that, is it? I mean, I'm just a guard."

Mr. Sy briefly closes his eyes and sighs, "Yes, that's right; you're just a guard."

Rolly notices the disappointment of the inspector and seems insulted.

The inspector, however, ignores it. "So, according to your entrance in the logbook, Mrs. Lee arrived shortly after. Did you also observe clearly what happened between them?"

"Nothing really happened, Sir. Ma'am Cornelia arrived around 5 PM and she stayed in the doorway all the time. They didn't even shake hands."

"Something must have happened, surely."

The guard shakes his head. "No, nothing happened. They talked a bit, but I couldn't understand from where I was sitting. Of course I asked Juan afterwards what they were talking about, but he didn't want to talk."

Then the guard's eyes light up: "But Ma'am Cornelia seemed very upset when she left; she had tears in her eyes!"

"Really? Why was that then, do you think?"

The guard seems to crumble and he mumbles apologetically: "I don't know and Juan didn't want to tell me."

Inspector Sy checks the logbook again and notices that he and Chief Arozo had been the last visitors shortly before 7 PM; there were no more visitors that night.

"Rolly, what happened after the chief and I left the jail?"

"Nothing really, Sir; I had a last look at him before I handed over to Alejandro, who was on night duty."

"Did you notice anything unusual when you checked on Juan?"

The overweight guard laughs briefly. "No, except that he wasn't looking too good. But who does after a few days in jail?"

When nothing follows, the inspector dismisses the man with a short nod. The guard presents his superiors with a smart, correct salute which makes his tight t-shirt creep up and expose a decent part of his hairless potbelly. Despite the graveness of the situation, Mr. Sy involuntarily has to smile, a gesture the heavy guard accepts gratefully, and he rewards Mr. Sy with an eye-blinding grin, which is not totally in line with the martial impression he had tried to make previously. After he has left, the chief and Mr. Sy look at each other in silence. Then Mr. Sy sighs: "Not a lot to go with, is there Chief?"

"Well... they all seemed pretty straightforward. Wouldn't put my hand in the fire for them, but they are a relatively honest bunch, these guards. Jerry and Willy are just too stupid to plan or execute such a crime, so I'll count them out."

Mr. Sy leans back carefully in his rickety chair and folds his manicured hands behind his tousled head. "So that leaves us with Teresa and her basket full of goodies and the unexplainable visit from Mrs. Cornelia Lee, who didn't seem to know Juan at all, but who still decided to visit him shortly before his death!"

"I hope you are not insinuating that Cornelia poisoned the boy, Inspector?"

Mr. Sy stares hard at the chief, who lowers his eyes quickly in embarrassment. "Don't let personal emotions cloud your judgement, Chief. We need to investigate all possible leads. Poison is traditionally the weapon of women, *and* Mrs. Cornelia could have a motive to kill Juan."

A small moan escapes from the chief. "You think she wanted revenge? You think that she thought that Juan killed her daughter?"

Mr. Sy looks satisfied. "We cannot exclude that possibility. But then… there is another woman who definitely could have administered the poison."

"Teresa?"

"Yes, correct! But, in case she did indeed do it, we do not know of her motive – if she had one at all. But," Mr. Sy pauses, "she does work for a man who might have a motive!"

"Robert Delsey!"

"Exactly; Robert Delsey. He might want to remove a contender or possibly a witness. This is still just speculation, of course. Just as we would still have to find out why Teresa would support him in his deeds – if she did so at all! Or maybe she acted on her own account after all…"

"Also revenge? You think she had been dumped by Juan and has now taken her revenge?" The chief moans: "Oh my God; so many open ends and so many suspects! My head is turning; how can you keep it all together?"

Mr. Sy smiles his small superior smile. "At the moment I am just gathering information and keeping all options open, but you are right, Chief – there are many options this time!"

The chief briefly buries his large head in his hands, rubs his eyes and then suddenly jumps out of his chair, frightening Mr. Sy out of his thoughts. "Right, there's no use wasting time feeling sorry for ourselves. Although I'm dead against it, let's interrogate Mrs. Lee. She is an early riser…" The chief ignores the raised eyebrow Mr. Sy so blatantly displays and continues, "As everybody knows. So it is no problem to visit her right away!"

FOURTEEN

For the second time in two days, Mr. Sy rings the ornate bell at the gatehouse of the Lee estate. Again, he is accompanied by the same gardener to the wide flight of stairs leading to the French doors that make out the entrance to the mansion. The same housemaid is waiting there for them; she gives an inquiring look to Chief Arozo and a brief nod to Mr. Sy before she leads them to the library. The doors and windows are still closed but the thick walls have an excellent insulating capacity, so it is not yet hot in the high, vaulted room. In the distance they hear the thin voice of the maid piping in the large hallway, interrupted by the warm cultured voice of Mrs. Cornelia Lee. The sound of clicking high heels on marble comes closer and Mrs. Lee enters the room. She is wearing her elegant black dress again, with its discreet cleavage that does full justice to her slim, well-shaped body. Almost reluctantly, Mr. Sy has to admit that he was impressed by the dark-clad lady; so elegant, so worldly, so… Yes, Mr. Sy had to admit it; despite her age, so attractive! Mrs. Lee nods in recognition to Mr. Sy and throws a warm smile at the chief, who, with a small, shy side look in Mr. Sy's direction, promptly blushes.

"Good morning, gentlemen; what can I do for you so early in the morning? Are there any new developments? Did you finally catch the murderer of my daughter?" The smile that has graced her serene face just seconds ago quickly disappears and is replaced by the harassed look of a grieving mother while she waits for an answer.

The chief lowers his head in an attempt to hide his discomfort and quietly says, "I'm sorry, Cornelia, but there's nothing firm yet. We are still investigating, all leads but I think we are getting a clearer picture –"

"The chief is possibly a bit too optimistic, Mrs. Lee," the inspector quickly interrupts. "There are indeed several promising leads, but it will take time to firm up on them. Until then we would like to keep all options open. In the meantime, something else has happened that is… How can I put this? Well, it has disrupted our investigation and opened up some other scenarios."

"Oh? And how is that, Inspector?" Mrs. Lee asks with raised eyebrows.

The chief answers instead: "The boy is dead, Cornelia. Juan was murdered last night!"

Involuntarily, Mrs. Lee raises one of her well-manicured hands to her mouth, now open in obvious astonishment: "Murdered? Juan? Last night? But –"

"Where were you last night, Mrs. Lee?" the inspector asks quickly.

Mrs. Lee seems in shock and for a moment she is speechless. "What? I… Well…" She looks at the chief, as if seeking inspiration, before she turns to Mr. Sy to answer his very direct question. "I hope you are not insinuating anything, Inspector. I was here, together with my husband and his brother." But she seems uncomfortable to look the inspector in the eye and again looks at the chief, as if seeking help. The chief turns his head away and develops a great interest in the book titles on the shelves opposite him.

With a shivering sigh, Mrs. Lee turns to the inspector again, "But I assume that you would like to know whether I visited the boy yesterday? Yes, Inspector, I visited Juan yesterday afternoon. But you obviously already were aware of that fact!"

The Inspector nods. "Indeed, Ma'am, we know you visited Juan yesterday afternoon around 5 PM; your visit has been logged."

Mrs. Lee has recovered her composure and asks: "Am I a suspect, Inspector? You just told me he was killed last night. *I* visited the boy in the late afternoon!"

The Inspector scratches his throat. "You are right, Mrs. Lee; the boy died last night around 4 AM, but this was after a long and painful death struggle; the boy was poisoned the evening or afternoon before!"

Her surprise seems genuine and a multitude of emotions flit over Mrs. Lee's face before she says: "So I *am* a suspect then?"

"Let's state it like this, Ma'am," the inspector replies, "we are obviously interrogating everybody who has had access to the boy before his death. We know from the logbook and witnesses that you visited Juan. What we do not know is *why* you visited him! Were you close to him?"

"Not at all, Inspector; I never met the boy before!" Mrs. Lee replies, more composed now she has decided to tell the full truth.

"Then it is even more surprising that you visited him!" the inspector states provokingly.

"You really think so, Inspector?"

Mr. Sy nods in reply but holds his tongue. It is better this way; he is sure Mrs. Lee will now tell him her full story without him prompting her.

"Yes, it must seem odd to you, me visiting a boy I didn't know. Well, it is not completely true. I have heard of him – not too many good things, actually – and even saw him from a distance once or twice. But we were never introduced and yesterday was the first time we talked."

Mrs. Lee briefly stops and walks to a *secretaire* to retrieve a crumpled package of cigarettes. She fumbles to get a long cigarette out, lights it with a heavy marble lighter standing on the desk and says apologetically, "I don't really smoke, Inspector. At least, not any more – not since I was about eighteen. But it seems to calm me down when I am in stressful situations." She shrugs her slim shoulders briefly, takes a long draw and adds while exhaling, "Like now."

Mr. Sy nods understandingly; he understands the complex irrational psyche of mankind perfectly well.

"Shouldn't we sit down, Inspector? Daniel?" She guides the men towards the small set of armchairs in the corner of the library and sits down opposite them, perching delicately on the front of her seat, her body bent forward, her left hand supporting the right arm with the cigarette. Mr. Sy can now fully enjoy the top of her heavy creamy white breasts inadvertently displayed between the unfolding layers of chiffon, while Chief Arozo quickly turns his eyes away, the slight blush reappearing on his cheeks. With some difficulty, Mr. Sy manages to tear his eyes away from the alluring view and is met by an amused smile on her delicately painted lips. The inspector smiles, embarrassed.

Mrs. Lee draws again on her cigarette and continues her story: "As I said, yesterday was the first time we actually talked. It was a very awkward conversation; we both didn't really know what to say." Mrs. Lee's eyes are staring into the distance while she remembers her moment with the deceased man. "He was a good-looking boy. I understand that girls were attracted to him."

Her mind seems to wander off, until she suddenly looks straight at the inspector: "But I didn't understand why my Elena was so fatally attracted to him, so I had to go and see for myself why my little girl fell for this good-for-nothing beach boy."

Mrs. Lee angrily stubs out her cigarette in the huge marble ashtray and lights the next one with the matching lighter. She inhales deeply, closes her eyes briefly and blows a large, bellowing, blue cloud towards the ceiling. "I think it was just a game for her, Inspector; she couldn't have been serious. Not with that boy."

There is a short pause before she continues: "But there was another reason why I visited him, Inspector. And I think you know why."

Mr. Sy does not like to be kept in suspense like this and just suffices with a short questioning, "Oh?"

"Yes, I wanted to see the man who apparently killed my little girl!" She sighs again, "Oh, I was so full of hatred, so… angry; in my mind, I had already killed that boy a thousand times before I went over to see him."

She sees the surprised look on the chief's face: "Does that really surprise you, Daniel? I am a mother too, you know! And somebody has taken my little girl's life. Do you think that, just because I am an educated woman, I can forget and forgive? Of course not!" The second cigarette is crumpled with an angry movement into the smooth marble surface of the ashtray. "But one look at that miserably pathetic young boy was enough to disperse all my anger; I knew instinctively that he hadn't done it." She lifts her hand as if to stop any comments: "Oh, I know, Inspector; you probably don't believe in instinct and probably not at all in feminine instinct, but I just knew!"

"Oh, dear Mrs. Lee," the inspector says, smilingly, "I *do* believe in instinct and gut feeling, since this, more often than not, is based on the instinctive perception by the human mind of a large variety and quantity of sensory inputs, which our brain then subconsciously puts together into a coherent picture without our conscious mind ever having been involved in the process!"

Both the chief and Mrs. Lee gape in obvious puzzlement at the triumphant-looking Mr. Sy.

Mrs. Lee shakes her head as if to clear a temporary blockage and continues: "If I understand you correctly there, Inspector, you understand my feelings then?"

"Yes, Mrs. Lee; I understand that for you it was abundantly clear that Juan could not have killed your daughter."

"Thank you, Inspector! I don't have any warm feelings for that boy; he is just the son of a local fisherman with all the deficiencies that the local male population so often displays; a Latino macho but with the heart and prowess of a rooster! I understand that very well. After all, I have lived among these people most of my life. And I think I can read them quite well by now. You know, Inspector, most of them are uneducated and have hardly been in contact with Western culture and true Christian values before; they still resemble the original nature tribes they stem from, as opposed to civilised people like you and me. And they have not yet learned to control their feelings, emotions and thoughts as well as you and I have, so I can read them quite well. Believe me, Inspector; I could read this boy like an open book. He did not kill my daughter!"

Mr. Sy believes her, although for a completely other set of reasons: "So if the boy did not kill your daughter, who did then? And who killed Juan? The key question actually being, *why* were they killed? Were there two separate reasons for the killing, or is there actually only one reason for their deaths?" It is obvious that Mrs. Lee has not yet come that far in her thoughts, so Mr. Sy apologetically adds: "I am sorry, Mrs Lee, to burden you with the problems of my investigation!"

"Not at all, Inspector," the lady replies while she rises and hold out her hand to the inspector to indicate that their audience is over.

Mr. Sy bends down, takes the slim fingers lightly in his hand, raises them to his mouth and presses a light airy kiss on them, just like he has seen many gentlemen do it in the romantic movies his mother used to watch over and over again. "You are too kind, Mrs. Lee. We must be going now and talk to some other witnesses."

Mrs. Lee nods graciously and the inspector and the chief take their leave. The chief, pounding the marble floor heavily with his army boots, leads the way, while Mr. Sy lightly walks after him, followed by the high-pitched tick-tack of Mrs. Lee's delicate heels.

101

"My apologies for bringing up the question again, Mrs. Lee," Mr. Sy turns around on the stairs, "but if you are so sure that Juan didn't kill your daughter, who do you suspect did it then?"

The attractive face of Mrs. Lee contorts into a painful grimace. "If I knew that, I wouldn't be standing here, but would probably have been sitting in one of your cells at the station, accused of murder!"

The chief laughs incredulously, but Mr. Sy is serious: "But you must have a suspicion, Mrs. Lee. Don't you have any indications? Haven't you heard any rumours?"

"You mean that my husband and his brother killed my daughter to prevent her from testifying about an imaginary drug deal? Yes, Inspector, I have heard that absurd rumour. Do you really think my husband would kill his own daughter? How *absurd*!" She almost spits out that last word.

"And what about his brother, Yunlin?" the inspector asks.

Mrs. Lee slim body tightens at this question and she replies in a deadly calm voice: "It would have been better if he had stayed away!" This sentence is so full of barely concealed hatred that the chief involuntarily takes a small step backwards. Cornelia notices the unease her statement has created and makes a conscious effort to put a disarming smile on again in order to weaken the harsh reality of her words. But it is obvious that she is shaken and far from composed. Then her face takes up a serious and thoughtful expression, and it almost looks as if she wants to address the inspector again. The inspector hardly dares to move, because he feels that her next words might be of considerable importance, but the moment passes; her expression changes and her facial expression slacks. Cornelia has her emotions under control again. "If I can be of further assistance, Inspector, you can call on me any time." The professional smile is back in place and she again offers her hand to Mr. Sy.

Her next words are directed to Chief Arozo: "Daniel, could I have a word in private with you?"

The chief nods and follows Mrs. Lee back inside. Mr. Sy takes his leave, makes a slight bow towards Mrs. Lee's disappearing back and descends down the stairs. The couple disappears in the cool darkness of the hallway again. And there Mr. Sy is, standing alone on the stairs, deep in thought, the hot morning sun burning his bare head. He is shaken out of his thoughts by a hooting hornbill and in the ensuing silence he becomes aware of the peaceful setting of the garden – the silence, only interrupted by the sound of crickets and the fluttering of an occasional bird – and the fresh air, which smells so much better than the polluted atmosphere in Manila. Then this countryside idyll is shattered when he all of a sudden notices a pungent smell; a smell he himself is emitting! In embarrassment, he suddenly realises that he has not had a chance to shower or straighten his sleep-tousled hair before he was abducted by the chief to race to the jail and inspect the body of young Juan. This is so unlike him; normally he takes great care of a groomed appearance. But then, this whole case is peculiar and thereby having an odd influence on his psyche.

What must Mrs. Lee have thought? He presses his discomfort to the back of his mind and tries instead to focus on the matter at hand; he strains his hearing to pick up the discussion between Mrs. Lee and the chief, but he can only distinguish the low murmur of her voice and an occasional surprised bellow of the chief. Mr. Sy is curious to know what they are discussing and whether the contents of their conversation have anything to do with his investigation. *Mrs. Cornelia Lee is definitely different from the local people surrounding her,* he thinks; *she is civilised and drenched in the values of Western culture.* And *she is definitely hiding something. But she seems to be fond of the chief; maybe she is confiding in him right now?* After a few minutes, the chief reappears, alone and visibly shaken and upset.

"A remarkable lady!" Mr. Sy exclaims, while the gardener closes the gate behind them. The chief initially doesn't answer. He drags himself to the car and slumps down on the driver's seat, immersed in his own private thoughts. The inspector slowly follows, clearly confused by the chief's behaviour.

It is clear that the chief has not heard the words Mr. Sy had directed at him; he is staring through the windscreen, his eyes unseeingly glued to the green wall of the surrounding jungle. Then, with a jolt, the chief sits up straight and brings the old engine to life. He puts the machine into gear and asked his companion, while the car starts its descent down the hill, "Do you believe her, Mr. Sy?"

"Believe what, Chief? That she is innocent, that Juan is or was innocent, that her husband is innocent, or that Yunlin is an unwanted guest? Which part should I believe?"

The chief clenches his teeth and concentrates on the road before answering: "She is sincere, Mr. Sy. Maybe she doesn't tell you everything she knows, but she would never lie; I would notice if she did!"

"So you know her that well, eh?"

A long silence follows, only broken by the occasional curse and honking of the horn when somebody or something doesn't move out of the path of the old Buick quickly enough. But finally the chief replies with a shivering voice, which does not seem to go with the huge man at all: "We were very close as teenagers. I mean, *really* close! We dreamt about a future together. You know how kids think when they are madly in love."

Mr. Sy keeps his silence, and the chief continues as if speaking to himself: "But her parents were dead-set against it. They are an old Spanish family and they had planned a different partner for her; not a guy like me, not a plain Filipino without pedigree." He laughs briefly: "No, they thought me totally unsuitable and sent Cornelia to some distant relative in Madrid, just so she could cool off and forget about me."

The chief seems to have forgotten all about the traffic around him and carelessly weaves the car through the thickening congestion back to town. Mr. Sy takes a firm grip on the doorpost of the old car, but doesn't dare to interrupt lest the chief break off his tale.

"Well, it didn't work. At least, she didn't cool off. When she came back, she was wilder than ever and completely convinced that she could only find happiness if she could marry me. But her parents kept a close watch on her and we only managed to meet once or twice during the months after her return. It was a desperate undertaking and I think we both knew it would never work out – not as long as her parents were set against it." The car swerves around a lorry, only to miss the ox-drawn cart in front of it by a mere inch. "Then one day, a business associate of her father's visited. Actually, her father owed him a lot of money; her old man had made lousy investments for several years by then. Anyway, this guy saw Cornelia and fell in love with her. That guy was Zhiheng Lee; by then, he was already an old man. At least *I* thought he was old; he was at least 20 years her senior! Her parents didn't exactly approve of him either; after all, he was Chinese nouveau riche. But then, he was *rich* and Cornelia's father was indebted to him, so they could hardly stop him from courting her."

They now approach the village and, without slowing down the heavy car, enters the narrow streets of the village. Mr. Sy now really gets worried. "Chief, please slow down!"

"What? Oh, sure!" He slams on the brakes, almost propelling Mr. Sy through the windscreen. The chief resumes their trip at a more leisurely pace. "The funny thing is that Cornelia obviously wasn't really interested in the guy. Sure, she liked the attention and the gifts, but she didn't love him. But when she noticed the disapproval of her parents, and combined with the impotence of our relation, the devil got into her and she slowly started to encourage old Lee, if only to spite her folks! He was thrilled, of course, and increased his efforts. Cornelia revelled in the discomfort of her parents, who were unable to stop old Lee. In that way, she punished them for their harsh treatment of our relationship. I think it was more like a game for her, you know, seeing her parents squirm. But when Lee finally proposed, Cornelia surprised herself and everybody else by accepting his proposal!" The chief turns the car off the road onto the driveway towards Bayun Resort. "I only met her briefly during that period and tried in vain to convince her that it was wrong; not only was she betraying our love, but she also made a fool of old Lee, who thought she had the same feelings for him as he had for her." The car slows down in front of the entrance gate of the resort and the chief switches off the engine. He doesn't seem to be in a great hurry to get out of the car, but simply sits there, both hands on the wheel, staring into the distance. "She didn't want to listen to me and started avoiding me. Not that we had a lot of opportunities to meet, mind you! But it did hurt when she returned all my letters at some stage. A few months later they were married and then Lee Jr. was born." The chief turns towards the inspector. "I am now going to tell you something that I want to be kept as a secret between you and me. I am only telling you because I want to dispel any doubts about my sincerity and honesty." He pauses before he continues: "It might otherwise confuse the investigation. But if I find out you spilled the beans to someone, I'll break your neck, all right?"

Mr. Sy is surprised at the turn the tale has taken, but manages to nod affirmatively.

"All right then." The chief returns into his previous position and starts talking while he stares blankly at the white-washed wall in front of him. "A few years into her marriage, Cornelia and I started seeing each other again; Cornelia was often alone and I think by then she had realised that there was no love between her and old Lee. She had married him to spite her parents and he had married her in order to buy some respectability."

Mr. Sy sits next to the chief in utter silence. As yet, he has no clue what the story is leading to, but feels that it will probably have an impact on his investigation.

The chief continues his tale in the same monotonous voice: "In the beginning, our meetings were innocent; we met by coincidence during social gatherings or in the streets, and once in a while we had coffee together. It became clear to both of us that we were again actively seeking each other's company, but we were always careful not to attract attention. I think we both knew it couldn't stay innocent very long; there was this electricity between us, you know? In a way, I was fighting it, but on the other hand I wanted to touch her and discharge that power between us; you know what I mean? Anyway, we started a relationship which lasted quite some time." The chief makes a long drawn-out pause, while he mentally seems to relive his escapades with his beloved Cornelia, and Mr. Sy almost prompts him to continue, when the chief resumes his story by himself: "But then, all of a sudden she broke it off again. She told me we couldn't meet any more; people would notice there was something going on between us. I was confused and didn't understand why all of a sudden she wanted to break up. I begged her to leave old Lee, but couldn't convince her; she had decided to stay with him." There is again a long pause in which the chief stares hard at the grubby canopied ceiling of the old car, trying to keep back the tears. "She told me something just now, Mr. Sy. It puts things into another perspective…" He swallows hard. "Although it doesn't make it easier to understand…" He swallows again before continuing, "Some months after our break-up, she gave birth to Elena. I had left the island by then, so I only heard of it much later and didn't really put two and two together at that point. Well… Cornelia just told me Elena was my child!" he blurts out.

"Elena was your daughter?" Mr. Sy exclaims in wide-eyed amazement.

The chief nods with tears in his eyes. "Yes she was, but I never knew, never even suspected it!" He slams his hand hard on the wheel so the whole car shudders. "Why didn't she tell me? Why did she hide it from me? And why couldn't she just have shut up now and kept it to herself!" He turns to the inspector, tears flowing freely now over his reddened cheeks. "I just found out I had a daughter with the woman I love, and three days ago that daughter died! I never knew her, Inspector! Never got a chance! Life is unfair. Oh, life is so unfair!" The chief's large body is shaking from the barely concealed sobs.

"Yes it is unfair sometimes. *And* cruel!" Mr. Sy says quietly. He turns towards the other man: "I am grateful you told me; it is easier for me to judge the situation properly. And you have my sincere condolences, Chief." He reaches out his hand and awkwardly pads the chief on his heaving shoulders. "But tell me honestly; are you sure you are able to continue the investigations?"

The chief swallows hard and looks at Mr. Sy: "I want to nail the bastard who killed my daughter just as much as you do, Mr. Sy. I know it's personal now, but if you remove me from the investigation, I will continue on my own!"

"Fair enough, Chief. As long as you stay objective and don't do anything without checking it with me, it's fine with me." Mr. Sy knows he can hardly demand Daniel Arozo to be removed without losing a lot of time and goodwill from the local authorities. It would be better to keep the chief connected to the investigation, and thereby under some form of control, than to take him off the case and have him run around like a loose canon. So Mr. Sy decides to play along, but has to admit to himself that from now on he has to keep a very close watch on the chief.

The chief climbs out of the car and stumps ahead of Mr. Sy onto the resort grounds. Mr. Sy follows at a distance, allowing the big man to compose himself again. Around a corner, they almost fall over a white-clad figure sitting in the shade of a big tree, his eyes closed, a pump gun slack in his hands, his chair precariously balancing on two legs against the trunk of the tree. The chief looks back at Mr. Sy and chuckles silently. Then a huge roar explodes from his chest: "ATTENTION. TERRORIST ATTACK!"

The white-clad guard topples from his chair and the gun drops to the ground, where it goes off with a loud bang, pellets tearing into the undergrowth. "YOU FOOL!" the chief bellows, "not only are you sleeping on guard duty, but you haven't even secured your weapon; you're an idiot,

Nonoy!" He grabs the gun from the ground and slams it into the chest of the little man, who by now is bright red below his suntanned skin.

"I am sorry, Chief Arozo, I was just thinking about the bad things that have happened and didn't hear you coming!"

This seems to enrage the chief even more. "Thinking, Eh? In order to think, you need brains, Nonoy! You were not thinking, you were sleeping! How, for fucks sake, could you have heard us coming, eh?"

"Oh no, Sir!" The guard puffs up his scrawny chest, "I would never sleep on duty; I am a good guard. I am loyal and –"

"Idiot!" The chief mumbles and waves Mr. Sy to come along. "That man is useless. I tell you, Mr. Sy; I don't know why Robert Delsey keeps him on. But he is probably afraid a new guard would be even worse!"

They approach the restaurant, where several waitresses are setting the tables for lunch. One of the girls points to the bar where Teresa sits on a stool, adding figures in an inventory book. Mr. Sy can see a small bulge slightly elevating the sarong she is wearing, but she still looks very slim for a pregnant woman. But then, most girls in the province are very slim – probably because their families lack the money for proper food. Mr. Sy has to admit that they look more graceful than most girls he knows in Manila, whose waistlines betray the fact that nutrition is of much better quality in the capital of the Philippines. The girl looks up and smiles. She is an attractive girl, in her twenties, with remarkably strong cheekbones, Mr. Sy concludes; taller than most of her colleagues, and has an enchanting smile.

She greets the two visitors and invites them to sit down. "Chief Arozo, so nice to see you!"

The chief smiles benignly at her: "Teresa, how are you doing? Do you know already; boy or girl?"

The girl giggles. "I don't know yet, Sir. My mother says it's a boy, but the doctor thinks it's a girl. Anyway; it is God's decision."

The chief nods gravely. The conversation takes place in English in order to accommodate Mr. Sy's lack of understanding of the Visayan tongue. Teresa's English is remarkably good, Mr. Sy notes; much better than of any of the other islanders he has met. Well, better than most *uneducated* islanders, who mostly only know a few words of the second official language of the islands.

After a brief exchange of more pleasantries, the chief gets to the point quite quickly: "The reason we come here, Teresa, is to hear about what happened yesterday at the jail. Can you tell me in your own words?"

The eyes of the girl grow big and flit between the chief and Mr. Sy.

"Oh, you can be frank, Teresa. This is Inspector Sy from Manila. He is helping with the investigation."

Mr. Sy nods kindly to the girl and says, "Nice to meet you, Teresa!"

The girl smiles nervously; her body is tense and she doesn't say anything. It will be difficult to get her to tell the story, so the chief tries to help her on the way: "We are only checking up on some statements of other witnesses. You brought Juan some food yesterday, didn't you?"

The girl nods affirmatively: "Oh oh!"

"Good. Who made the food?"

"Well, that was Ate Maria. You know, the auntie of your neighbour, Pablo?" The chief obviously does not know, but still nods. "She is the cook now at the resort. She started two months ago. You know Teodoro, her husband, had this accident half a year ago when he fell out of a tree? He hurt himself really bad and he still cannot walk? And the boys are still in high school? So they have no income and Mary May, her sister, she cannot help either, because her daughter Ara is so poorly and needs medication. She was in Holy Child hospital already twice and..."

Her voice keeps droning on and on. *Why do the islanders have to talk so much about family relations and other unimportant matters that only muddle up the picture?* Mr. Sy thinks. The chief, for his part, does not seem to mind and is listening attentively to the monologue, once in a while throwing in a nod or understanding grunt.

"... So Ate Maria made the food. It was quite good; dried fish and rice. I only brought it to Juan." Though Mr. Sy likes the girl, he is greatly relieved when she finally focuses on the essentials again.

The chief nods understandingly: "So why did the cook make the food for Juan? Wasn't that a bit odd, now that Juan was in prison?"

Teresa looks as if she doesn't understand it: "But everybody has a right to a staff meal, Chief Arozo!"

"Really?" The chief raises one eyebrow in surprise.

"Yes!" Teresa says: "Sir Robert specifically instructed Ate Maria to make two meals a day for Juan. I also thought it was strange, so I asked him personally. But Ate Maria was right! And Sir Robert also told me to make sure Juan got his food every day!"

"That's interesting!" the chief says, with a small look at Mr. Sy. "So you packed the food. And then?"

"I took it to Juan in the late afternoon. He asked me to stay and keep him company while he ate. Juan is my sister's boyfriend's cousin, so I felt obliged to stay. And I felt a bit sorry for him, Chief; I am sure he didn't kill Ma'am Elena and he was sitting in this cell all alone!"

"Yes, yes, Teresa! So you stayed while he ate?"

"Yes," the girl replies eagerly, "and he ate it all! He was very thankful, especially because he also got Sir Robert's special coffee! It was a big honour; he loved it!"

"Sir Robert's special coffee? What's that?" Mr. Sy interrupts.

Teresa laughs, "Oh, Sir Robert has a special coffee; it is imported from India and it is meant only for him. He only drinks brewed coffee, never instant. I don't like brewed coffee; it is far too strong. My father and mother, God bless their souls, didn't like it either. They said they once had it when they went to Luzon to visit my mother's sister in Banaue. There they drink it all the time because my uncle works on a coffee plantation and they get one pound of coffee every week for free!" She beams proudly before continuing, "Juan never had brewed coffee before; I could see it on his face! He was so proud when he got the thermos and then took his first sip…" The girl laughs out loudly now, "He almost spit it out again! And twisted his face like this!" She made a successful imitation with a completely contorted face and her bright pink tongue stuck out far between her widely parted lips. "And then he said…" She laughs again, "It is *nice*! But he was lying; I knew right away, because Juan is just like us!" Slowly her laughter abates and she looks at the two smiling men with tears still in her eyes. "It was *so* funny!" She giggles again behind a raised hand: "So he drank the coffee anyway and even told the guard it was bitter, but good. And *very* special and *very* expensive brewed coffee." She nods sagely with every exclamation.

At this point, Mr. Sy has completely changed his opinion of this pretty girl. Sure, she is talking a lot, but he is by now quite taken by her; Teresa is very outgoing and really funny! And she isn't intimidated by the policemen at all any more; it seems as if she is having a good time in their company!

"Well, that was funny indeed. And it was kind of Sir Robert," the chief finally manages to say, trying to make his smiling face more serious again. He then continues more thoughtfully, "Maybe, Mr. Sy, it is time to talk to Sir Robert. What do you think?"

"Yes, Chief, that's a good idea!" Mr. Sy replies, although he is somewhat reluctant to leave the company of the girl so soon. But maybe they will meet again. With a friendly nod to the charming waitress, he follows the chief towards the administration building where they are told where they can find Robert Delsey.

They find the Englishman bent over some ledgers. He seems glad for the distraction and pushes the books away. "A real pain in the you-know-where, the tax guys from *BIR*. They want everything triple and four-fold and everything on bloody paper! Doesn't matter that we have it all on our computer!" He pats the brand-new Apple desktop computer that proudly sits on the heavy wooden desk. "No Sir; all on paper! They probably don't even know what these babies can do!" He fondly pats the computer again.

"Anyway! Gentlemen, what can I do for you?" With a flourishing movement, he motions for the men to sit down. "Cigar? No? They are locally made, but not too bad!" Robert Delsey takes one of the huge cylinders, snips off the head and ignites it with a match. With squinted eyes, he pierces through the billowing clouds that quickly fill the small room and asks again, "Well, what can I do for you? It is nice to see you again, but I assume this is not a social call and you have business on your mind?"

"Correct, Robert," the chief replies, "we are now investigating two murders; you probably heard about it already?"

"Yes, darn uncomfortable business, I would say," Robert Delsey says. "Any idea what happened?"

"We're trying to find out. At the moment, we are interrogating all possible witnesses."

"And then you come to me?" the resort manager says incredulously to the chief. "I haven't seen that boy for three days now!"

Mr. Sy replies, "That might be so, uhm… Robert. But your waitress, Teresa, is a witness; she was one of the last people who saw the boy alive and we are checking up on her story now."

"Teresa?" Robert Delsey is clearly taken aback. "She couldn't harm a fly! Sure, she had a fling with Juan, but which girl hasn't? It's no reason to kill him!"

"Excuse me Robert, did you say that Teresa had an affair with Juan?" the chief interrupts quickly. "I didn't know that!"

"Well, yes; you didn't know? Some rumours even say that he is the father of her child, although she denies it, of course."

"Interesting!" Mr. Sy murmurs, truly intrigued but also somewhat disappointed. The chief continues, "So who is the father of her child, according to her?"

Robert Delsey answers, with a twinkle in his eyes, "She claims it is Wilfredo, a worker on the farm next door. But since he is already married, he can hardly admit that he is the father, can he?"

"And what do *you* think, Robert?" The chief observes the man closely while he poses the question.

But the Englishman seems unperturbed: "Hmmm, it's hard to say. She *did* hang out with Wilfredo a lot after her fling with Juan. Who knows?"

"I think, Chief, we should look into this later," Mr. Sy says decisively. "Let's get back to the food basket Teresa brought Juan. Teresa claims that you had ordered her to bring him food twice a day?"

"Well… yes!" the resort manager replies, "anything wrong with that?"

"Did you have a specifically warm relationship with the boy?"

"No!"

"Did you feel sorry for the boy, then?"

"No, not really. I think he killed the girl, so why should I feel sorry for him?"

"So why did you tell your staff to bring him food then?"

"Oh, I understand! Yes, that does look a bit odd, doesn't it?"

Mr. Sy nods in affirmation.

"You know the labour laws of this country, Mr. Sy?"

"Not really," Mr. Sy admits.

"Right! Well then! Let me explain it to you; all employees at the Bayun Resort have a contract which states that they have a right to two staff meals a day. Juan had such a contract."

"So you brought him food, even though he was in prison and didn't work for you anymore?" Mr. Sy asks in amazement.

"Sure! He was still employed, wasn't he? We even had to pay his salary. We could hardly fire him, I mean, we would have had to have given him three valid warnings before we could have done so. That you lot incarcerated him is no valid reason, according to his lawyer. After all, he might have been innocent and locked up without a reason. He might have sued us if we stopped his staff meals or his salary. We might even have been charged for libel, because by stopping his staff meals and salary we would have indicated that he is guilty. And that wasn't proven yet, was it?"

"But... that is *absurd*!" Mr. Sy protests, for once at a loss for a proper reply.

"Exactly! Utterly absurd! But it is the law, unfortunately."

Mr. Sy looks at the chief, who only shrugs his shoulders in resignation.

"So you sent him food out of fear of being sued – is that it?"

"Bang on, Inspector. That's exactly the case!" the resort manager replies triumphantly. "It is unbelievable, isn't it? Anyway, it was not specified what kind of staff meal he should have gotten, so we kept it simple."

"So why did you order the staff to serve him your special coffee?"

"Did they do that? Strange; I never told them to do that! It's my private stock and not meant for anybody else. Anyway, they don't know how to make a good coffee. I normally let Nonoy make it; that's probably the only reason that fool is still employed here. He's from Mindanao and somehow seems to be the only one capable of brewing a good cup." Then he adds with a grim laugh, "Anyway, I'll talk to them about that, Inspector. Thanks for the tip!"

Mr. Sy nods before continuing, "Don't you think it is odd that the boy was killed, Robert? I mean; who could have a motive? Teresa is, according to you, out. So who else might have had a motive?"

Robert Delsey thinks briefly, then his expression changes and he starts to splutter: "Wait a minute; I never said she didn't have a motive. I merely said that she is a sweet girl. How should I know whether or not she killed him?"

"All right, Robert. But let's assume you are right and the girl is innocent. Who, according to you, might have a motive to kill Juan? Any ideas?"

The resort manager thinks deeply while drawing on his cigar: "Hmmm... Let's see.... Hmmm." But he seems to be unable to come up with a name.

"Robert, you must have heard that Juan claimed to have seen a crime that night down at the beach. Could there be, according to you, a relation between the crime both Juan and Elena might have seen, and their premature deaths?"

"Hmmm… difficult to say…" Robert Delsey focuses on the glowing end of the brown cylinder. "It's possible. If they indeed saw a crime, the drug dealers might want to eliminate witnesses. Although I still don't understand how they could so easily have gotten rid of the boy. I mean, he was under close supervision by your guards in your jail, right?"

"That's right, Robert," Mr. Sy admits, "so you assume that they didn't see anything – because the drug dealers could never have been able to arrange the killing of the boy so quickly."

Robert Delsey confirmed this reasoning with a brief nod.

"Well, if that is the case," Mr. Sy continues, "Juan and Elena were not eliminated because of what they saw, and hence there must be other motives – and therefore other killers, correct?"

"Humppf… I suppose so. Let me think…"

"No ideas?"

"Well…" the resort manager seems hesitant to speak his thoughts, "I always suspected Juan killed Elena. I told you so yesterday, right?"

Mr. Sy nods.

"I still think we cannot exclude this. So if this is true, maybe we should look at someone who got really mad when it became known that Elena was killed by Juan!"

"Someone like yourself?" The chief interrupts.

Robert Delsey throws an angry look at Chief Arozo. "Don't be ridiculous, Daniel! No, I mean her parents! Would you not get flaming mad if your daughter was killed?"

"Oh yes, I would!" The chief answers, deadly calm, while his black eyes fire deadly darts at Robert Delsey. "I would go over to him right away, rip off his arms and legs and then I would tear his heart out. But I wouldn't calmly plot to poison him. No Sir, I wouldn't!"

The resort manager, though almost a head bigger than the chief and ten years fitter, involuntarily leans backwards. "Calm down, man; we are all here to try to solve this mystery. No need to get all worked up!"

Mr. Sy raises his hand towards the chief: "He's right, Chief; let's keep a cool head. So, you think it might have been the grieving parents?"

Robert Delsey turns towards the inspector again. "Yes, why not? I mean, isn't it obvious! They are, like most people, exceptions given…" he looks nervously at the chief, who has resumed his menacing stance, "… convinced that Juan is guilty. And some even fear that he would have been set free. That seemed unjust to all of them, and it was not unlikely to happen. Now, Mr. Lee is too old and frail to do justice himself; he would be totally unable to storm a prison to tear out the arms and legs of a young man…" he throws a provocative look at the chief and continues, "but the mother, Cornelia Lee, is still a fit woman and she loved her daughter dearly. She might seem composed all the time, but really, Chief, under that quiet surface beats a fiery and emotional heart!"

Involuntarily, the chief nods slightly, so Robert Delsey continues somewhat more at ease, "Anyway, any mother would be upset, right? So maybe she went bonkers; who knows? Being a weak woman, she would resort to weapons other than brute strength to kill the boy. And what is a typical female weapon?" He looks triumphantly at both men, "Well? No? *Poison*, of course!"

"You try to tell me Cornelia *poisoned* the boy?" The chief shudders with anger and almost chokes on his words.

"Chief!" Mr. Sy rings out his warning. "If you please!"

He turns to the resort manager: "Any proof for your allegations?"

Robert Delsey laughs bitterly. "Of course not! How could I? I don't think you would believe me, even if I *had* evidence!"

"Oh?" Mr. Sy asks, surprised, "What makes you think so?"

The resort manager nods towards the chief. "I think Daniel here assumes that I have far better motives to kill the girl *and* Juan, so he would never believe me." He now speaks directly to the chief: "Isn't that right, Daniel? Just because I liked Elena, you think I would kill her out of jealousy because she had a fling with that boy, Juan? And the fact that I am a foreigner makes it even easier for you to suspect me, right? How ridiculous! Maybe you just want to implicate me, because you want to defend your beloved Cornelia!"

With a roar, the chief throws himself upon Robert Delsey, only to find himself painfully crumpled against the wall a split second later. Robert Delsey looks in amazement at Mr. Sy, who calmly straightens his jacket, and exclaims: "Incredible, Inspector; how did you do that?"

"Jujitsu," Mr. Sy replies calmly. "Comes in handy once in a while."

Mr. Sy goes over to the chief to help him up. "I am sorry, Chief, but you were about to do something very foolish."

The chief does not reply. He seems deflated and all aggression has left him. He gets up and, with a vacant look, walks out of the office.

"I apologise on behalf of the chief. This matter is very difficult for him, you must understand; two killings so quickly after one another, and still no firm suspects. Well, you understand, don't you? There's no need to make anything more out of it."

Robert Delsey nods eagerly. "Sure, sure, Inspector. No problem. I hope that my input will help you with your investigations."

Mr. Sy nods and stretches out his hand. "Thank you, Robert. If anything else comes to mind, please contact me; I'm staying at Uncle Joe's place."

"I know. If anything springs to mind… Goodbye, Inspector."

FIFTEEN

When Mr. Sy gets outside, the chief is nowhere to be seen. The guard, who is lingering just outside, notices his questioning look and points up the pathway towards the gate. Here he finds the chief already sitting in the car. With a sigh, Mr. Sy lowers himself onto the passenger seat beside him. "That was unwise what you did back there, Daniel. I personally sympathise with you and can to a large extent understand your emotions, but you must surely see that you displayed very unprofessional behaviour."

"As if I didn't know!" The chief mumbles apologetically, "I just don't know what came over me; I tried to control my anger, but it just burst out of me. Did you ever experience something like that? I mean; in a way, I was no longer of this world and I saw that man, that pompous arrogant Englishman, standing at the end of a tunnel, tempting me, challenging me. I could think of nothing else but: *I want to strangle that guy!*"

Mr. Sy has personally never experienced something like that, but had heard similar stories from suspects before; an uncontrollable rage directed at one person that came over one without warning, surprising the victim and perpetrator alike. But he had suspected the chief of irrational and emotional behaviour before. He has, from the start, considered Daniel an unhappy man; he drinks too much to drown the disappointments in his life. The incident with Cornelia Lee has confirmed Mr. Sy's suspicions and he had seen the chief unravel emotionally afterwards. According to his best understanding, Chief Arozo is presently unfit to participate in the investigations and Mr. Sy wants him to withdraw. But the chief has to do so voluntarily, since Mr. Sy cannot force him. Mr. Sy decides to apply some of the psychology his American teachers at Quantico imposed on him during his training there.

"Daniel, I understand. It is a common phenomenon for those who have endured heavy emotional stress." He continued in the same soothing voice, "And you have been exposed to many stress factors lately. No man, not even a strong man like yourself, can endure such stress indefinitely. You have done your part. It is time to take a step back… Relax. You need to be strong to continue, so get strong again!"

The chief looks up, emotions boiling under the tanned surface of his broad face, but is calmed by the understanding that shows on Mr. Sy's placid face. "You think so? I feel like such a failure; unable to solve the murders, unable to control my temper –"

Mr. Sy quickly interrupts him: "Nonsense, Daniel! Look at me; I have been investigating murder cases for almost fifteen years now. I am successful – probably the most successful investigator in the force! And you know how many cases I have solved?" He made an artificial pause to highlight the importance of the following statement: "Only about forty percent!"

"You are kidding me!" The chief recovers some of his composure.

"Yep, a mere forty percent! And you know how this sometimes makes me feel? I'll tell you; lousy, miserable and angry. Especially when I know a suspect is guilty, but I can't prove it; I then feel like taking justice into my own hands."

"My God, Sy, I hadn't thought you had that in you!"

Actually, Mr. Sy doesn't have it in him, but sometimes a slight exaggeration could further a good cause, so he continues his spin and put a slightly embarrassed look on his face: "Don't tell anyone. It's bad enough my boss knows about it. He's actually the one who saves me every time I am in that mood and he tells me: 'Jonathan, it's time for you to take a step back. Take a holiday and come back when you are ready again.' Yes, I have a good and understanding boss."

Actually, Mr. Sy's boss does nothing of the kind, and can in truth barely remember the first name of his key employee. But again, a small lie once in a while will not hurt a good cause.

The chief lets out a small giggle: "You know, I actually already feel much better. Imagine that the great Inspector Sy also has emotions and is not infallible!"

"Don't push your luck, Daniel. I admitted small flaws in my character;

there's no need to make fun of me!" Mr. Sy adds with a forced smile; he does not like to be laughed at, not even about his imaginary flaws. "So Daniel, do yourself and the force a favour and stay home. Sleep in, work on your hobbies – whatever!"

"And the investigation?"

"I'll deal with that and inform you if anything important happens. I'll manage until you are back in a few days. Just give me a guy who can drive me around, so I am not dependent on these smoke-belching Jeepneys."

The chief is laughing by now. "All right, Jonathan; I assume you'll be alright and I think a small break will do me good. But promise you'll keep me posted!"

"I will!" Mr. Sy says, but he has kept his true intentions hidden behind his immobile smile.

Chief Arozo and Mr. Sy agree that the chief will take his leave immediately. He would usually have to ask his superior for permission, but the local mayor is his cousin so this is an unnecessary formality. He will go to the station to drop off the car and inform his second-in-command, then send an agent to pick up Mr. Sy.

Just like his father, Mr. Sy had never learned to drive, since a true gentleman has a driver, after all. While he is waiting for his driver, Mr. Sy has some time to kill, so he decides to talk to the guard, who might have some knowledge about the events. He finds the guard standing behind the restaurant, observing the girls working the tables. When he hears Mr. Sy approaching, he quickly turns around, salutes and smiles: "Inspector, good afternoon!"

"Good afternoon! Nonoy, isn't it?"

The man's English is very good, though a bit pompous: "Yes Sir! Well actually my real name is 'Eulogio' – Eulogio Negrito Junior, that is. But my army commander thought that was too difficult in a crisis situation when we had to react quickly. So he asked me whether he was allowed to call me 'Nonoy'." The guard shrugs his shoulders: "What could I do? I accepted and later my comrades also started to call me by that name; I suppose to show me the same respect as my superior did."

"So you were in the army then, Nonoy?"

"Yes Sir; I volunteered. First I was normal infantry, but my captain saw my potential and proposed me for the Army Rangers! That was a hard bunch, Sir. We traced terrorists and Muslims all over Mindanao. I was decorated several times!"

"So why did you become a guard?"

"Oh, that is a sad story, Sir. While on a night patrol, a flare exploded close to my eyes, so my eyesight is not so good any more."

"But good enough for guard duty?"

"Oh yes, Sir! No problem! And if the light is very bright, I have these sunglasses given to me by Ma'am Elena." He points at a pair of expensive Ray-Ban glasses perched on top of his broad nose: "It was a present, because she likes me. She saw I was sometimes suffering when the light was very bright!"

"That was very kind of her! Speaking of Ma'am Elena, can I ask you some questions?"

Some of the guard's eagerness disappears and is replaced by a slight suspicious look. "I don't know much about it, Sir. I am just the guard and mostly keep to myself. You have to keep a distance from the other workers in a position like mine."

Mr. Sy tries to make the guard relax again: "Of course Nonoy; I understand. I only have some innocent questions. You know; background information and the like."

"Well, that's all right then!" the guard exclaims, relieved.

But the man seems to know little to none about the relationship between Robert Delsey and Elena, and even less about Elena and Juan. "I am sorry, Sir, that I cannot help you better. Ma'am Elena was always very kind to me, but she was the daughter of my boss and we did not communicate daily. Juan I knew even less; he was just the son of a fisherman, you know? Of course I know Sir Robert much better; he is here every day and I have his trust and confidence. He sometimes even asks my advice and help with marketing!"

"I'm sorry, Nonoy; 'marketing', you say?"

"Yes Sir," Nonoy replies proudly, "he sometimes gives me money and sends me to the market to buy vegetables; he trusts me completely with big amounts. I sometimes get as much as two hundred pesos and he trusts me so much that he never asks for receipts!"

"Right; that kind of marketing!" Mr. Sy smiles inwardly; this was a simple soul! "But speaking of helping Sir Robert, I understand you normally make special coffee for Sir Robert?"

"Yes?" comes the suspicious answer.

"I mean, Sir Robert has special coffee and you seem to be the only one who can make a good cup of coffee out of it."

"Ah, yes Sir," Nonoy replies brightly again, "they are specially imported coffee beans and Sir Robert only trusts me to make coffee from it. I learned it from my auntie in Mindanao. It is real brewed coffee, you know! Not the instant stuff the locals drink!"

"Yes, that's what I heard. The odd thing is that Juan apparently also got some of your special coffee!"

The guard seems shocked. "My coffee, Sir? Who said that?"

"Well, Teresa confirmed that it was the coffee you made that she brought to Juan and I initially wondered why Sir Robert allowed her to bring it to him, because Sir Robert was in no way close to the boy. Sir Robert told me he knew nothing about it, so I am just curious as to why Juan got this coffee. You obviously know as well as I do that Juan was poisoned and it is possible that either the food or the coffee was poisoned!"

With a pensive look, the guard lowers his eyes. It takes a while before he looks up again and answers, "This is very difficult, Sir. I am a good and loyal guard. But I also want to be honest to the police." He stops and looks straight at the inspector now.

"Yes, go on!" Mr. Sy would love to look the man right in his eyes now, but the dark green glasses of the Ray-Bans prevent him from doing so.

"Well, yesterday I helped Teresa pack the food for Juan. It was still early and the cooks were not yet there…" The guard pauses again, as if finding it difficult to continue.

"Yes, and?"

"You know, she is pregnant, so at present she does not like the smell of food and coffee. So I helped her… The coffee maker was on the table with the ground beans next to it, so I supposed she had planned to make brewed coffee. I only came when she had almost finished, so I don't know what she did before or that it was right I made the coffee…"

The constant breaks are starting to irritate the inspector: "Go on, Nonoy."

"Yes, so I quickly made the coffee and then when all was ready I placed it in a basket standing on the kitchen table, with the rice and fish. Somebody was going to pick it up, I didn't know who. So then I went outside, back to my duties. I went around the office buildings and passed the kitchen door again… Then I saw Sir Robert coming from the kitchen. He seemed startled…"

"How so, Nonoy?"

"Well, he made a small step, like this." The guard mimes a poor and exaggerated imitation of a surprised person. "Like he was caught doing something wrong. You understand?"

"But you did not see him in the kitchen doing something with the food or drinks?"

"I only saw him coming from the kitchen. But he looked like a very guilty man!"

Mr. Sy thanks the guard, who salutes and wanders off. Mr. Sy is left alone with his thoughts again. It is quite obvious that Juan died of poisoned food or drinks. It seemed obvious that it must have been either in the food or the coffee from the resort, but then, is that so likely? Maybe not; after all, someone else could have given Juan something laced with arsenic. The guards probably wouldn't have noticed, because despite their confirmation of the opposite, Mr. Sy is not convinced they had kept a good eye on the prisoner all the time. But maybe someone else, someone like Cornelia Lee, could have given him something; chocolate, maybe? The autopsy would probably confirm what was in the stomach, but obviously not how it had gotten there.

But if the poison had indeed been in the coffee or the food, who had put it there? Teresa, the waitress? Betrayed lovers do odd things once in a while, especially if they get pregnant and the father does not acknowledge his responsibility. Or maybe Robert Delsey? Mr. Sy is sure that the man has not been completely honest in their conversations and there are some arguments that could be used to incriminate him for the murders. But still… It could also have been somebody else; a hired killer maybe? Maybe one of the villagers who wanted to earn a few quick pesos on the side for a quick killing? That would not have been unusual at all. They didn't even have to visit Juan to kill him; they could just as easily have given him the poisoned goods through the barred window. But hired by whom? Acting on behalf of the Lee brothers? Or maybe somebody completely different, who had a grudge against the local Don Juan?

It is quite exasperating; there are just too many leads and too few hard facts. This case might turn into one of the hardest cases he has ever encountered! Mr. Sy decides to call it a day and return to Uncle Joe's place.

During dinner, which he enjoys with Uncle Joe alone, he avoids the subject of the murders and they chat instead about the present political situation, recent films – of which Uncle Joe knows an awful lot – and the precarious economic situation of the majority of the Philippine population in contrast to the enormous wealth of the happy few. And of course, the all-permeating corruption that has blossomed under the Marcos regime is discussed with obvious gusto. In this respect, Uncle Joe has become a true Filipino; he knows all the details about local and national corrupt officials and politicians, but apart from mocking he does not do anything to get rid of the parasites. Nevertheless, it is an enjoyable evening and Mr. Sy is sad to hear the old man say goodnight a few minutes before 10 PM. But he is also looking forward to a good night's rest, during which his overburdened mind might present him with some clues he has overseen in the daytime.

SIXTEEN

Contrary to his normal routine, this particular night has brought neither relief nor relaxation to Mr. Sy. Despite the open windows, the air had been stifling, hot and humid, while the incessant chirping of the crickets and the occasional repetitive calling of the resident gecko had kept him awake all night. Well, Mr. Sy has to admit, it might also have been the loose threads of the case, which he seems unable to tie up, that kept him awake. It is so exasperating! This has never happened to him before, but he has to face the truth in the eyes; he is at his wits' end! He always had some ideas – or rather suspicions – and his well-developed police instincts would then guide him towards a solution. But not this time. No, definitely not this time. With a deep sigh, Mr. Sy reluctantly opens his eyes after many hours of restless tossing back and forth and blinks against the glaring light that, despite the early hour, already fills his bedroom. He tosses the blanket aside and places his feet on the sticky linoleum that covers the floorboards of his bedroom. Stretching his aching back, Mr. Sy hobbles across the landing towards the bathroom, while the delicious fumes of a cooked breakfast whiff around him. He hurriedly makes himself ready, checks his by now immaculate appearance in the mirror and goes downstairs.

In the kitchen, he is welcomed by the two men eating in absolute silence. Uncle Joe rises to get another plate while Chief Arozo raises his head with a resigned look: "Didn't want to wake you, but we just got the news that old Lee has been murdered."

"What?" Mr. Sy is unable to suppress his surprised and angry outcry. "When did this happen? Who did it? Why didn't you wake me?"

Chief Arozo seems as surprised by this unprofessional outburst as Mr. Sy himself. "I don't know, Jonathan; one of my men just came by a few minutes ago to tell me the news. They apparently found the old man shot in his garden."

Uncle Joe hands Mr. Sy a plate laden with food: "First eat, young man; five more minutes won't make a difference."

Mr. Sy has recovered from the surprise and thinks otherwise; within five minutes, a bunch of buffooning local officials could spoil a crime scene completely. But there is, at this stage, probably nothing he can do anyway, so he resigns himself to his fate and hurriedly starts working on his plate. Ten minutes and two mugs of strong coffee later, he rises and hurries, the chief in his wake, to the car where the police driver is already waiting. Mr. Sy sits down on the passenger seat and the chief opens the back door. Mr. Sy's forthcoming comment is interrupted by a sharp intermission: "No, Jonathan; don't even think about stopping me. I'm alright now; last night's sleep did me well. And besides, it is my island, my people. I appreciate your help but it is *my* investigation!"

Mr. Sy just shrugs and tells the driver to leave. With an abrupt jolt, the heavy car starts to move down the hill, picking up speed in the process.

They have difficulties getting to the gate of the estate; throngs of curious onlookers, stretching their necks and babbling excitedly, prevent the car from proceeding. They get out and the chief uses his impressive bulk to create a path towards the gate. Despite incessant ringing, the gate is not opened, and the futile efforts of the chief to make himself heard above the continuous chattering of the crowd and attract the attention of the people inside fail to show any effect. With a resigned movement, Chief Arozo opens his leather holster and retrieves his .45. A young man right beside the chief notices the huge gleaming gun and, with a nervous shriek, jumps aside. This causes a ripple effect in the crowd that starts to flow back and forth, accompanied by a crescendo of surprised and angry shouts. The chief raises the gun into the air and looks questioningly at Mr. Sy. With a slight nod, the gun goes off with a terrific bang. The following abrupt silence is only disturbed by the thin wailing of a frightened infant.

"Step back, everybody! Or even better, go home. There is nothing to see here!" the chief bellows into the now silent crowd.

Looks are exchanged and then low murmurs break out of the previously silent crowd. A few shuffle their feet, but apparently their curiosity is too big to allow them to go home. The chief glares angrily at the spectators closest to him and hushes them away with a casual waving movement of his gun: "Go on; move! Back! Back, I tell you!" Slowly, the first spectators turn around and start moving away.

"Go on! That's right! Go home! There's nothing here to see!" The chief keeps on moving back and forth amidst the crowd, uttering forceful encouragements. After a few minutes, only a few lonely onlookers are left sheltering in the shade of the huge Balete tree opposite the gate. The chief returns to Mr. Sy: "Sometimes they are like cattle!" He laughs and continues, "And then I just treat them like cattle!"

He approaches the gate again and hammers against the dark wood with his gun. "Hey, you lot in there; this is Chief Arozo. Open the gate!"

The creaking of a badly oiled lock is heard as a key is turned around and the gate slowly swings open. Inside, two policemen, brandishing old battered Garant rifles, are eying the area behind the chief with worried and suspicious looks.

"Lock the gate again, boys. And don't let anyone in or out without my permission!" The chief instructs both men while he enters, Mr. Sy in his wake.

They continue to the mansion and are welcomed by a distraught housemaid, who quickly guides them into an office. It is obviously the office of old Lee; the walls are decorated with purely male ornaments, like trophies of extinct animals, prizes of long-forgotten tournaments and a few delicate Chinese figurines. A slim, well-dressed man bends over the huge writing desk behind which Cornelia Lee is sitting, leafing through some papers. Once she spots the visitors, she rises quickly, a small shaky smile on her distraught face, and approaches both men with outstretched, welcoming arms. She has obviously been crying, but otherwise seems quite composed. "Mr. Sy, Daniel; I am so happy you are here. It is dreadful, so horribly dreadful!" Chief Arozo takes her outstretched hands while fighting with his contradictory emotions. Cornelia Lee quickly retracts them again and points towards the politely smiling Chinese man standing next to the huge desk. "Do you know my brother-in-law? This is Yunlin, the younger brother of my husband."

Yunlin smiles in an aloof manner and bows slightly, obviously without any intentions of shaking the hands of the visitors. Mr. Sy smiles back and presents a mere shadow of a bow, all the while keeping his eye on the small man, who seems less than disturbed by his attention. The chief just nods distractedly and concentrates on Cornelia instead.

"I don't know what to do, Daniel! First Elena and now Zhiheng! What is happening, Daniel? What's going on?" She turns around and sits behind the desk again, her delicate fingers intertwined in something resembling a prayer: "I was still in bed this morning when I heard a bang. Not a big bang, just… you know, a bang. I didn't think anything of it then. But a few minutes later, I heard my personnel running through the house, shouting and crying. So I got up and they told me Zhiheng had been shot in the garden. I just couldn't comprehend it. He normally takes a stroll just after sunrise, you know. And someone just shot him close to the back wall. They took me there and it was awful! There was so much blood; his whole chest was covered in it. I just couldn't stand it. Thank God Yunlin was there too and he took over."

The chief drags out a chair and sits down on the opposite side of the desk: "When exactly was this, Cornelia?"

She raises her beautiful, almond eyes towards the ceiling and answers softly, "Oh, I think around six, maybe six fifteen. Definitely not later!"

Mr. Sy is still staring at the small man and asks: "What did you do when you took over, Mr. Lee?"

A thin smile flits over the face of the small Chinese man: "Oh, nothing special; just the obvious. I approached my brother but was careful not to touch anything. There was so much blood and I was pretty sure he was dead. But I still felt for his pulse. But my first impression had been correct; he was definitely dead," Yunlin Lee nods sadly.

"And where were you when you heard the shot?" Chief Arozo asks.

A small eyebrow twitch disturbs the otherwise placid calmness of Yunlin's face: "I didn't hear a shot, Chief Arozo. I was having my breakfast in the dining room. The doors were closed and the air con was on. One of the girls was serving me breakfast when a gardener came in to tell me the horrible news. That was the first time I heard about a shot. The girl and the gardener can testify."

The chief nods: "And you, Cornelia; can anybody testify where you were when Lee was shot?"

"Am I a suspect, Daniel?"

The chief blushes. "Of course not, Cornelia. We merely want to establish the whereabouts of all persons when the shot was fired, that's all!"

"Honestly, I don't think anybody can vouch for my whereabouts. I was still in bed. It was still early. And I tend to sleep alone, if you must know!" she replies haughtily. "My husband and I had separate bedrooms. We have for many years now. You know, our rhythms are so different: he went to bed early and rose at dawn, while I am somewhat of a night bird and normally sleep till nine or ten."

"I understand, Cornelia; I didn't want to pry," the chief replies.

Mr. Sy, annoyed by the chief's consolatory tone, takes over: "I would like to talk to you later in private, Mrs. Lee. For now, could you gather all personnel who were on the premises this morning? We would like to interrogate them. Could that be arranged, Mrs. Lee? We would like to see them all gathered outside in half an hour."

Yunlin is quick to answer: "I will see to it, Cornelia! That is, unless you have any more questions, Inspector."

Mr. Sy nods his approval and the small man leaves the room silently.

"But before that, we would like to see the crime scene. Can you ask somebody to show us the way, Mrs. Lee?"

"Of course, Inspector!" She rings a small silver bell and the housemaid appears instantly to guide the two men to the crime scene where old Lee had bled to death.

In death, the once powerful Zhiheng Lee has been reduced to a small crumpled Chinese doll with a blood-splattered silk kimono. A small gun is lying close to the body, a silk slipper lying next to it; the other one is still on his foot. A few footprints are discernable in the wet soil and the long grass around the body is flattened in some areas. The body itself is lying on its side; Lee's legs are stretched out, one arm is flat in a blood puddle in front of his dead unseeing open eyes, and the other is crammed under his torso. The kimono has partly fallen open to reveal a scrawny chest with sparse grey hairs and a multitude of tiny ragged wet holes encircled by crusty dark red rims. The small rivulets of blood that had poured from the holes are now dry; brownish streaks lead to the large red puddle in front of the body.

"Hunting gun, or more likely pump gun; there's plenty of them around."

The chief concludes with an expert look. Carefully avoiding the red puddle, he bends down and opens the kimono further with a small stick: "The killer must have been quite close to create such damage. Look at that; the poor guy got the full load in his chest!"

Mr. Sy nods in agreement; he has seen many shotgun wounds, but never one where the pellets have hit the body in such a concentrated manner.

"Old Lee must have died instantly from shock," the chief continues while he gets up again. "Well, let's see what Dr. Gonzales has to say about it."

As if on cue, the coroner appears next to the two men, panting slightly. "Well, Chief, it seems that a serial killer is on the loose on our island. This is the third death in three days!" He smiles wryly and then focuses his attention on the body. The other men silently observe him going through the motions. After ten minutes, the coroner rises and approaches the policemen, stating in a dry, factual manner: " He was shot at close range with a pump gun from probably less than, oh… let's say one to two metres. There is hardly any spread; the full load hit him in the chest. He seems to have died of heavy haemorrhaging within a couple of minutes, but he probably lost consciousness long before that. Look there; can you see the marks behind him?" Dr. Gonzales points at a flattened piece of grass a few decimetres behind the body: "I think he was standing there when he was shot and fell backwards. You can see a few splatters of blood right there. Then he tried to get up, but he didn't manage to and just rolled over on his side to die."

"What about the other gun, Dr. Gonzales?" Mr. Sy asks, while pointing at the small four-barrelled pistol.

"That's a .22 Mossberg Brownie, which apparently belonged to old Lee," the coroner mentions casually. "Haven't seen one in ages. Anyway, I haven't investigated it properly; that's a job for your guys, but I could smell that it hasn't been used today."

The two policemen nod understandingly before the coroner continues: "Well, I'll have to do a proper autopsy before I can say anything conclusive. Daniel; please have the body bagged up and brought to my office." And with a small bow, the coroner leaves the crime scene.

The next couple of hours are spent on interrogations of all the witnesses. Mrs. Lee has ordered a small desk to be set up on the veranda, where the policemen can do their work. It is a painstaking process; there are fifteen witnesses in all – housekeepers, gardeners, kitchen maids and drivers – and most statements do not correspond with each other. Some inconsistencies are not uncommon, but this case is exceptional. One of the reasons is that most witnesses had left the estate to report on the latest developments to friends and relatives outside, so by the time they are finally called back in, their statements are tainted by some appalling gossip that has developed like a brush fire on a cork-dry savannah. Several witnesses present, without blushing or a bad conscience, some of the half-facts or plain lies that they have picked up from 'authoritative sources' outside. One witness claims to have seen Robert Delsey 'swinging below a *wog wog*', who dropped him off inside the estate, just before dawn, whilst another claims that she had heard, from a reliable source, that Mrs. Lee had been chasing old Lee through the garden with a rake until the old man was too exhausted to run and she finally killed him by repeatedly hitting him with the same garden instrument! Chief Arozo and Mr. Sy note everything – even the most ridiculous comments – faithfully in their report, but they agree that none of the statements shed any more light into the how and why of the murder.

But there seems to be a general understanding among most workers that Robert Delsey had behaved suspiciously; he wasn't at his home when the night guard had gone to fetch him and when he, after a long delay, finally arrived at the crime scene, he had started shouting aggressively at the workers. But the sight of the murdered Lee must have triggered his guilty conscience, because he was seen running away almost immediately and had apparently withdrawn to his house.

Mr. Sy and the chief both know that they probably will benefit most from a proper interrogation of Yunlin Lee, Cornelia Lee and Robert Delsey. The former because both policemen agree that the three murders could have something to do with this infamous and unproven drug deal, the latter because he had an emotional motive to kill all three, and the recent widow is also still in the picture; she is a valuable witness in both cases and might even be a suspect for one or more killings. The chief resents the fact that 'his' Cornelia is still suspected, but cannot deny Mr. Sy's calm and rational reasoning. No matter how the men turn the facts, all three persons seem to have a motive for the killings. In their next steps, they have to validate their alibis and check their statements for inconsistencies. Mentally, Mr. Sy throws his eyes towards heaven and asks the support of the Almighty One; this is going to be a long and complex process! Both policemen agree that they are not only investigating three separate murders, but now have to investigate a complete string of events; from Elena's death until the death of her father. Three consecutive killings in three days are just too much of a coincidence and there just *has* to be a connection!

SEVENTEEN

"So you never saw Elena after you arrived on the island and only heard about her death from your sister-in-law? Is that correct, Mr. Lee?" Chief Arozo asks while he tries to retain his polite composure. He, Mr. Sy and Yunlin Lee have withdrawn to the intimacy of the library to proceed with the interrogation of the younger and only remaining Lee brother.

Yunlin Lee crosses his thin legs, which are clad in immaculately pressed trousers, before he smilingly answers: "I already told you that thirty minutes ago, Chief Arozo; I arrived late at night on the island with my yacht and, considering the tropical depression that was churning up the sea, was happy to have made it alive! My captain had notified my brother by marine telephone that I would land at the cove and he was there to receive me. I had not seen him in many years and the reunion was, as you can imagine, quite emotional. We returned to the mansion and, after a small nightcap, turned in at around 12 o'clock. And no, Inspector, as I told you before, neither Elena nor Cornelia were there to verify the facts I have just presented. Normally I would say that you should ask my brother to confirm my statement, but unfortunately he has been murdered by a killer you seem unable to apprehend. Just as you are unable to apprehend the killer of my niece and that young Filipino dive guide. But of course, my employees can confirm my statement. I must prepare you both, however; they only speak and understand their local Chinese dialect and their English is virtually non-existent! Of course I could interpret, but that would reduce the validity of their statements somewhat – wouldn't you say so, Chief Arozo?"

The chief mumbles something incomprehensive so Mr. Sy continues: "We will look into that, Sir. Now, to your relation with Juan Aldones –"

"I'm sorry, Inspector; who? Oh, I see; the young dive guide. I never met him in my life!" With a satisfied smile, Yunlin Lee leans back in his chair.

Normally Mr. Sy achieves good interrogatory results by letting the silence continue, thereby 'encouraging' a witness or suspect to reveal further details in order to bridge the uneasy pause, but Yunlin seems oblivious of any discomfort and just sits there, smilingly reclined in his chair, viewing the Inspector with evident satisfaction. After a full minute of uncomfortable silence, it is Mr. Sy who feels compelled to continue: "Yes, it seems like that, Sir. But you must have heard about him in the recent days, have you not?"

"Of course, Inspector. But you, better than anybody else, should know that one cannot put too much value on third party revelations; isn't that what they teach you at the police academy, Inspector?"

It is extremely rare that Mr. Sy loses his temper, but this is one of the only occasions that he almost does. It is so obvious that this man knows much more than he reveals, and he makes it quite obvious that he knows that Mr. Sy knows. Such arrogance! Only ten years earlier, Mr. Sy could have thrown him into jail and lost the key without bothering about a proper process and let him rot away in a stinking moist cell at the back of police headquarters. But those days are gone. Besides, Mr. Sy prefers to nail his opponents with fair and sound evidence. He will make sure that this obnoxious representative of the criminal society he loathes so much will get the punishment he deserves. So he only smiles at the drug lord's quip and answers, "You are absolutely right, Sir. So if I understand it correctly, you did not meet the two victims while you were on the island, nor do you have any idea who could have murdered them?"

"That is correct, Inspector. I don't dwell on speculations; I gladly leave this to the police."

Mr. Sy looks briefly at the chief, who is visibly fuming by now, and decides it might be useful to let him put some heat on Yunlin. With an almost imperceptible nod, he allows the chief to take over. Chief Arozo takes a step forward and now towers threateningly above the drug lord: "Let me sketch a scenario for you, then; maybe that will refresh your memory. Let's assume you and your older brother were landing drugs at the beach –"

Yunlin raises an eyebrow and starts to say something.

"Don't you interrupt me, *Mr.* Lee," the chief utters menacingly. "Your turn to speak will come, and when you finally do, you will sing like a Chinese canary!"

Yunlin shows obvious irritation at this provocation, but is wise enough to hold his tongue.

"And let's say Elena and Juan were there by some coincidence, observing your illegal activities. When they ran away, they were probably noticed by you or your men. You chased them and got hold of Elena, who then met with an 'accident'. Juan managed to slip away, however, and you couldn't reach him; he was by then enveloped by his neighbours and family. Then he was arrested and for a while was out of your reach. But you couldn't take the risk and have him testify against you, so you had him poisoned. I don't know by whom, but I will find out. Unfortunately for you, he managed to tell us what had happened before you got to him."

Yunlin Lee keeps his silence and his arrogant little smile forces the chief to continue: "Your brother, however, didn't agree with the killing. He might have been a drug dealer, but wouldn't go so far as to kill his own daughter. He probably found out you had killed her, so you had a fallout. But you reacted quicker than he did and you decided to eliminate him before he could take revenge. Don't you think this scenario has a plausible ring to it, *Mr.* Lee?"

If Chief Arozo had expected a violent reaction from the drug lord after this verbal attack, he is proven to be wrong; Yunlin merely smiles up towards the angry chief and says: "As I said; I leave speculations to the police. I think the inspector agrees with me that it is just that; speculation! Where is your proof, Chief? These are all just rumours you picked up on the street. Besides, I have an alibi for all occasions, if you would only bother to check it!"

The chief just stands there, trembling with suppressed anger.

Yunlin Lee continues, unperturbed: "And talking about rumours, what is this rumour that a certain foreigner – eh… what was his name? Yes; Robert Delsey – that he is also implicated? And have you already checked out *his* alibi? No? That is really a shame! Sloppy police work, Chief! Besides, who says it is only one killer? Maybe your cases are not connected after all. Have you thought about that?"

Mr. Sy can see that this discussion is going the wrong way, and that the chief, unstable as he is, might do something foolish. So Mr. Sy puts his hand calmly on the shoulder of the other policeman and says, "We are done here,

Chief. There is no need to bother Mr. Lee any more at this stage." With a wry smile towards the sitting man, he continues: "I am sure Mr. Lee is still overcome by grief over his dead brother and niece and we should allow him to mourn."

An angry expression flits briefly over Yunlin's face, but he recovers quickly and replies smilingly: "You are a kind and perceptive man, Inspector. If you need further information, you know where to find me."

Mr. Sy has started moving the chief towards the door, but at this last remark the chief pulls himself free and bellows at the still sitting drug lord: "Yes, we know where to find you, because you will not move your yellow ass from this island until I allow you to do so!"

Mr. Sy gets hold of the struggling chief again and together they leave the library.

When they enter the dome-like hallway, the chief is still breathing heavily but no longer resists Mr. Sy guiding him towards the exit. They stop however when they recognise Cornelia Lee leaning against the balustrade of the first floor, beckoning them to come up. She chimes: "Ah, gentlemen; don't leave yet. Please come to my room. I was just going to have some coffee. Will you join me?"

The men enter an airy, sunny room with a terrific view over the gardens towards the sea. The room consists of two areas separated by sliding doors that currently stand open. Through the opening, the men can see a large, king-sized bed with lots of overstuffed pillows in a shady retreat decorated with typical female paraphernalia. The room they are standing in is cosy and equipped with a writing desk, sofa, tea table, two cosy chairs and shelves with lots of porcelain figurines. Cornelia Lee beckons the men to sit down while she instructs the housemaid to fetch two more cups. She pours the coffee for the two men, adds sugar and milk without asking and opens the conversation with a sad smile: "I know you wish to interrogate me about what has happened and of course I will oblige you. But before we start, I have to get something off my chest, Inspector. You are probably wondering how I am bearing up so well. After all, a few days ago my little girl died and a few hours ago my husband was slain by some bandits. If you would have asked me some days ago how I would react if something like this happened, I would have said that I would probably break down completely and cry without stopping. I have not only surprised you with my reaction, Inspector, but also myself."

Mr. Sy wants to say something, but Mrs. Lee interrupts him: "No no, Inspector, there's no need denying it; I saw it on your face when you entered and I poured your coffee."

It is true; Mr. Sy *had* been surprised that Mrs. Lee was so composed after the loss of her daughter *and* her husband so shortly after each other.

After both men decline a refill, Mrs. Lee pours herself another coffee and sighs: "When I heard that Elena had died, I thought my heart would break. It was as if a part of me had died and the world looked cold and colourless all of a sudden. I tried to keep my composure, because this is expected from me. It also gave me a way to cope with the loss; if I had lost myself in mourning, I probably would have collapsed completely. But believe me, the loss of Elena is deeply felt and I was... I *am*, devastated!"

She lifts the fine porcelain cup to her slightly trembling lips again and takes a small sip before continuing, "Strangely enough, the death of my husband has not touched me as deeply. Of course I was shocked when my husband was ripped away from this life so suddenly, but to be honest, we had been growing apart for a long time now and it sometimes felt as if I was living under the same roof with a stranger. We met occasionally during lunch or dinner or at formal occasions, but we no longer actively sought each other's company."

All of a sudden, tears appear in Cornelia's eyes. "He was not really a bad man, Inspector, but he was misguided. You know, he was the eldest son and his father expected great things from him. His father's family had built up a trading empire in China, but they lost everything in the Revolution. After that, his father impressed on Zhiheng that it was his obligation, as the eldest son, to resurrect the family business. And Zhiheng did as his father had expected him to do; he started in a small way in Hong Kong and then expanded in a big way in the Philippines. His father died some years later, but Zhiheng kept acting in his spirit. I knew of most of his business; trading, banking, shipping. But I suspected there to be a less legal part of the business, which Zhiheng never introduced to me. He wanted to protect me and I think he was also embarrassed."

"Do you have any idea what the nature of that illegal business was, Mrs. Lee?" Mr. Sy asks.

Cornelia Lee shakes her head. "I am sorry, Inspector; I don't know for sure. To be honest, I didn't want to know it either!" She smiles apologetically, "I am a bit like an ostrich here, I'm afraid!"

Mr. Sy nods understandingly while the chief sits on the edge of his seat, battling with mixed emotions.

"Anyway, I no longer loved my husband, Inspector. I cared for him as a good friend, but there was no longer the companionable warmth of love – if there ever was." She turns towards the chief and whispers: "Dear Daniel, this must be so difficult for you. I told you I would bring you nothing but trouble!"

She straightens up, turns towards Mr. Sy and looks sternly at him as if to discourage him to disapprove with what she has to say next: "I would like you to know that my heart, in truth, belongs to Daniel; it always has. We have known each other since before I got married and, truth be told, I should have married him instead!"

The chief lets out a small gasp and stares at his beloved with wide eyes. Cornelia rises and bends down towards him to touch him tenderly on his cheek while she continues talking to Mr Sy in a low voice, her eyes tenderly caressing the broad face of the chief: "I was stupid, Inspector, and listened to my family back then. When Zhiheng asked for my hand, I accepted to please my family and to prevent the bankruptcy of my father's business. I did not love Zhiheng. Oh, he was kind and considerate and showered me with gifts, but he never managed to conquer my heart. My heart belonged to Daniel then and it still does!"

All of a sudden, she breaks down in tears, throws her arms around the broad shoulders of the chief and sobs: "And now I am free from him, but we lost our daughter!"

Mr. Sy calmly observes the emotional spectacle. "With your daughter, I assume you mean the daughter of yourself and Daniel."

With a snap, Mrs. Lee head flies up: "How did you guess?"

"I didn't; Daniel told me!"

"Oh Daniel!" Mrs. Lee sniffs before she collapses again in the arms of the chief, who can barely keep back his tears either.

Mr. Sy allows the couple a few minutes to compose themselves again before he starts his interrogation of Mrs. Lee. She more than willingly answers all of the inspector's questions, but in a distracted way, as she seems to be too much absorbed in the love for the only person still left to her. Nothing conclusive comes up in the course of the interrogation. They go through the events surrounding Elena's death and the killing of Juan again, but nothing new comes up. When Zhiheng was shot, Cornelia had been in bed, a housemaid had fetched her after the shot had been heard and she could not supply any conclusive evidence about the identity of the killer, although she had a bad feeling about her brother-in-law.

"How come, Mrs. Lee?" The inspector asks.

By now, Mrs. Lee is sitting on the armrest of the chiefs' chair with her slim legs crossed, holding hands with him: "He should have been the successor of his father and not Zhiheng. Yunlin is ruthless and has a dark soul, Inspector. He thinks he is unreadable and never shows emotions. But I can see through him; he cares about only two things: money and power! He will do anything to protect and enlarge his empire. As I said, Inspector; I have no firm evidence, but it would not surprise me if he had his hands in all three killings!"

Mr. Sy only nods. Cornelia Lee might be right; her string of thoughts is logical. By now, he has received a better impression of Cornelia Lee; deep down she is an emotional person, but she is also a person able of planning and executing actions in a rational way. However, he still cannot shake the thought that Cornelia could calmly have planned the poisoning of Juan in order to avenge the death of her daughter. And the course of events could possibly have made her mentally so unstable that she planned yet another killing; the killing of her husband! In a twisted way, it does make sense; she has lost the one thing she had loved; her daughter. Maybe she thought her husband had been involved in the killing, or maybe she just wanted him out of the way to make sure she would not lose the second love in her life: Chief Daniel Arozo! Another uncomfortable thought crept into the mind of Mr. Sy. What *is* the role of Daniel Arozo? He has also lost his daughter *and* proven himself to be a man who is guided by strong emotions too! Had the chief not suspected that old Lee might be implicated? This is strong circumstantial evidence and Mr. Sy knows he can no longer ignore the fact that Chief Arozo also had good motives to kill old Lee. *And* he has easy access to weaponry and knows how to use it! He had not thought about this before and makes a mental note to check the chief's alibi carefully.

That night, Uncle Joe and Mr. Sy get little pleasure out of the company of Daniel Arozo. Mr. Sy disapproves of the unprofessional attitude the chief had displayed at the estate and he vents his displeasure quite clearly. The chief doesn't seem to notice, however; he is in a pensive, distracted mood and Mr. Sy can guess why. He is therefore not surprised when the chief gets up straight after dinner and says goodnight. It suits his plans well, because he intends to verify the chief's alibi for the past few nights. But Uncle Joe's statements are inconclusive; the old man did not know when the chief got up the previous mornings, but assumed he had been in the house all night. Mr. Sy doesn't dare to query any further, lest he raise Uncle Joe's suspicions. Knowing how close the old man and the chief are, the risk would be high that the chief would get wind of the inspector's misgivings. The inconclusiveness of his investigations frustrates Mr. Sy and makes his mood broody and grim. He does not want to burden the old man with his bad moods, so Mr. Sy also retires quite early and slips between the cool, starched sheets of his bed in the hope of a long and relaxing good night's sleep.

EIGHTEEN

Mr. Sy is disappointed yet again, however; the next morning is similar to the previous ones and he is again woken with a new development in the case.

"Hurry up; there is a witness at the police station who claims that he can prove that Robert Delsey killed old Lee. Maybe this is the breakthrough we were hoping for!" the chief exclaims excitedly. The old car brings them to the station in record time and they hurry towards the door of the station, which they find bolted.

"Open the door, Ramos; it's me!" the chief bellows.

They can hear the heavy steps of army boots inside, a bolt is pushed back and the sergeant opens the door. The chief storms in, followed by the inspector. Inside, they find the resort guard Nonoy sitting on a wooden chair. His shifty eyes take on a worried look when he recognises the officers. The chief takes a step towards the guard, but Sergeant Ramos holds him back with his hand. "Chief; a word in private, please."

With a brief look at the resort guard, the sergeant goes ahead of the chief and the inspector towards the cell block. Inside, Sergeant Ramos looks around to make sure no one is listening in before he says in a low voice: "Nonoy here claims that Robert Delsey has shot old Lee. He's says he's got pretty good evidence, but he wants to tell you himself."

The chief is already heading towards the guard when Sergeant Ramos stops him again: "Wait Sir, there's something more!" The sergeant doesn't elaborate, but instead retrieves a piece of paper from his chest pocket and presents it to the chief and the inspector to read.

Mr. Sy quickly scans the papers and says: "Don't touch it, Chief; there might be fingerprints on it that we can use to identify the author of this letter." Mr. Sy instructs the chief, "Just hold it in front of us, Sergeant, so we can read it."

Mr. Sy despises anonymous tips, but also knows that more often than not there is a good portion of truth in them. If this is also the case with the anonymous letter the sergeant is carefully holding by its corner, there might be a breakthrough of a sort after all. The letter says the following:

'This is an anonymous tip from a concerned and loyal citizen of the Republic of the Philippines. We have observed that the foreigner Yunlin Lee, of Chinese origin and presently residing at the Lee estate, has illegally and unlawfully hidden heroin in the library on the right-hand side of the entrance door, third shelf, behind some leather-bound books. Remove the books and the wooden panel behind it and you will find ten packages of heroin. He was not alone in this crime but was helped by other foreigners residing on this island.
Signed: A Concerned Citizen'

The language is pompous, but clearly written by a Filipino with some kind of education. Sergeant Ramos sees they have finished reading and asks: "What do you think, Chief; is it genuine?"

"Hmmm, maybe. We have to keep this a secret, Sergeant; if it is true, we don't want to warn the criminals and allow them to escape!"

Ramos squirms unhappily and mumbles something with downcast eyes.

"What's that, Ramos?" The chief demands.

"I am sorry, Chief, but Nonoy has already read it!"

The chief utters an angry snarl and throws a fuming glare at the unlucky sergeant. Then he glares at the resort guard with a scorching look that forces the man to cast down his eyes. Both he and the sergeant shrink when the chief bellows, "You let that idiot read it?"

Ramos nods unhappily and adds: "Somehow he also touched the paper and I think his fingerprints are on it now."

The chief groans: "What a mess! Not only do we have at least two sets of fingerprints smudging the evidence, but soon the whole village will know about this letter! You could just as well have written an article in the newspaper!"

141

The resort guard looks distinctly unhappy about all the negative attention he is attracting, not to mention Sergeant Ramos who looks like a little boy whose favourite toy has just been taken away from him. Then the chief shouts at the guard: "You there, Nonoy! A word of advice before I listen to your story; don't mention to anyone what you read on that piece of paper, OK?"

The guard nods solemnly: "Of course Chief; I understand that it is a confidential police matter!"

"Right you are! And it will remain a confidential police matter. So if I hear even the slightest rumour, I will know that you were indiscreet," the chief now smiles wolfishly, "and I will make *you* into a police matter; understand?"

The guard nods unhappily.

"Right, so tell me about the murder of old Lee; what's that all about?"

With a sly look on his broad, dark face, the guard starts talking: "You know I am the duly appointed head guard of the Bayun Beach Resort and have always done my duty to the fullest and earned the trust of the owners and management, who –"

"Yes, yes, yes, Nonoy," the chief interrupts impatiently, "we've heard all that before; get to the point!"

The guard is clearly annoyed by the interruption. "I am sorry Chief, but it is important, because I have always been a loyal worker and now Sir Robert has fired me!"

"I thought you had something to tell us about the murder of old Lee and now you bother us because you are fired?"

"But it all goes together, Chief! I think he fired me because I suspected that he killed poor Mr. Lee!"

"Chief, please let Mr. Negrito continue his story at his own leisure; I think we will get most out of it that way!" Mr. Sy says forcefully.

The chief waves his hand to indicate the guard to continue.

"Thank you both, Sirs! Well, as I said, I am a loyal servant of the resort and its management, but of course cannot close my eyes to illegal activities. I think something illegal was done by Sir Robert. First I did not think of it, but after the killing of Mr. Lee I started to think –"

"Think, eh?" the chief mumbles, nearly inaudibly. Mr. Sy shushes him to be quiet.

The guard hears the quip, as he was intended to do, and has difficulties swallowing his indignation. Only an encouraging look from the inspector makes him continue: "Yes, I had my thoughts. When I started my shift two nights ago, the night before poor Mr. Lee was killed, I went into the back room behind the office, where our guns are stored. There are several guns in the cabinet: Sir Robert's private hunting rifle, two revolvers as back-up for the guards and two pump guns; one for the day guard and the one with the long barrel for the night guard. Only two persons have the keys for the cabinet and that is Sir Robert and me. Normally I hand out the guns when the reliever guards take over, and Sir Robert only uses his key to retrieve his hunting rifle. So this time I took, as always, the pump gun off the day guard and went to the cabinet to place it there and take out the night gun."

The guard now lowers his voice and looks around, as if he is afraid of being overheard: "Strangely enough, the night gun was missing, so I held onto the day gun for my night shift. But I was not worried; the last days were very confusing, so maybe Sir Robert had received the gun from the night guard and just forgot to put it back. When I heard that Mr. Lee was killed with a pump gun, I was still not worried. But last night I took the night shift and suddenly noticed a person creeping through the bushes. He did not notice me, so I closed in on him and I apprehended him!"

He makes a small artificial pause before he continues with a triumphant tone in his voice, "It was Sir Robert and he looked guilty! I did not know what he was doing there; it is unusual for the manager to creep through the bushes and I could have shot him. I am a very good shot, you know!" he adds proudly.

"Please continue," Mr. Sy urges the man.

"Yes. But it was a strange situation and something in Sir Robert made me nervous. So I spontaneously asked him whether he knew where the other pump gun was. I was so surprised by his reaction; he got very angry and shouted at me that I was an insolent and stupid person who should mind his own business!"

The guard looks at the three policemen indignantly, as if expecting a supportive reply. But the policemen keep their silence, forcing the guard to continue: "But I am not insolent or stupid; I was only doing my duty! He made me very unhappy but I still apologised, although there was no need to. But he was in a rage and did not listen to reason. He kept on insulting me and then he just fired me! I did not know what to answer, because it was so unjust. But of course I had to accept his decision, although I will go to the Department of Labour to complain and get compensation!"

The policemen are getting impatient with Nonoy's lengthy tale but Mr. Sy obviously does not want them to interrupt him, so they let him ramble on. The guard has gained some confidence when he is not contradicted anymore by the chief and continues with a stronger voice: "I did not leave the resort right away but walked to the office and waited for one of the girls who were on night duty to note down my time in the Daily Time Registration. While I waited there, I saw Sir Robert walk by with the missing pump gun in his hand! Fortunately he didn't see me, but I saw him! He took the gun to the gun cabinet. I checked later and found it there! I didn't touch it, but I could smell that it had been fired recently!"

The guard looks around in triumph and this time there is an immediate reaction from the inspector: "Are you willing to testify this, if needed in a court of justice, Mr. Negrito?"

Solemnly the guard places his right hand on his heart and replies: "Of course, Inspector; it is the truth and as a law-abiding citizen I am not afraid to say the truth and nothing but the truth, so help me God!"

At first a puzzled expression appears on the inspector's face, but then he smiles at the obviously rehearsed reply and then directs himself to the chief: "Time is of the essence in both cases now, Chief. I suggest that you go to the resort to secure the gun and have it checked for fingerprints, while I go to the estate to follow up on the other matter. I would need a squad of armed men, though!"

"Of course, Mr. Sy; Sergeant Ramos will round up our best shooters to accompany you," the chief replies. Then to another officer who has just arrived: "You; keep Nonoy here and take his statement."

"But the Remington is stuck again, Chief!" the man answers whiningly.

"Well, get the machine from Doc Gonzales then!"

The officer nods unhappily; his typing skills on the old mechanic typewriter are limited to say the least, and he will now have to spend several hours in the stuffy office to take Nonoy's statement. The guard does not seem to mind a prolonged stay in the office and, head lifted high on his scrawny neck, is obviously enjoying his new role as star witness.

Chief Arozo barks some commands to his men to gather the shooters, before he leaves in a hurry with his own squad in the direction of the resort.

Inspector Sy's shooters gather ten minutes later and troop into the surplus army truck. Mr. Sy mounts an old army jeep and the small convoy shoots off in the direction of the Lee mansion.

NINETEEN

The old Buick thunders through the resort gate, throwing up huge clouds of dust, and comes to a screeching halt just inside the grounds. The chief jumps out, followed closely by three junior police officers, and hurries towards the office buildings. A surprised guard has to jump aside in order to avoid being run down. The chief chases through the office, leaving an utterly surprised secretary behind, and enters the back room where the guns are stored. His assistants take up position in the office itself, challenging anybody who might want to crash their blockade. Chief Arozo tries to open the gun cabinet, but finds it locked. He runs back into the office and shouts: "Keys! Where are the keys to the gun cabinet?"

The secretary has risen halfway from her chair and gapes at the chief.

"Come on, girl; I haven't got all day. Where's the key?"

"Aaah, with Sir Robert, Chief," comes the drawn-out answer.

"And where is Sir Robert?"

"Out, Sir; he's out. He's gone to town," the girl replies while she slowly falls back into her chair again.

"Bloody hell!" the chief utters under his breath. Loudly, he instructs one of his officers: "Boboy, get some tools to open that cabinet!"

Boboy salutes and runs outside, returning after a few minutes with a crowbar and hammer. He enthusiastically starts to attack the cabinet, but it is harder than first thought as the front and door frame of the cabinet are reinforced with heavy steel plating. The chief observes the spectacle for a while before instructing his assistants to drag the bulky cabinet away from the wall. But here the cabinet is also not co-operating; it has been mounted into the wall with thick bolts, so they have to use brute force to break them out of the cemented wall with the crowbar – a sweaty business in the cramped room. Now they can finally attack the back wall of the cabinet, which is made of much thinner plating, and within minutes they break through. Now the chief dons some gloves and carefully lifts the pump gun out by the top of the barrel. He then wraps it in a plastic waste bag and the four of them depart as hastily as they had arrived, leaving behind a handful of surprised staff with unanswered questions.

They bring the gun back to the police station in a short time and one of the assistants, who had participated in a special course at the National Bureau of Investigation on the lifting of fingerprints, manages to retrieve some good prints from the gun. Now they only need to take Robert's fingerprints to ascertain whether Nonoy's statement is true.

In the meantime, Mr. Sy has arrived at the mansion in a patched-up army jeep driven by Sergeant Ramos, closely followed by an old 2-tonner crammed with twelve policemen toting ancient WWII Garant rifles.

He impatiently rings the bell several times. When a surprised gardener finally answers his urgent calls and opens the gate, the policemen pour in and fan out into the grounds. Mr. Sy walks leisurely towards the main entrance, accompanied by a grim-looking Sergeant Ramos who is carrying a shining M-16 over his shoulder. Suddenly, one of Yunlin's men appears in the doorway. He immediately recognises the danger the uniforms pose for his master, quickly turns around, pushes an astounded housemaid aside and runs inside, slamming the heavy door behind him. Mr. Sy beckons Sergeant Ramos to stop; he has an unpleasant feeling about this.

The sergeant un-shoulders his gun and releases the safety catch when he sees the same man appear in an open window next to the front door pointing a pistol at him. But the sergeant has reacted too slowly; the Chinese lets off three rapid shots and the sergeant stumbles backwards, like a boxer punched in the gut, blood pouring from wounds in his chest and stomach. On the steps, the screaming housemaid throws herself against the closed door before slumping down onto the marble steps. Mr. Sy is briefly distracted by her, then quickly ducks, rolls sideways and throws himself flat on the lawn. Next to him, Sergeant Ramos grunts and tries to get up again. His attacker tries to get another shot at him, but he is distracted when the panicking maid suddenly appears at his window, screaming at the top of her lungs. He shoots at the maid instead and the bullet throws the woman backwards onto the lawn. Ignoring the multiple wounds that are bleeding copiously and rapidly colouring his khaki uniform crimson red, the sergeant picks up his gun and aims at his attacker. A volley of high-velocity projectiles speed towards the open window and the man standing in it. The M-16 has been switched to automatic and the walls around the window are peppered by shots, which blast large chunks of plaster through the air, covering the by now silent housemaid in dusty white powder. The sergeant had been slightly off-aim, but some bullets still find their way towards the Chinese man, who had been switching his focus to the inspector. The bullets slam into the shooter's torso, turning him around and propelling him backwards into the room.

Suddenly, more gunfire erupts from the mansion, as several other Chinese hoods start shooting at the policemen who are carefully advancing towards the house with their guns raised to their shoulders. Mr. Sy can see one policeman go down as a shot shreds his throat, blood spouting liberally over his uniform, and another one stumbles as he is shot twice in the legs. By then, all the other policemen have ducked for cover and start a raggedy return fire.

Mr. Sy makes sure that no more fire is coming his way and crawls back to Sergeant Ramos. He finds Ramos lying on his back, breathing heavily while blood bubbles out of his chest wound with every breath. The sergeant has become very pale and seems to be in great pain. Despite his urge to help, Mr. Sy knows there is precious little he can do for the man in this situation, apart from pressing his jacket on the wounds in an attempt to stop the bleeding and utter some comforting words. The sergeant, waving the meaningless words aside, pulls Mr. Sy's hands from his chest and presses his gun into Mr. Sy's hands. The inspector seems at a loss, so the sergeant groans: "I'll be OK. You get these assholes, right?"

Mr. Sy nods grimly, grips the M-16 firmly and pulls some spare clips out of the holster on the sergeants' belt.

Mr. Sy might not look very intimidating, but he had, after his ROTC-stint, enjoyed excellent combat training with the Philippine Special Forces Airborne Regiment, a crack unit that had seen service in Mindanao, fighting the Muslim insurgents, so he knew very well how to handle a weapon. He has extensive experience with the Colt CAR-15, which basically is an M-16 rifle with a shorter barrel, and had excelled with this weapon, both on the shooting range and in the jungle. The routine immediately comes back to him and he loosely holds the gun in his right hand while he runs towards some policemen, who are hiding behind a low wall, to organise the attack. He quickly issues his orders; while two policemen give covering fire, the other policemen, divided into two groups, will carefully approach the mansion from the sides. They should take no risk, use any possibility for cover, and take their time. In the meantime Mr. Sy, will approach the back of the building alone. The policemen nod; they had all served in the army and understand the tactical approach Mr. Sy proposes.

Mr. Sy moves back into the bushes while the first cracks of the Garants tear through the fetid air. He slowly makes his way to the back of the house, all the while making sure that he is not in the open. A few minutes later, he is at the back of the house and carefully moves through the bushes until he is only a stone's throw away from the building. He makes sure to stay low and in the shadows. This is probably an unnecessary precaution, since he also has the sun in his back, and the defenders would have difficulties seeing him anyway, but Mr. Sy is a careful man; he has seen many soldiers die because they underestimated the dangers ahead. He feels uneasy going in alone; he is not a coward, but does not feel the urge to be a dead hero either. But he does not want to expose these inexperienced country policemen to the dangers he expects in the mansion, either. Not only are there at least four to five armed and desperate Chinese hoodlums, but they also have to take care not to shoot any of the innocent civilians – housemaids, cooks, workers and, of course, Mrs. Lee. Mr. Sy has therefore decided to go in by himself. Besides, it seems that the Chinese are even less experienced than his squad, so he convinces himself that his tactics might probably work.

The M-16 is heavier than his old CAR-15, but the grip is still familiar and he gets the feel for the weapon surprisingly fast. Within seconds, the heavy gun feels like a natural extension of Mr. Sy's limbs. Careful not to make any hasty movements, he slowly rotates his head to examine the building in front of him. There! A single figure is posted behind a first floor window; an impassive Chinese face peers down intensely into the garden. Mr. Sy takes a deep breath, exhales slowly, carefully takes aim and, in one smooth movement, pulls the trigger. He barely feels the recoil of the gun, but can clearly observe its effect; the window shatters and the figure falls backwards out of sight. Immediately after, he hears the man cry in agony. A second face appears in the shattered window, but disappears before the inspector can fire.

From the front of the house, he can distinguish the thudding fire of the attacking Garants and the lighter cracks of the defenders' pistols. But here at the back, all is quiet, save the moaning of the injured Chinese on the first floor. The second man is surely waiting for him, but where? Is he still on the first floor? Mr. Sy crawls several metres to the left where the bushes almost reach the wall. He then gets up and quickly runs the last few metres towards the wall. Mr. Sy is panting slightly, all the time expecting the impact of a bullet, but he manages to reach the safety of the wall unscathed. His back to the wall, he ejects the almost empty clip and quickly reloads. Moving the gun to his chest, he slowly moves towards the back door. With his left hand, he opens the door, moves quickly forwards and drops on one knee, the gun pointing straight forward. For a split second, he can see nothing in the dark hallway, and then a blinding flash erupts only a few metres away; Mr. Sy can feel a bullet singe his left ear as he instinctively pulls the trigger of the M-16. The gun shudders in his hands and, in the bright light of the muzzle fire, he can clearly see the person opposite him being thrown backwards against the wall before slowly sliding down into a sitting position, his black eyes open in amazement that his prey had gotten the better of him. The man is rapidly dying and Mr. Sy doesn't waste any time on him. Instead, he swivels his gun towards the inside door, which opens only a fraction of a second later. Instinctively, Mr. Sy lets off an ear-tearing volley at the figure that jumps inside. He catches the person in full flight and the bullets tear up the victim from the pelvis to his neck before he lands on top of Mr. Sy. He quickly pushes the corpse aside, stumbles to his feet and points the M-16 towards the door opening again. Mr. Sy forces himself to breathe slowly and deeply while he carefully listens for sounds that might betray another attacker. But nothing moves on the other side.

Mr. Sy looks down at his once-white suit that is now completely ruined; the knees are caked with mud, the jacket is torn and covered with the blood of his Chinese attacker. Distractedly, he wonders whether the department will cover the expenses for a new suit; probably not. He ejects the near empty clip and reloads the gun with shaky hands while trying to remember how many men Yunlin actually had with him. Was it four or five? And how many guards had there been in the house originally? He isn't completely sure, but he guesses that there are no more than two or three defenders left, including Yunlin. The gunfire outside is slowing down and the return fire has nearly subsided; everybody is probably trying to save on ammunition now.

Then there is another rifle volley, followed by a high-pitched scream from behind the door. Mr. Sy starts moving carefully through the kitchen, opens the door to the huge hallway and silently slides along the walls; in front of one of the windows, he sees a silent, crumpled-up body and next to it a slouching figure, breathing heavily. The Chinese thug is still alive, but judging by the copious bleeding he will not live for much longer. Mr. Sy approaches him carefully, his gun constantly swivelling through the room. He picks up the man's gun, a Chinese Type 77 pistol, and stuffs it into his pocket; he might need it later. Then he starts moving silently towards the stairs, all the while swivelling his gun from side to side. Suddenly there is movement from upstairs, followed by a shot that does not even get close to the Inspector. Mr. Sy jumps forwards, rolls around and fires three shots up the stairs, hitting the gunman right in the chest. The man slumps down on top of the stairs and his pistol clatters to the marble floor below him.

For a while, the inspector just stands silently while listening intently. Nothing moves and he can only hear some muffled sounds from outside.

Then, suddenly, Yunlin's voice comes from above: "Inspector; can you hear me?"

"Yes, I can hear you. I order you to give yourself up!"

His command is met by laughter: "Why should I give myself up, Inspector? The game is not over yet!"

Now Mr. Sy can hear the shuffling of feet and the sounds of a struggle, cut short by a low thump and a woman's sob.

"I think we all want to get out of this mess alive; don't you think so, Inspector? Especially our lovely Cornelia, up here in my arms, is anxious to be united with her police lover again!"

Now Mr. Sy can clearly distinguish the voice of Cornelia Lee, pleading with her brother-in-law to let her go. Apparently Yunlin has taken her hostage and intends to use her as a shield to get away. The inspector grits his teeth and moves backward a few paces to get out of sight again.

"Now, Inspector; I don't want to harm anyone, but if you or your men try to stop me, I will shoot Cornelia and anybody else who stands in my way!"

Mr. Sy has only once experienced a hostage situation; he had been a rookie cop and a bank robbery had gone awry. That particular hostage situation had not been handled well; in the end, all robbers, three of the hostages and one policeman had been killed. Mr. Sy does not wish to repeat history.

"What do you want, Yunlin?" he shouts upwards.

"There is something that belongs to me in the library. I want that *and* free passage to my ship!"

"Will you release Mrs. Lee then?"

Yunlin laughs derisively: "So you can order your coastguard to blow me out of the waters? No Sir, I will release her when we are out of the country. You have my word!"

In the meantime, the remaining policemen have trooped in; they had overcome their opponents without further casualties. With quick hand signals, Mr. Sy indicates where they should take up position in order to cover the impressive hall completely with their guns. Then he moves forward and can now clearly see Yunlin standing at the top of the landing with Cornelia Lee held tightly against his body and a gun held against her head.

"I'm coming down, Inspector. Tell your men to drop their weapons." He doesn't wait for a reply but immediately starts moving down in a rapid and controlled manner.

Mr. Sy is, against his will, impressed by the man; Yunlin is in a difficult situation and still manages to keep his cool and, using the indecisiveness of his opponents, take the initiative. Mr. Sy beckons the policemen to lower their guns and take a step back so that Yunlin can pass. Yunlin does not let the barrel of his gun trail from the head of his sister-in-law for even a split second; he obviously realises that he can never shoot himself free against the overwhelming force opposing him and that his only way out is his female shield. Yunlin has by now reached the bottom of the stairs and is slowly walking backwards, trying to keep his vulnerable back free from the guns of the policemen. He pushes the library door open with his foot and, trailed by

Mr. Sy and his policemen, shuffles towards the bookshelf that apparently contains the heroin. He releases his grip on Cornelia but keeps pointing the gun at her head and says to her: "Pull out the books; do it now! That's right! Now remove the panel. Just pull the lever down there; good! Just throw it on the floor!" He directs the frightened woman while making sure to keep her body between him and the policemen and maintaining his aim on her head. "Now take out the package... slowly!"

Cornelia does as she is told; she pulls out the package and shows it to Yunlin. His narrow dark eyes open a fraction wider in surprise and involuntarily he lowers his gun; the package is torn and obviously missing some of its contents: "What...?"

And then a gun goes off with a roaring crash. A massive slug pulverises Yunlin's right shoulder. The gun flies out of his hand while he drops away from Cornelia and lets out a piercing animalistic scream. Another shot in the chest pins him to the bookshelf. All faces turn towards the open window where Chief Arozo calmly stands with his massive chrome Colt .45 held in his outstretched hands. Yunlin looks at the gaping hole that used to be his right shoulder and, in a futile movement, presses his shuddering left hand onto the gaping chest wound to stop the bleeding. Cornelia sobs, takes a few steps away from her brother-in-law and falls to her knees. Two policemen hurry forward to drag her away further while his colleagues keep pointing their guns at the drug lord. But their vigilance is unnecessary; by now, Yunlin is clearly in shock and unable to do any harm. Copious amounts of blood are flowing through his fingers down his side towards a bright red puddle that has formed around his feet and starts to soak into the expensive leather books that had been discarded so carelessly just seconds ago. Then Yunlin's legs buckle beneath him and he slowly slides down the bookshelf into a sitting position. He looks at Mr. Sy, blinks his eyes several times and seems to try to say something. Mr. Sy approaches the dying man and squats down beside him: "Any last words before you meet your creator, Yunlin?"

Yunlin swallows several times, his head lolling powerlessly, before he whispers: "It was incomplete..."

The dying man coughs and slumps sideways. Mr. Sy drags him up again and says: "What was incomplete?"

"The merchandise..." Yunlin's chest heaves up and down mightily while his heart tries to pump the declining amount of blood faster and faster through the body to feed its dying cells: "The merchandise is incomplete… Somebody… Somebody stole it!"

Then the man laughs crazily and his head jerks up. His face is unnaturally pale, his brow glistening with sweat. His wide, open eyes stare at the inspector and he whispers, almost inaudibly: "I didn't kill these kids; somebody else did…"

Then his eyes glaze over and the head slumps sideways. Mr. Sy rises and looks into the impassive faces of the policemen around him. Had he heard the last words of Yunlin correctly? Had the drug lord indeed said that he had not killed the kids? Meaning who; Elena and Juan? Or maybe some completely different kids?

Heavy running feet announce the arrival of the chief and the sobbing Cornelia throws herself into the arms of her saviour.

It transpires that the chief had had a bad feeling about letting Mr. Sy go after the drug dealers alone, so immediately after his return from the resort, he left the police station again after he had instructed his staff to check the gun for fingerprints. He had hurried towards the estate and had from a distance heard the gunfire. Driving his car through a throng of curious onlookers, he had crashed the gates and ploughed his heavy car into the bushes surrounding the mansion. The gunfire had died down by then and he had initially thought that he was too late, and that the police had lost the battle. He misgivings felt confirmed when he discovered the immobile body of Sergeant Ramos and the bleeding bodies of two of his badly wounded men on the lawn, so he had been extra careful when he stole towards the building. By coincidence, he had moved towards the library window first and had briefly peeked inside, to see the back of Yunlin with Cornelia in his grip, the gun at her head. He had felt a great calm come over him and had rested his heavy gun in his outstretched arms on the windowsill, waiting for the right opportunity to take Yunlin out. Some of his men had seen him, but had wisely kept quiet. Then, when Yunlin briefly lowered his gun after he saw the package, the chief calmly squeezed the trigger and fired the first massive slug into Yunlin's body.

Mr. Sy feels awkward and embarrassed in the presence of Cornelia and her chief. Their distress had vanished and is replaced by the sentimental

154

sugar-sweet behaviour of two puppies in love. The chief ignores his duties and replies to Cornelia's doting look with a broad, oafy smile. This only increases Mr. Sy's irritation about the chief's unprofessional behaviour. Fair enough, he had taken out the drug lord in a most efficient manner, which displayed his cool and good marksmanship, but his general actions in recent days seemed to have been guided mostly by personal emotions, rather than by professionalism in his working field. Moreover, Mr. Sy had hoped to take Yunlin Lee alive. Not that he is troubled about the violent death of the drug lord; on the contrary. But he *had* hoped that Yunlin would have been able to help him with his primary investigation – the death of Elena and the subsequent killings of Juan and Zhiheng Lee. Yunlin would not have volunteered the information, but the inspector had a good way of convincing him; in the Philippines, the normal sentence for drug trafficking is execution and it is rare that a man would refuse an opportunity to save his own life.

But it is now apparent that it is not going to be like that and Mr. Sy is even further away from achieving his goal. Having discovered drugs in the possession of Yunlin Lee would certainly convince some people that Yunlin probably was the mastermind behind the killings, but Mr. Sy is not completely convinced. Sure, Yunlin had the motive, the ruthlessness and the means to execute the killings, and his personal dislike for the drug lord almost swung the inspector's opinion. But his dying words indicated that he was not responsible for the killings, and, as a wise man had once said, why should a dying man lie? So this insecurity keeps nagging at his mind as he tries to deduct a probable truth. Would Yunlin have gone as far as killing his niece? Yunlin was not an impulsive person and the inspector does not think that Yunlin would have condoned a rash killing. No; he most likely would have settled the matter in a different way and if, for one reason or another, he would have been forced to kill his own niece, he would certainly not have left the body as evidence.

The inspector does not believe that Juan had killed the girl either; it just doesn't fit the picture, although he cannot completely reject the option either. After all, the boy had been there around the time of death, and the motive, killing because of rejection, although remote, was not unlikely. But there had been skin under the girls' nails; and although Juan had the same blood type as found in the skin sample, and he had some light scratches, he did not have any open wounds and it was therefore unlikely that the blood stemmed from him. So, logically, it had come from somebody else when Elena had scratched this person in her dying struggle.

And what about the semen in the girl's vagina? Mr. Sy had believed Juan when he claimed he had not made love to the girl, but there had been no signs of forced entry either, so Elena must have volunteered. And the coroner had stated that the girl had had sex around the point of death. So who, if not Juan, had been this mysterious lover? And was that person possibly the murderer of the girl? Could it have been Robert Delsey after all? The man had a motive, and lacked an alibi, but would Elena have condoned having sex with him? After all, she had rejected him clearly before and had avoided his company during the weeks before her death. And why would she have sex voluntarily and then scratch him? It didn't make sense!

And who killed Juan? There was, of course, the remote possibility that Teresa, the head waitress at the resort, had killed him as revenge for her impregnation and subsequent abandonment by Juan. But this idea does not make sense to Mr. Sy; why would she have waited so long? There must have been ample opportunity before!

If Yunlin had killed Elena and assumed that Juan was another bothersome witness of his drug operation, this might be his motive to kill the boy. But did he have an opportunity? Mr. Sy doesn't think so.

However, Cornelia Lee had an opportunity *and* a motive! The inspector looks at the happy couple and wonders whether she possibly even had *two* motives; the first being revenge on the assumed killer of her daughter, the second being the removal of a bothersome witness of the drug deal between her husband and his brother; maybe Cornelia Lee had known about her husband's illegal activities all along and had, contrary to her previous statement, supported them anyway. Which one was it, if she was involved at all? But deep down, the inspector has already removed Cornelia Lee from his list.

Finally, who had killed old Lee? It could not have been Juan, obviously. Cornelia had been in bed and Yunlin had been in the breakfast room; these facts were supported by independent witnesses. But of course, Yunlin had several loyal soldiers, all probably with a criminal background and, as the recent events had proven, not adverse to using weapons. One of them could very well have sneaked up on old Lee and shot him. So this option could not be excluded, although all possible suspects were dead now; the investigation was a definite dead-end.

Even though he is bothered by the notion that he could even have thoughts like that, Mr. Sy still has a nagging uncertainty that the chief possibly had a motive *and* an opportunity to kill old Lee.

And then there is Robert Delsey. The guard had incriminated the Englishman and they had secured the weapon on which they hoped to find his prints. If the prints on the gun were his, this would be a powerful indication, since Robert Delsey had a motive to kill all three victims; Elena because she had rejected him, Juan because he was a contender, and old Lee because he had taken away the resort from him. *And* he apparently did not have an alibi in any of the cases! It further corroborated with the initial thoughts of the inspector that the killings were in one way or another connected. He dearly hopes, when he returns to the car, that the prints will show a conclusive result!

TWENTY

A few hours later, the small police force that Chief Arozo had sent to the resort has taken Robert Delsey into custody and accompanies him to the station to have his fingerprints taken. The tall Englishman protests and asks for the reason of this treatment. The policemen shrug their shoulders and referred to their orders; he should just wait until the chief or Mr. Sy return.

Mr. Sy had decided not to confront Robert Delsey until the result of the prints was available. Since the chief had finally decided to take a leave of absence, a fact Mr. Sy greatly approved of, the inspector now sits alone on the covered terrace of the local inn, once in a while sipping a bottle of coke, impatiently waiting for the fingerprint specialist to finish his work. Lots of people pass his table during his long wait and Mr. Sy has to endure many curious looks from the locals; by now, they all know about the gun fight at the Lee mansion and most of them had also seen Robert Delsey being taken into the police station by an armed troop.

Finally he sees a police officer run towards him. Mr. Sy gets up and meets him halfway. "The results are there, Inspector; it is positive!"

Mr. Sy nods and grimly starts off towards the police station. Here he meets the fingerprint specialist, a boyish man with an intelligent look in his jet-black eyes. The man has returned from the coroner's office where he has made the comparisons with the coroner's microscope: "They are identical, Inspector; I had a match on eight points, there is no doubt about it!"

"Thank you, Officer; good job!"

The officer beams, salutes and returns to the coroner's to collect his gear and return to his daily duties.

Mr. Sy enters the police station, ready to confront the fuming Englishman who is marching back and forth in the confined space of the front office. Several police officers are looking on impassively: "So there you are, Inspector! What's this all about?"

"Please sit, Mr. Delsey, and I will explain it to you."

Reluctantly the Englishman sits down, his eyes flaming with righteous indignation.

"Mr. Delsey, you have been accused by a witness of having shot and killed Mr. Zhiheng Lee. The witness observed you when you returned a shotgun to the gun cabinet at the resort. Our officers have retrieved this gun and established that it had been fired recently. They furthermore compared the fingerprints on the shotgun with your prints and found a perfect match. Now, if you could bother to explain this to me, I would be obliged!" Mr. Sy concludes his explanation with a brief smile that does not reach his eyes.

Robert Delsey just stares at the inspector for a moment and then explodes: "This is absurd! Me, killing Mr. Lee? Utter nonsense! And how do you know this particular shotgun was the killer weapon? And why should I have done that? And *how* could I have done it? I only arrived at the estate much later!"

Mr. Sy chooses to ignore the referral to the murder weapon, because of course Robert Delsey is right; although the facts established around the gun are good indications, they would never hold up in court on their own. The police are unable to match the pellets that killed old Lee with a specific gun as, contrary to rifles, whose fired slugs are engraved with an unmistakable pattern by the barrel of that specific gun, shotguns do not leave such marks. So Mr. Sy decides to play his next trump card: "Oh, but we think you did have the opportunity, Mr. Delsey. Is it not correct that you arrived late at the crime scene, because the person who went to fetch you, did not find you in the house? Where were you when they came to get you, Mr Delsey?"

Robert Delsey's face turns red and he stutters slightly when he answers: "Who said that? I *was* there! I was there all the time until Nonoy rang the bell!"

"That's odd, Mr Sy; our witness, who indeed is Mr. Negrito, testified that you were *not* there. Do you have any witnesses who can indicate the contrary, Mr. Delsey?"

Robert Delsey opens his mouth and starts to say something, but closes it again quickly.

"No? No witnesses to support your story, Mr. Delsey?"

Robert Delsey looks up to Mr. Sy with a pleading look on his face: "Look, Inspector; it's somewhat complicated and I am not sure whether I can disclose it."

"Disclose what, Mr. Delsey? Come on; you are presently under suspicion for murder, so I think it would be wise to come clean, don't you think?"

Robert Delsey feels distinctly uncomfortable under the prying look of Mr. Sy while the local policemen clearly revel in his discomfort. "Oh, damn! Well… You see… Damn… It's somewhat embarrassing…"

Mr. Sy verbally prods the man to continue: "Yes?"

Robert Delsey sighs deeply: "Oh, what the heck! Very well then; I spent the night with Teresa, our head waitress, and was still in bed with her when Nonoy rang the bell!"

The policemen smirk and exchange meaningful looks while Mr. Sy exclaims in surprise: "The pregnant waitress?"

Robert Delsey nods shamefully.

"So she can support your story?"

Robert Delsey sighs: "Look, Inspector; I am not proud of what I have done. As you probably already guessed, I loved Elena dearly and I am surprised myself that I betrayed her memory so shortly after her death. But Teresa… Well, she is a lovely girl and she was abused and abandoned by Juan, so I felt obliged to comfort her. Did you know that Juan is the father of Teresa's unborn child? No? Well, he is, but he never acknowledged it! Just as he refused to acknowledge the fatherhood of at least three other children in the village! He was just a scoundrel and that scoundrel then tried to put his fingers on Elena!"

"You hated him, Robert?" Mr. Sy asks quietly.

Robert Delsey sighs again: "Yes, maybe I did, Inspector. But I would never have killed him. Give him a good thrashing, yes. But killing him, no!"

Instinctively, Mr. Sy believes him. He interrogates Robert Delsey for several hours on end; he asks him about his background, his life in the Philippines, his relation to old Lee, Juan and, again and again, his relationship with Elena. Robert willingly answers all questions. They have a few breaks, when the officers present go to the local inn to fetch food and refreshments, before they continue again. It is obvious that Robert is tired; not only with the investigation, but also tired with his life and the bothersome circumstances it presents now. At some stage, his walls break down; Robert Delsey, the big, proud man who had tried to present an image of a brash, strong-willled and aloof superior, breaks down and, with tears in his eyes, spontaneously shows all the emotions that he had, until then, kept bottled up inside him. Mr. Sy finds himself in the position of a priest, the confessant wanting to receive absolution. This Mr. Sy obviously cannot give, but he can allow the man to come clean with himself. In the course of events, remarkable facts come to the fore and Mr. Sy listens in silent amazement as Robert Delsey outlines everything that preceded Elena's murder and the role he himself played in the ensuing events. The story Robert tells is incredible but totally convincing. The only thing that it lacks is evidence; the only person who can bolster at least part of his story is the head waitress, Teresa. *Even then*, the Inspector thinks grimly; *who says these two did not commit the killings together?*

After four long hours, Robert Delsey speaks his final words and then slumps down onto the uncomfortable chair he has occupied for so many hours. Mr. Sy stretches out and gets up to loosen his limbs, followed by Robert's moist eyes: "You are so silent, Inspector; don't you believe me?"

"I believe in facts, Robert. Your tale sounds convincing, but it needs to be supported by evidence."

"So why don't you go and ask Teresa? She will tell you the truth!"

Mr. Sy nods distractedly; his mind is already several steps ahead. If the story of the two unlikely lovers corroborates, who then had killed Lee? The testimonial of the guard regarding the gun could easily be rejected in court. Besides, Robert Delsey had convincingly explained why his fingerprints had been on the gun; he had fired the guard for incompetence and taken the gun into his care after he had chased the man out of the resort. But why had the very same guard told the police that Robert had *not* been in his house when he came to fetch him? Was the man involved in the killing, or did he merely have a grudge against an assumed brutal employer?

Mr. Sy sighs; all in due course. First he is going to interrogate Teresa, because she is the only witness that could actually defuse some of the accusations against Robert Delsey. Once that has been done, he can look at the case with fresh eyes.

TWENTY-ONE

Despite the late hour – it is already past 8 PM – Mr. Sy has asked an officer to take him to Teresa's house. The girl lives alone on a small compound behind the resort after both her parents had died of diphtheria the year before and left their house to her. They cannot reach the compound by car – the road is simply too bad – and they have to walk the last half-mile along a muddy track. There is only a small, watery moon that does little to disperse the darkness in the compound. Some huts are badly illuminated by an occasional oil lamp or stark light bulb. In the dark, Mr. Sy and his driver stumble over invisible roots as the occasional snarl of a frightened dog, and the friendly greetings of the few villagers that are still awake, accompany them on their way to Teresa's hut. Fortunately, the officer knows where Teresa lives (he is her cousin's neighbour) and they can easily find the small bamboo and Nippa hut standing alone at the edge of the compound, bordering on the surrounding jungle. From a distance, they can see the yellow light of an oil lamp cast eerie shivering shadows and can faintly distinguish muffled sounds from the house. As they approach the house, the rickety door opens and a small shadow slides out. It makes a tentative step forward in the direction of the men, apparently unaware of them being there, but when it notices them it quickly turns around, runs in the opposite direction and disappears in the jungle behind the hut.

It takes Mr. Sy a split second to react and then a troubled thought hits home: *this can't be true!* He starts running while shouting to his companion to follow the unknown person into the jungle. Mr. Sy reaches the hut in no time, throws open the door and is confronted with the unsettling sight of Teresa half-sitting, half-lying on the bed, her legs on the floor, with blood oozing out of a terrible gash in her throat, while her quivering hands ineffectively try to close it. The girl, her surprised wide open eyes directed at the Inspector, is completely naked and Mr. Sy now notices her pregnancy by her swollen nipples and the slight curve of her protruding belly above the small triangle of dark, curly hair. Her begging eyes plead Mr. Sy to help her while her mouth makes futile gurgling noises. The inspector looks around and finds a sheet crumpled at the foot of the bed. Hurriedly, he tears it into several large pieces, pushes Teresa's hands aside and tries to avoid looking at her nakedness while he takes hold of her neck with his left hand. His right hand presses the material firmly onto the terrible wound while he lowers Teresa back onto the bed, where wet strings of her freshly washed hair soak the small pillow immediately. *Strange*, Mr. Sy thinks, that he can distinguish the smell of the shampoo – a mild coconut odour – in a situation like this. Within seconds, the improvised bandage is soaked with blood and Mr. Sy takes the next dressing and places it on top. Teresa's breathing becomes arduous and the gagging sounds vex the inspector; he knows he is probably fighting a losing battle, but he doesn't want to give up. He tries to comfort and relax the girl: "It's OK, Teresa. It's not as bad as it looks. Nothing we can't fix. I'm here." He uses the next dressing and then the last one, but he is unable to stem the pouring blood. Panic starts to develop in his normally composed mind as he fumbles in his pocket to drag out his handkerchief. He presses it onto the wound: "Don't worry; I'll take care of you. Just relax. It will be OK!"

But he knows the girl is not going to be OK at all; there is just too much blood and he has no way to stop it. Mr. Sy grits his teeth in futile frustration; the one witness who could vouch for the innocence of Robert Delsey, and who possibly could finger the real murderer, is dying beneath his hands!

"Who did this, Teresa? Who did this to you, girl?"

But Teresa is already too far gone to answer him. Her body convulses, so he has difficulties keeping the dressings on the wound, and after a few very long moments he feels her body go limp below him. Her dead unseeing eyes glint in the warm light of the oil lamp as Mr. Sy carefully lets go of her and she slumps back onto the bed. The inspector rises, quite composed again; he realises that his investigation has reached another dead end.

Of course, the perpetrator had gotten away. The policeman apologises profusely and blames it on the unusual darkness of the night and his unfamiliarity with the surrounding jungle. Mr. Sy does not bother to reply, but just tells the man to fetch assistance; he will, in the meantime, stay with the corpse and keep the curious onlookers at a distance. This proves not to be necessary; apparently nobody has yet noticed that the girl's life has been brutally ended by an unknown attacker, so Mr. Sy is alone with the body and his thoughts. He tries to ignore the presence of Teresa's body and goes through her belongings. She does not have much; a few dresses, jeans, some t-shirts, pots and pans, cutlery, a kitchen knife, a romantic novel with a stamp, 'This book is property of the public library of Morgantown, West Virginia', some legal papers and a few pictures. Mr. Sy goes through the latter; a black and white picture of a serious couple in wedding attire, another one of the same couple, now quite a few years older, with a young Teresa in between them, a few colour photographs of Teresa with smiling foreigners, obviously taken at the resort, and two pictures of Teresa with Juan. One has been taken on the beach; Juan embracing Teresa, with three smiling girls making peace signs in the background, and another one of Teresa and Juan holding hands in a restaurant. *So it is true that they had had an affair*, Mr. Sy thinks. But did she also have an affair with Robert Delsey – and was she indeed with him that morning old Lee was killed? Well, she wouldn't be able to tell him now, but Mr. Sy believes it; Robert would never have taken the risk of sending him to the girl if he would not have been absolutely sure that she would corroborate his story. But unfortunately for Robert Delsey, it does not so much matter what Mr. Sy believes, as much as what he can prove.

TWENTY-TWO

The next morning, Mr. Sy wakes up and does not feel refreshed at all. He has hardly slept; the occurrences of the recent days have kept his mind in turmoil and he has been unable to put the image of the dying girl out of his mind. The fact that he had not gathered any conclusive evidence irritates him and he is bothered that his clear judgement will start to be clouded by instinctive and emotional sentiments. He knows that his professionalism is presently impaired and that bothers him. He reluctantly pushes the crumpled sheets aside and drags himself towards the bathroom. While he shaves, he can hear the engine of a small plane in the distance. The sound grows louder and when Mr. Sy peeks through the narrow bathroom window, he sees a small Piper fly by, obviously preparing for a landing on the beach. Mr. Sy dries his face and quickly dresses. A feeling of dread comes over him and he has a premonition that the arrival of the small plane is connected to his case and therefore to himself. He skips breakfast – he has no appetite anyway – and goes outside. His driver is already there and stomps out his cigarette before opening the door for his superior. The driver knows how to handle the old car and brings the inspector to the police station in no time. Two sheepishly grinning policemen are posted at the door and several more are squatting or leaning against the outside wall. When Mr. Sy enters, he finds the office empty, apart from a small pudgy man sitting behind the chief's desk. The man is well-dressed, although his body shape prevents him from looking elegant. Now the slightly ridiculous man loudly exclaims with a nasal voice: "So there you are, Sy; just the man I was looking for!"

Mr. Sy is not fooled by the looks of this man; he knows that there is a sharp political mind behind the fleshy façade. He therefore is distinctly unhappy to see this specific person, who happens to be his immediate superior, Commissioner Yong 'Glenn' Teves. He understands why the man is here, but cannot imagine how he had been informed; as usual, Mr. Sy has made sure not to report anything of his, in this case impotent, investigations to his boss before their conclusion.

Glenn Teves puts his short arms on the desk and, with his double chins pointing vaguely in the direction of Mr. Sy, he adds: "You made a true mess of it this time, didn't you? Four people murdered and not a clue who's done it. Then a shoot-out between the police and a drug gang, leaving two policeman and six hoods dead on the estate of one of the most esteemed persons in the country – and you don't even bother to notify me? How do you think I look in the eyes of my superiors, eh?"

Mr. Sy drops his eyes and refuses to look at his boss.

"Well, you made me look like a damn fool, Inspector, that's what you did. I look like an incompetent superior who doesn't know what's going on in his own department! Yesterday I was summoned by the interior minister, who had received a worrying phone call from the governor of this rotten island. He asked me all kinds of questions and I couldn't answer one of them! Not one!"

Mr. Sy feels ashamed. Ashamed because he has not yet solved the case and has not been able to present an open-and-shut case to his boss, as he usually did. But he is even more ashamed that his apparent incompetence has now attracted the attention of officials at the highest levels; now it is almost unavoidable that somebody will leak information to the national press and he will become the laughing stock of the department! How will he ever be able to look his family in the eyes again?

But Mr. Sy's professionalism keeps the upper hand and he decides to report his findings in full. Obviously the commissioner gets upset to hear about yet another murder, but to Mr. Sy's great relief the commissioner has the decency to hear Mr. Sy out; the only interruption is a query into a possible inconsistency in Mr. Sy's narrative. Mr. Sy had never thought high of the police qualities of the man, but considers him bright enough to appreciate the capabilities of his staff; this is the main reason he normally had completely free rein to handle his own investigations.

When Mr. Sy finally concludes his presentation, Commissioner Teves sighs and leans back. "A difficult situation, Inspector. As I understand, there are two separate cases; the first being a drug deal gone awry and the second one a case of a deranged jealous foreigner killing his ex-mistress, her lover, his boss, and finally a waitress he had been banging."

The Commissioner warningly lifts a pudgy finger when Mr. Sy tries to interrupt, "Bear with me for another minute, Inspector. Now, I will report to the minister that you did commendable work in apprehending a dangerous Chinese drug gang. Unfortunately they resisted arrest and in the ensuing gunfight, all criminals were killed. Sergeant Ramos played a fundamental part in the arrest of the gang, but was sadly killed while leading his men in the attack. I will recommend him for a decoration for valour and will make sure his family is looked after. It's never bad to present a real, dead hero to the masses. Now; to the second case regarding this Englishman. To me, he seems to be the most likely candidate for the killings. Besides, nobody will shed a tear when a foreigner is arrested on allegations that are possibly not completely fool proof. We must close this case quickly, Inspector, and show positive results!"

"But I am not at all sure he is responsible for the killings!" Mr. Sy cries out. "He is innocent at least in the case of the waitress' death, who was also his only defence witness. Don't you think it is odd that the girl was killed? Could it not be that Zhiheng Lee's killer got wind of the fact that the waitress would testify in favour of Robert Delsey and decided to get rid of her, so that Robert would be left as the only suspect?"

Glenn Teves only smiles slightly derisively: "It almost sounds as if you *want* this foreigner to be innocent, Inspector!"

"No Sir!" Mr. Sy exclaims vehemently. "I don't even like the guy, but I still think justice should be done!"

"Justice, Inspector? Why does the notion that someone else killed the girl make you think that Delsey is innocent? Could it not be that his whole yarn about him and the waitress being lovers was told to make you believe that the man had an alibi after all? And that Delsey ordered someone else to kill the girl before she could tell the obvious truth?"

Mr. Sy is impressed by the agile mind of his boss, but thinks the whole concept is too far-fetched. No; after his interrogation of the man, the inspector is convinced that Robert Delsey had spoken the truth.

But his boss leaves him with no alternatives. "I want you to arrest the man, squeeze him properly and present me with his confession in the coming days. I will handle the politicians until then! We understand each other, Inspector?"

Mr. Sy understands very well what the commissioner means and nods miserably.

Commissioner Teves leaves immediately afterwards and thirty minutes later Mr. Sy can hear the little flying machine roaring past, heading north in the direction of Manila.

Mr. Sy has never before been in a position where he has had to sacrifice his professional integrity on the altar of political convenience and he has to admit to himself that he doesn't like it at all. But he can understand the reasoning of his boss and he even tries to convince himself that his boss is, in a way, right in his assumptions. Anyway, it is an easy way out, since, as the commissioner had said, who cares about the fate of one foreigner?

His mind burdened with heavy thoughts, Mr. Sy absentmindedly instructs a police squad to pick up Robert Delsey and bring him back to the police station. The waiting time drags out endlessly and Mr. Sy has ample time to battle with his inner demons. Finally, the policemen enter with a subdued Robert Delsey.

"She's dead, isn't she, Inspector?"

Mr. Sy nods silently.

The tall Englishman lets out an exasperated sigh: "So it is true what they said; she is really dead!" The big man sinks to his knees and covers his face in his hands: "Oh my God, oh my God! This can't be true!"

He looks up at the inspector. "How could this happen? You told me you would ask her about us. She would have testified to my innocence. How can she be dead now?"His voice rises an octave and tears though the silent station: "Now you think it is me, don't you? You think I killed them all! But you must know I didn't kill Teresa! Your men were with me all night! How could I have killed her? She would have testified that I didn't kill old Lee!"

Mr. Sy does not dare to look at the man as he mumbles, "It doesn't matter, Robert. The fact is, it could have been you and you are the most likely candidate." Then the inspector stiffens his back and formally declares, "Robert William Delsey-Cauloyne, you are hereby arrested for murder of

Elena Lee, Juan Aldones and Zhiheng Lee and instigation to the murder of Teresa Zampata. You have the right to remain silent, but anything you say can be used against you in a court of justice. You have the right to an attorney. If you are unable to afford an attorney, the state can provide one for you."

Robert Delsey's expression changes from shock to disbelief. "You can't do that! I am innocent!" He gets to his feet and approaches Mr. Sy, who wisely takes a step backward, and declares vehemently: "I AM INNOCENT! And you *know* it! Who set me up to this, tell me! Who is behind this? Is it this oaf, Arozo? Or that spiteful good-for-nothing guard Nonoy? Or that bitch Cornelia Lee? You must tell me! I want to confront them!"

Mr. Sy feels cornered as Robert Delsey gets closer and closer. He looks at the irresolute policemen and bellows: "Get hold of this madman, before he does something stupid!"

Immediately, the men leap forward and push the Englishman roughly to the ground, pinning his arms behind him. Robert Delsey howls in pain and frustration and the men have difficulties holding him down. Then an officer finally gets hold of his handcuffs and clicks them around the wrists of the accused. Unconcerned about Robert's discomfort, they drag him up by his backward twisted arms and prod him forcefully to the cell block with their batons. Once or twice, their hands accidentally slip and a truncheon lands hard and painfully on the accused man's kidneys.

Mr. Sy looks at the disappearing man with a thoughtful look in his eyes before he directs himself to the officer on duty. "When does the ferry to Dumaguete leave?"

"It just left, Sir. The next ferry is tomorrow."

"That's too late; I want you to arrange special transportation for the accused, one officer and myself to Dumaguete. There we will board the ferry to Manila. I think it leaves the day after tomorrow. "

The officer salutes, turns around and quickly leaves the station to arrange the transportation. Mr. Sy then calls another officer, gives him some money and tells him to pick up his belongings at Uncle Joe's and pay the bill; he does not feel like meeting the old man in this situation and having to explain himself. He sits down at the chief's desk, takes the Cross pen he had received at his graduation from the police academy from his breast pocket, retrieves a sheet of paper from the drawer and writes a note to Chief Arozo – yet another person he does not want to be confronted with in this embarrassing situation. After finishing it, he folds the paper, put it in an envelope, marks it 'private and confidential' and places it on top of the pile of papers in the chief's in-tray. Then he makes some telephone calls and afterwards patiently waits for the officer to return.

Shortly after, the officer on duty returns and reports that a *banca* has been chartered and is waiting at the harbour. Silently, Mr. Sy rises and beckons the guards to fetch Robert Delsey. He requests a handgun and holster from the officer and attaches it to his belt. Then the prisoner is loaded on the back of the old 2-tonner truck, guarded by four heavily armed guards, and leaves for the short trip to the harbour, closely followed by Mr. Sy driven in the old Buick.

A thick throng of curious onlookers have already gathered on the pier and are gaping at the miserable-looking shackled Englishman. While he is slowly helped on board of the rocking vessel, Mr. Sy can clearly hear the derisive remarks hurled at the defenceless man: "Murderer! Rapist! Stinking foreigner! Exploiter!"

It is good that the small vessel casts off its lines before the mood of the mob grows violent. Mr. Sy is distracted by a small group of people, who are following the vessel to the end of the pier and have started throwing rotten vegetables, and hardly notices that the firm underground of the pier has given way to the moving planks of the vessel. When he does finally notice, the pier is already a considerable distance away and the ship is moving forward on the long swells of the ocean. Quickly, Mr. Sy sits down and tries to suppress his sudden nausea. It doesn't work, of course, and bile starts to claw its way up his throat. Opposite him, Robert Delsey, unaffected by the movement of the little ship, smiles wryly at him, while the accompanying policeman and the ship's crew ignore the inspector's discomfort.

The one-hour trip seems to take ages and several times Mr. Sy wishes he was dead. The sight of the small bay of Dumaguete, with the pier jutting out into the sea, is balm to his tortured mind. Shakily, he disembarks, helped by a grinning crew. Robert Delsey is roughly dragged off and hobbles behind the inspector, his pace impaired by the old-fashioned shackles around his ankles and wrists. Several times, the police officer has to support him to prevent him from falling. At the end of the pier, the three men mount a tricycle that takes them to a small guesthouse off Perdices Street, where they will spend the night before leaving for Manila the next morning. The officer is surprised that they do not progress towards the city jail, but when he notices the comfort of their room he decides not to complain. The room they occupy is quite large, with sufficient space for three beds, a large cupboard, a table with two chairs, some side tables and a washbasin. It furthermore has an excellent air con unit. Mr. Sy tries all beds and finally chooses the one with the hardest mattress. Then he orders the police officer to take off the prisoner's shackles and use the handcuffs to tie him to the smallest bed, which conveniently has a sturdy wooden grille as a headrest.

"We will stand guard at turns, Officer. I will take the first shift, so you can go out and have a bite in town. You know Dumaguete?"

"Oh, yes Sir!" comes the eager answer: "It is a big town, lots of things to do and good restaurants!"

"All right then. Let's see; now it's nearly 4 PM, so be back at eight!"

"Yes Sir! Thank you Sir!" The police officer salutes and quickly leaves the room.

Mr. Sy leisurely unpacks his case, takes off his jacket and his shoes, slips the gun out of its holster and places it on the small side table. He sighs and lowers himself carefully onto the bed, all the while observed by the man on the other bed.

"Are you tired, Robert?"

"What? No, not really. Mentally exhausted, perhaps. But that's not surprising, isn't it?"

"No, probably not..." There is a long pause before the inspector continues, "You think you are securely tied to that bed?"

"What? I don't understand."

Mr. Sy pushes himself up onto his elbows and looks at his prisoner: "I mean, you don't think you could break loose, do you?"

Robert Delsey laughs. "You are kidding, right? I'm attached to this bed by handcuffs and that grille looks pretty solid. Besides, one move from me and you could shoot me for trying to escape!"

"How could I do that?" Mr. Sy answers sadly. "You have been so compliant until now that I have lost my vigilance! I could never reach that gun in time, if you would make a serious effort to grab it first!"

Robert Delsey looks utterly puzzled and doesn't know what to say.

"Robert, could we just test the stability of that grille?"

"Huh? Are you trying to set me up, Sy?"

"No, not at all; I just want to make sure that the grille will hold, that's all!"

Robert Delsey starts pulling lightly at his handcuffs.

"Come on, Robert; is that how a desperate criminal behaves? Give it a good tug!"

Robert Delsey looks in surprise at the inspector, but starts yanking his hand back and forth more vigorously anyway. The grille holds out, however.

"Let me help you, Robert!" Mr. Sy gets up and places both hands on the strut that holds one side of the handcuff. "When I say pull, Robert, you pull!" And with one mighty concerted heave, the strut splinters and the handcuff comes free.

"See, Robert; this grille is no good to hold a prisoner cuffed. Lousy Filipino quality; broke with just one little tug! Ah well!" Mr. Sy sits back on his bed again and lowers himself on his mattress, hands folded behind his head, and closes his eyes.

Robert Delsey is sitting on his bed, holding the splintered strut in his hand. "Why are you doing this, Sy?" The tall Englishman asks, with doubt seeping out with every word. "You want me to escape and catch me later? Is your man waiting outside to shoot me?"

Mr. Sy sighs without opening his eyes: "You are so suspicious, Robert; if I had wanted to do you harm, I could have done it long ago! Have you ever considered that I might believe you? Have you ever considered that there are also Filipinos with some kind of intelligence and honour? If they put you in front of a court, you will certainly be convicted, because my boss will have made sure to put you in front of the right judge! So don't insult me any more, but grab your chance. Grab the gun, man! Threaten me, empty my wallet; you'll find your passport there and almost 1,500 dollars in cash. Don't thank me; it's your own money! And then leave!"

Robert Delsey is goggling at Mr. Sy with big surprised eyes.

Mr. Sy opens his eyes and sighs again: "I prepared some help for you. Take a bus to Sibulan. It's too late to take a ferry, but there's a *banca* waiting for you at the harbour, called the *Joshua*. It belongs to a friend of a friend of mine. It will take you to a beach on Cebu Island near Tampi. There is a beach house there with a tool shed. In the shed you will find a motorbike with a full tank, enough to take you to Cebu Airport. You should be there before midnight. The first plane out of the country doesn't leave until 8 AM, so you need to wait a bit. But don't worry; I'll make sure they will concentrate the search on the area around Dumaguete and I won't alert the airports until tomorrow noon. By that time, you will be far away. You know, you hit me on the head quite hard and I needed medical attention, so it is reasonable that I didn't react quicker!"

Robert Delsey smiles warmly. "How can I ever thank you?"

"By moving your big foreign ass out of this room and doing as I told you!"

Robert Delsey pockets his passport and the money. Then he takes the gun and tosses it around in his big hands: "Do I really have to hit you with this?"

"Yes; make it look convincing, but don't hit too hard!"

Mr. Sy turns around on the bed while Robert Delsey lifts the gun over his head. The gun slams down and hits Mr. Sy on the left side of his head. "Owww! That really hurts!" Mr. Sy inspects the result in the mirror over the washbasin. A small trickle of blood is running down his collar; very convincing! He turns around and stretches out his hand: "Goodbye, Robert!"

The big Englishman takes the outstretched hand and shakes it violently. "Goodbye, Jonathan! And thank you ever so much! Although I am a wanted man now, I feel as if I got a second chance in life. I won't squander it this time, I promise!"

Mr. Sy slowly retracts his hand. "Yes, you indeed have a second chance! Who knows; maybe one day we'll meet again and even find out who killed all these people. Please send me a postcard once you are safely out of the country; just a local postcard to my office saying, 'wishing you were here'. Then I will know you are OK!"

Robert Delsey nods, pulls up his shirt and puts the gun down the back of his trousers. He lowers the shirt again to conceal the weapon and opens the door.

"And Robert?"

"Yes?"

"Do get rid of the gun once you are at sea; we don't want any more killings, do we?"

Robert Delsey laughs sheepishly: "Of course."

The door closes behind him and Mr. Sy stretches out on the bed again and tries to sleep. A few hours later, he hears heavy boots on the landing and prepares to tell an utterly convincing, untruthful tale.

EPILOGUE

The sun is slowly setting behind the extinct volcanoes of the island of Negros and small waves are softly slapping against the dark sand of a beach just south of Dumaguete. It is a soothing sound that calms the two men sitting in their deck chairs just a few metres away from the sea and removes any stress they might have felt when they met for the first time in six months only hours before. They had checked in at a small resort on the sea, ordered some cocktails and retired to the undisturbed privacy of the deck chairs lined up at the seaside. It is off-season and the only other guests are an American couple, he obviously ex-army, having served in the Philippines, and she patiently listening to his tales from occurrences and people long gone. The wife had tried to involve the two Filipinos in their conversation, but the men had just smiled politely and left for the beach.

It takes a while before the oldest of them, a large thick-set Filipino wearing only some wide Bermudas and flip-flops, addresses the younger man: "You wrote me this note; it made me curious. And now I am here!"

The younger man nods. He is well-groomed, wearing long linen pants and a white shirt. As a compromise to the laid-back surroundings, he has removed his shoes and socks, and now his white toes are wriggling in the warm sand.

They speak Tagalog, although the younger man obviously is of Chinese origin. "Thank you for coming. I have a lot of explaining to do, but I wanted to wait until I got this message." He retrieves a folded postcard from his breast pocket and gives it to the other man. The older man unfolds it and sees a colourful picture of some European-style buildings next to squat buildings

175

of obvious Chinese origin lining a harbour with tall ugly concrete buildings in the background. He turns the card around. It says: 'Macao harbour with Portuguese warehouses'. The handwritten text says, 'Wishing you were here...'

"What is this supposed to be?" The older man says, slightly annoyed, as he returns the card.

The younger man pockets the postcard again. "You surely remember Robert Delsey?"

"Sure, how could I forget him?"

"Well, it's his card; he's in Macao now. I telephoned him recently and he is well; he has opened a small gambling hall and makes a living from blackjack and poker."

The older man's eyes open wide in surprise. "You have contact with Robert Delsey? Have you reported him? Have you informed Interpol?"

The younger man smiles, relaxed: "No, Daniel; I haven't. Actually, I was the one who helped him escape!"

"What!" Chief Arozo rises out of his chair abruptly and the contents of his cocktail swashes over his round, hairy stomach: "You are kidding me! You helped him escape?"

Mr. Sy nods: "Yes, and I wanted to tell you for a long time, but I was afraid that you would react in the wrong manner." Then the younger man abruptly changes the subject: "How's Cornelia? You still plan to marry in January?"

"Sy, don't change the subject!"

"Well?"

Daniel Arozo grumbles: "She's fine. She has sold her part of the Lee business empire to some Indian guys; didn't want anything to do with it any more. She wanted me to resign, so I did. February 29th will be my last working day and in March my new life will start. It will only be a small ceremony; nothing much. We don't want to upset the locals; you know how they are. Afterwards, Cornelia wants to travel; she was surprised I had never been to Spain, so she wants to introduce me to her family. They still live in the old country; vineyards and the like."

Mr. Sy smiles. "I envy you, Daniel; you finally found your true love and a life of leisure is beckoning..."

"Yes, I *am* lucky, I suppose…" The chief replies: "But tell me; what has happened to you?"

Mr. Sy shrugs his shoulders: "Oh, I suppose that what could have been expected; my boss was furious that Robert Delsey had escaped. He didn't quite buy my story, though, and convinced me that it would be best for all if I resigned."

"So you are no longer with the force?"

Mr. Sy nodded: "Correct. I was complimented on the destruction of the drugs cartel, but was officially reprimanded that I had let a prisoner escape with my gun. My career in the force was over by then, but I don't regret it."

"Why not?"

"He was innocent, Daniel! Robert Delsey was no friend of mine, but he was, at least according to me, innocent of the murders of Elena, Juan and Zhiheng Lee."

"What makes you so sure?"

Mr. Sy elaborates on his ideas and Chief Arozo, being of sounder mind than ever before, can understand the rationale behind it. He starts nodding his head ever more vigorously: "It makes sense, Jonathan, but can you prove it?"

"Sadly, no! But if we find the real murderer, it will prove our thesis, wouldn't it?"

"It certainly would! Tell me; have you any suspicions?"

Finally, Mr. Sy smiles broadly. "I have indeed. And that is exactly why you are here!"

- To Be Continued -

177

GLOSSARY

Amacan: Native Filipino building material made of woven natural fibres.

Ate: Filipino word for auntie.

Bangus: Filipino word for milkfish.

Barangay: Native Filipino term for a village or district.

BIR: Bureau of Internal Revenue.

Cabana: A small hut built with a thatched roof.

Calamansi: Also called Golden lime or Philippine lime.

Dumaguete: Capital city of the Province of Oriental Negros.

Jeepney: A small bus that carries passengers on a regular route with a flexible schedule. Originally made from US military jeeps.

Ma'am: Polite form of address for women of higher social standing than the person addressing her.

Maayong Buntag: Visayan for "Good morning".

Marcos: Widely corrupt Philippine President/Dictator who ruled from 1965 to 1986.

Mindanao: Second largest and southernmost major island in the Philippines, parts of which are home to a Muslim minority.

Nippa: Leaves of the Nipa Palm, used for thatched roofs.

ROTC: Reserve Officers' Training Corps. Mandatory service for men at all universities and colleges.

Shabu: A slang term for the drug methamphetamine.

Sir: Polite form of address for men of higher social standing than the person addressing him.

Tagalog: First Filipino language spoken by a quarter of the population (amongst others in Metro Manila) and as a second language by the majority.

Tuba: Filipino palm wine.

Visayan: Filipino language spoken in the Visayan region, to which Siquijor belongs.

Wog wog: Also called "Wakwak". Vampiric, bird-like creature said to snatch humans at night as prey.